Nothing had changed. Not about this.

Suddenly, kissing Nick was not enough. And somehow Abby had forgotten to be careful. Her body had forgotten why it should maintain a distance. Overcome by a more powerful need, it reached for his, seeking the once-familiar contact. Needing it. Needing him. She had existed for too long with nothing but memories. Now she had to cling to him, allow his arms to enfold her, embrace her, hold her close, to…

She was aware of the enormity of her mistake as soon as he stiffened, but by then, of course, it was too late. His hands on her shoulders again tightened, this time pushing her away, and obeying, as she had always obeyed him, Abby took a step back.

His hands fell to the bulge of her pregnancy, the palms cupping the unmistakable contour of it.

"What the hell?" Nick said, the question so soft it was almost a whisper. "What the hell is going on?"

ABOUT THE AUTHOR

Gayle Wilson is the award-winning author of fourteen novels written for Harlequin. She has lived in Alabama all her life except for the years she followed her army aviator husband—whom she met on a blind date—to a variety of military posts.

Before beginning her writing career, she taught English and world history to gifted high school students in a number of schools around the Birmingham area. Gayle and her husband have one son, who is also a teacher of gifted students. They are blessed with warm and loving Southern families and an ever-growing menagerie of cats and dogs.

You can write to Gayle at P.O. Box 3277, Hueytown, Alabama 35023

Awards and Nominations:

Harlequin Intrigue

Echoes in the Dark—	1995 Award of Excellence winner, Colorado Romance Writers
	1995 Maggie finalist, Georgia Romance Writers
Only a Whisper—	1996 Award of Excellence finalist, Colorado Romance Writers
	1996 Holt Medallion finalist, Virginia Romance Writers
	1996 National Readers' Choice Award finalist, Oklahoma Romance Writers
The Redemption of Deke Summers—	1997 Award of Excellence finalist, Colorado Romance Writers
Heart of the Night—	1997 Award of Excellence finalist, Colorado Romance Writers
	1997 Holt Medallion finalist, Virginia Romance Writers

Harlequin Historical

The Heart's Desire— 1994 RITA Award finalist for Best First Book

Never Let Her Go
Gayle Wilson

HARLEQUIN®

TORONTO • NEW YORK • LONDON
AMSTERDAM • PARIS • SYDNEY • HAMBURG
STOCKHOLM • ATHENS • TOKYO • MILAN • MADRID
PRAGUE • WARSAW • BUDAPEST • AUCKLAND

For Aunt Jenny and Aunt Bess, for "adopting" me,
for sharing your love and your wisdom with me
for the past thirty years.
I love you both more than you can know.

ISBN 0-373-22490-7

NEVER LET HER GO

Copyright © 1998 by Mona Gay Thomas

This edition published by arrangement with Harlequin Books S.A.

® and TM are trademarks of the publisher. Trademarks indicated with
® are registered in the United States Patent and Trademark Office, the
Canadian Trade Marks Office and in other countries.

Printed in the U.S.A.

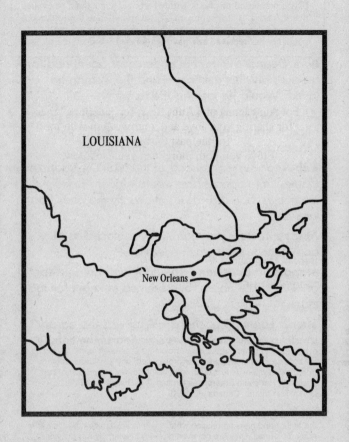

LOUISIANA

New Orleans

CAST OF CHARACTERS

Nick Deandro—The FBI undercover agent had lost his eyesight, his memory—and the woman he loved. Would he lose his life as well?

Abby Sterling—When she was assigned to protect Nick, no one—not even Nick—knew that they shared a past, and the baby she carried.

Rob Andrews—The head of the NOPD Organized Crime Unit hoped Abby would trigger Nick's memories. She did—but not exactly the ones Rob was after.

Mickey Yates—The man Abby replaced as Nick's bodyguard. Why was he leaving?

Maggie Thibodeaux—The cook and housekeeper of Nick's safe house. She seemed to know far too much.

Sheriff Lannie Blanchard—Why was the parish sheriff so interested in the situation at the safe house?

Prologue

He was watching from the shadows when she opened the door of her apartment. From the moment he heard the key in the lock, the feeling of anticipation had been too strong, almost unbearable. Almost uncontrollable. He was, however, a man who valued control, so he forced himself to stay hidden in the darkness. Forced himself to wait, just as he had planned.

She had been out running, despite the late-afternoon heat. That was obvious from the black shorts and the gray knit tank top she wore. The top had a semicircle of dampness around its low neck, marked with the sweat he could see glistening on her throat and shoulders and even on the front of her legs.

He studied her body as she bent to untie her shoes, pulling the laces up a little in the first two eyelets. She pushed the shoes off, each in turn, with the toe of the opposite foot and then tugged off her socks, balancing gracefully on one foot and then the other. She walked across the cool wooden floor on bare feet, high-arched and narrow, as shapely as the tanned legs.

She turned the air conditioner on high and adjusted the vent upward. Then she stood for a moment in front of the softly chugging window unit, eyes closed in indulgence, letting the cold air blow over her face and neck.

Finally she turned, at the same time unfastening the barrette that confined the mass of blond hair at the nape of her neck. She shook her head a couple of times, the long curls breaking apart and drifting like strands of silk around her neck. A few caught in the perspiration, gleaming there in the low light until she pushed them away with her fingers.

She put the barrette between her teeth and used both hands to hold the sweat-dampened hair high on her head, letting the air reach the back of her neck. The position pushed her breasts into prominence under the tight knit.

Despite the confinement of a sports bra, he could see them clearly through the damp fabric. The nipples had pebbled with the change from the thick outside heat of New Orleans in spring to the relative coolness of the small, dark apartment.

She released her hair and, in the same motion, lowered her arms, crossing them over her stomach to catch the hem of her top. She pulled the tank over her head and threw it toward a chair. It missed, sliding off to lie in a pale mound against the ancient wood of the floor, almost lost in the shadows.

She didn't stop to pick it up. Instead, she moved out of his sight, going farther into the interior of the apartment. He leaned back against the wall and took a deep breath, feeling the roughness of the bricks behind his head.

At least it was another sensation. A different one. A distraction. Something else to think about besides the hard ache in his groin. An ache that never seemed to go away, never seemed even to diminish anymore. Especially if he allowed himself to think about her.

He heard the water turn on, and he visualized it running, saw steam rising to fill the rust-stained tub in her tiny bathroom. In his mind's eye he watched her strip off the rest of the sodden garments, holding on, just as she always did, to the freestanding lavatory as she bent to remove her shorts and panties.

She would drop those on the black-and-white ceramic-tile floor with the same carelessness she had displayed when she threw the tank top at the chair. After she had undressed, she would stand there nude, examining her face in the age-clouded mirror, perhaps holding her hair up again to get it off the heat and dampness of her neck. And when she did, her bare breasts would lift, pushing upward in small peaks, just as they had before.

Fighting the undeniable power that image had over his body, Nick Deandro allowed his eyes to move around the dim, cluttered kitchen he was standing in. The sink was full of dishes. There was a mug beside it that had held her morning coffee, and probably still did, he guessed, black and cold now. A box of cereal was out on the table, just as she'd left it this morning, in a hurry because she was late. She was always late.

Neatness wasn't her strongest attribute, Nick acknowledged ruefully, smiling a little at the understatement. But she had so many others that one weakness really wasn't important. Not important to him. But then, he had never believed *she* would become important. Not like this. Not this…obsession.

No one who knew him would have believed it either. Slender, blond and slightly vulnerable weren't things that Nick Deandro had ever before been attracted to in a woman. Anyone who knew him could vouch for that. So this had surprised him. Taken him unaware and unprepared. Not only that it had happened between them, but how strong it was. Almost fierce. And he knew it had surprised her as well.

She was probably in the tub by now. He closed his eyes, allowing himself to imagine that. Not resisting the picture forming in his mind. After all, it didn't do any good to resist. He had tried that a lot before he'd called her the first time.

She had been surprised by his call. He had clearly heard the shock in her voice. Of course, she had been thinking that it was something official. Something important. That had been in her tone as well, briskly businesslike and professional.

What he had been thinking, as he held the car phone against his ear, driving through the thick steam of a Delta night, had been anything but professional. *Anything* but.

And what had happened when he'd showed up here that first night… He still had a hard time believing the strength of the immediate chemistry between them. Something they both had felt. Apparently the open animosity had only been an aspect of the heat that flared between them. So strong it had overpowered all the cautions. When she had opened the door that first night and moved into his arms, he knew that nothing about this assignment would be anything like the others he had worked. And it hadn't been, of course.

The quick visit he had planned wasn't going to happen, he admitted. Not tonight. *Out of control,* he thought again as his fingers fell to the buttons that fastened his aged jeans.

He took his loafers off, exactly as she had discarded her running shoes, and by that time he had the jeans undone. He pushed them and his briefs down and stepped out of both, and then, reaching over his shoulder, jerked off the navy polo he was wearing and dropped it on top of the pile.

She wouldn't fuss about them or pick them up, folding them into neatness. He would give her that. And a whole lot more besides, he thought, grinning at the one-track-minded direction of his thoughts.

He needed to think of something that might distract him. Because if he didn't, he admitted, this was going to be short and sweet. Incredibly sweet, he knew from experience, but maybe as incredibly short as well.

But she had never complained about that. Or about anything. Of course, exhaustion and satiation don't lend themselves to conversation. It was usually real quiet when they were through.

She hadn't closed the bathroom door, and despite the omnipresent and oppressive humidity, there was a whiff of steam in the hallway, drifting through the dark air toward him, like heat waves shimmered from the asphalt of a summer road.

He could even smell whatever she had put into the water. It was familiar. This was the way her skin smelled as he made slow, endless love to her. Then, the scent rose from her body, just as it did now from the bath.

She had been dipping her cloth in the hot water and languidly squeezing the liquid out of it, letting it stream down over her breast. Her head was back against the rim of the tub, but she was watching the water run over the skin of her shoulder and trickle off the end of the rose-brown nipple.

She had pinned her hair loosely out of the way on top of her head, and the gathered curls gleamed silver-gilt in the low light. Some of the strands were again caught in the moisture that covered her throat, but this time she ignored them.

Nick hadn't made any noise. He was sure of that, moving carefully down the dark hallway on bare feet. Suddenly, however, she glanced up from whatever solitary game she was playing, seeming to sense his presence.

Her eyes widened in shock, the expanding black of the pupils almost swallowing the rim of emerald green that surrounded them, and she began to scramble out of the water. A small flood of it lurched over the side of the tub to puddle on the tile before recognition clicked in.

"God, Nick," she said. The gasping inhalation she had taken whooshed out in relief. "You scared me to death." She took another breath, shock easing.

The hand that had been holding the washcloth suddenly raised and threw it. It didn't come close to hitting him, landing instead with a sodden splat somewhere in the hallway behind him.

"Nice shot," he said. His eyes were examining the slim perfection of her body.

"What are you doing here?" she demanded. Her arms had automatically crossed over her chest, the gesture protective and modest, yet somehow provocative at the same time.

Nick grinned in response. "Too late," he said. "I've already seen it all. All of you."

She smiled at him finally, apparently appreciating how ridiculous had been the urge to hide her body from his eyes. She certainly knew he had seen it all. Not frequently enough, however, that he didn't enjoy looking. Not often enough that it wasn't still exciting to him.

Her eyes moved downward to that excitement, and then came quickly back to his face. Her smile had changed. It was softer, somehow. Maybe anticipating. He knew he sure as hell was.

"You shouldn't be here," she said.

"You know what they say about all work and no play."

"Is that what you're here for? To play?"

"Maybe," he admitted. "If you're not too tired."

"I'm not too tired. Hungry," she said, "but not too tired."

He nodded. "We could order out."

"Cheap date," she chided, amusement rich in her voice.

"Want me to wash your back?" His question was slightly suggestive, intended to be, but she didn't respond to the tone.

"If you can find the cloth. It's somewhere in the hall."

Nick didn't even look around. Instead, he stepped into the room, and suddenly the tiny bathroom seemed smaller. He was a big man, and he seemed to fill up all the space.

His father's family were Sicilian, but Nick's maternal ancestors had been tall, blond and Nordic. The combination made for an unusual mix of features, but not one that he could ever remember anyone complaining about.

He was almost six foot two, and there wasn't a bit of fat in any of those inches, not even around the middle where men his age usually put on a little weight. That he hadn't was also unusual for a man who spent so many hours sitting behind a desk. He worked out, but not enough, he knew, to justify that flat belly.

That was another undeserved gift of his heredity, just like the contrast between the pale blue eyes and the gleaming, raven's wing hair. Black Irish, people usually guessed, despite the strong, almost roman nose and the olive skin, covered now with a fine dew of perspiration and nothing else.

It was at least ten degrees hotter in the bathroom than it had been in the hallway. Hotter and wetter. Which wasn't a bad combination, Nick acknowledged. Not in this situation.

Her eyes had followed his movement into the room, and they were still directed up at him now, holding his as he stood beside the tub, looking down at her. Her body was completely revealed by the transparency of the cloudy water, and he reacted. The hard rush of desire was almost as overpowering as the sense of anticipation had been when he had heard her key turn in the lock.

"You want to join me?" she invited.

"I don't think I'd fit," he denied, but it was tempting as hell. *She* was tempting. She had been from the beginning. Far more temptation than he had been prepared to resist.

"We could find out," she suggested softly.

"I've got a better idea," he said.

"You usually do."

She smiled at him again, the slow seductive one. At some point in the conversation, she had uncrossed her arms, willing now to have him look at her.

He supposed she was over the initial shock that he was here when she hadn't been expecting him. Here where he sure as hell shouldn't be. But he'd worry about that later. And based on previous experiences, it would probably not be until much later.

He knelt beside the tub, and her eyes followed him, focused on his face. He put his left hand into the water, surprised at how hot it was. It seemed they had been talking a long time, but the steam was still drifting off the surface. Still fragrant.

He cupped a handful and held it out over her chest, tilting his big hand until the moisture ran out of it onto her breast. It was the same mindless game she had been playing when he'd come into the room. Except it wasn't, of course. It was a much different game now that there were two players involved.

And suddenly her eyes reflected that. He lowered his hand, and with his thumb he traced the path the spill of water had taken. The thick pad slid across the moisture, finding no resistance over the slick skin. When he reached the darker tip of her breast, he used the side of his thumb to push the nipple down and then back up.

He heard the small breath she took, liked hearing it, and so he repeated the motion. Down and then up. "Good?" he asked softly, watching her eyes.

"Yes," she breathed. Her hand lifted, bringing droplets of water up with it. They fell like tears on his forearm. She put her fingers over his, holding them, and the abrasive movement of his thumb hesitated.

"What's wrong?" he asked.

"Nothing," she whispered. She guided his hand, pushing it open over her breast, the small, perfect globe fitting into his palm as if it had been made for him to hold. He tightened his fingers and watched her eyes close slowly and her lips part, the breath again sighing out between them.

"Tell me," he urged. "Tell me you like me to touch you."

"You know that," she said, her voice slightly hoarse.

"I want you to tell me," he said. "Tell me you like it."

"I like it," she repeated obediently. She took a breath, the softness of her breast moving within the hard, callused roughness of his confining fingers. He closed them again, a slightly stronger compression this time.

Her inhalation was broken. Almost a gasp. And her head had fallen back to rest again against the rim of the tub. The long, ringed column of her neck was exposed and suddenly the urge to press his mouth over it was irresistible. The need to taste the moisture there, both the salt-sharp tang of her sweat and the soapy bath water, was overpowering. Nick raised his body, leaning awkwardly over the tub.

Her skin was moist and scented. The fragrance was evocative of the nights they had spent in that disordered bedroom, making love through the heat-drenched hours, the only sound the distant noises of this city that never slept and the efforts of the window unit to add a breath of coolness to the conflagration that had ignited between them.

Two people who should never have been attracted to each other. Two people no one else would ever believe were here in the shadowed darkness together. Two people…

His mouth had found the small hollow at the base of her throat, and he licked the moisture that had collected there, touching it with the tip of his tongue, tasting it. Tasting her.

Her hand cupped the back of his head, holding his mouth against her body. Inviting what he was doing. Welcoming it. His lips slipped lower, across the shadowed valley between her breasts. His hands shaped the outside of them, bringing their heat against his cheeks. He turned his head, the movement small, his tongue laving from side to side, his late-afternoon beard gently abrading her skin.

A moan this time. Stronger than the breath she had drawn before. He liked hearing her moan. He liked making her moan. He liked all the noises she made when he made love to her. And that had been surprising, too. He would never have thought she was the kind of woman who made those particular sounds.

He turned his head, allowing his mouth to fasten over the small bud of her breast that his fingers guided to it. He suckled, hard and strong, giving in to the need to take her into him, a part of her, anyway. Some part of her within him, just as he would soon be within her. Soon.

He turned his head and devoted his attention to the other

breast, his mouth caressing there as well. Demanding. He was aware that she had moved. Her fingers fastened again over his. This time, however, she pulled them away and the nipple he had been suckling almost slipped out of his control. Almost.

She held the hand she had captured, carrying it with hers under the water. He knew what she wanted. She was very good at that. At letting him know what she wanted. What she needed. And he wanted to know. Every need. Every desire.

His fingers were guided to the soft curls. *A true blonde,* he thought again, remembering his initial surprise in discovering that. Only the first of the many things he'd discovered that night. Like this. How much she liked this.

Another moan, this one low and deep in her throat. Almost guttural. The sound of it so damn sensual. For all her soft fragility, so incredibly sensual.

She put her head against his, pushing her forehead into his hair. His mouth was still examining her breasts. Her breathing deepened as he continued to touch her. Small, quick inhalations, building now. Building as they always did. So strong that they created an answering strength and an answering need in him.

"Yes," she whispered.

He could feel her mouth moving against his hair. He wanted it on his body. She did things to him that no one else had ever done. And Nick Deandro had known a lot of women. Never one like this. Never anyone like this particular woman.

He felt the shivering response begin within her. So quick. Always so responsive. And that had surprised him, too. He had never expected her to be like this. Of course, he had never expected her to want to be with him, either.

He raised his head, so he could watch what was happening in her face. "Open your eyes," he commanded softly.

She obeyed, but the reaction had been delayed, overpowered by the demands of the other. When the long lashes finally drifted upward, it was already over. Her eyes were soft, distant, almost too far away. Too solitary. Like the bath game she had been playing when he entered the room.

Two players, he thought. He rose, and her eyes widened in surprise, their focus coming back a little from the lonely place he had taken her. He reached down and picked her up out of the bath. Her arms automatically fastened around his neck. Her body was slick, slippery with whatever she had put into the water. It was warm and wet against the coolness of his skin.

He carried her out of the low light of the bathroom, down the dark hallway and into the shadowed dimness of the bedroom. As he walked, her breasts moved, sliding like satin over the hair-roughened skin of his chest. The bathwater ran in hot rivulets down his stomach and thighs, fingers of sensation trying to caress his growing need.

The disorder of the unmade bed seemed inviting. He laid her down in the nest of the tangled sheets and immediately lay down on top of her. Her legs opened, welcoming him.

He was so hard he was mindless with wanting her. He wanted her with him. He wanted to watch her eyes as he pushed into the sweet heat of her response. He wanted to see it happen in her face again while he was there with her. Together. Not a solitary game. Together.

He thrust downward, burying himself in her. Another moan, low and intense. Not protest, he was aware on some level. And he lifted and lowered again. Deeper this time. Searching the depths of her. Seeking the bottom of what he felt. Wanting all that she wanted to give. More than willing to take what she had offered. So willingly offered him. As it had been from the first. As if it had always been meant to be.

His hips drove against hers. Too hard, he thought, feeling the small, fragile bones of her pelvis under the grinding, pounding movement of his. Too hard. But he couldn't stop. He wanted her so much. So much. So much.

The explosion rocked them both. He had wanted to see

her, to read her eyes, but he couldn't. He couldn't do anything but ride the waves of sensation. Mindless with it. But even in the throes of that exultation of sensation, he tightened his arms, holding her to him.

And when he finally raised his head, the effort it took to accomplish that small movement enormous, her eyes were open, watching him. Slowly, a single tear slipped out of the pools of moisture they had become and tracked over her temple.

He brushed it away with his thumb. He shook his head, ashamed and embarrassed. "Sorry," he said softly, pulling the words from the unfunctioning morass of emotion his mind had become. "So sorry I hurt you."

"No," she whispered. "You didn't hurt me. It's just…" She hesitated, and her eyes moved over his face, and then she smiled at him. "You always surprise me," she said finally.

He didn't understand. He didn't know how he had surprised her. Other than the fact that he was here. That they were together again. "Is that bad or good?" he asked, his breathing easing a little, and his body beginning to soften. Still within her. Still joined.

She smiled again, and then her fingers touched the perspiration that had gathered on his upper lip. She wiped it off with the tip of one finger and then put that finger in her mouth. "Always good," she said. "So good," she whispered.

"We're going to have to do something about this," he said, surprising himself. It wasn't that he hadn't thought about it before. He had. A lot. But he hadn't planned to say anything to her. Not yet.

He didn't even know if she had had any thoughts in that direction. And he was cautious by nature. That's why he'd survived in this business so long. Cautious except, of course, for this.

"Something?" she repeated. Her eyes examined his face.

"Something permanent," he suggested and held his breath.

She was quiet for a long time. The quietness scared him. He'd never before suggested anything permanent to a woman, and he wasn't sure that silence was a promising response.

"Permanent like…?" she asked finally.

"Permanent like…mortgages, kids, rings," he said. *Way to go, Deandro,* he jeered silently. *Some damn romantic proposal.*

Again, silence. And he waited, holding his breath.

"I think you got the order of that wrong," she said softly.

"Whatever."

With one of those mercurial changes he loved, her eyes lightened. The heated, heavy sullenness of passion and even the seriousness of his suggestion were both wiped quickly away. She laughed, loud and unrestrained.

He realized that he loved hearing her laugh. The open joy of it always surprised him. Like the sounds she made when they were making love. So different from how he'd expected her to be. In every way different.

"I love you," he said softly.

The laughter faded, from her eyes and from the quietness of the room. It was gradually replaced by wonder, the dark pupils expanding again into the rim of green. And then she nodded.

"I didn't think you knew that," she said.

"Slow," he agreed. "But usually I get there."

"I know," she said softly. "I knew you would. Eventually."

"You think babies and mortgages are going to work for us?"

"Eventually," she repeated, but it hurt him this time to hear the word in that context.

"Why eventually?" he asked. He brushed an errant curl

off her cheek with his fingers. They looked dark and hard against the smooth alabaster of her skin.

"When this is all over," she said.

There was a hint of a question in her voice, but he knew she was right. Now wasn't the time for any of this. It was too complicated. His life was such right now that he couldn't do anything about this. Anything other than what he had done tonight. Come to her when he could. A stolen, hidden hour or two in the middle of the other.

He nodded, almost regretfully, despite knowing all of that. Understanding it, even. It didn't make it easier to walk away from her. Back into the darkness of the night in which he'd been living for the last few weeks. Even this furtive meeting might screw everything up.

"I have to go," he said, remembering.

"I know."

He didn't move, unable to physically separate himself from her. Unable to force his body away from the heat and wetness of hers. He realized with a sense of wonder that just thinking about leaving was having an undeniable effect on him. An effect that shouldn't be happening now. That wasn't supposed to happen.

"Hmm…" she said, her lips tilting slightly and her eyes again lightening.

"Hmm…" he repeated.

"Interesting phenomenon," she suggested.

"Phenomenal phenomenon," he breathed, lowering his mouth to hers. It was the first time he had kissed her tonight. Her mouth opened, aligning with his. Her tongue found his.

She tasted so good. She shouldn't. Not after running in this heat. Not after a long day of endless cups of black coffee. But she did. She always did. Honey-sweet tongue moving hotly against his, his arousal growing as they kissed.

And this time was slow. Measured. So wet and hot from

the first that it felt almost like the bath. Like the rich, humid air of the night that surrounded them. Endlessly slow.

His mouth tasted. Nibbled. Caressed. His fingers explored. Reacted to her reactions. And all the time his hips moved, lifting and sliding in and out of the heat and scent and wetness of her body.

A long time. Longer than he had time for, but that didn't stop either of them. Nothing stopped this except exhaustion and satiation. He had known that before. And he knew it now again. As slow and dark and powerful as the movements of the old river. As the weight of humidity in the Delta night. Surrounding them as they surrounded and enfolded each other.

A long, long time.

HE DRESSED in the kitchen without turning on a light. He thought she would be asleep, but she sat up in the shadowed bed as he came back into the room.

"When will I see you again?" she asked.

He couldn't see her face in the darkness, only her shape, a darker black than the rest. "When I can," he said. That was the absolute truth. He would come back here when he could. As soon as he could. Because he couldn't do anything else.

"Take care of yourself," she said softly.

"You know me," he answered, pushing the nonchalant words out of a throat suddenly constricted again with need. He didn't have time for that. He had already spent too many hours here. Dangerous even in the darkness.

"I do," she agreed. "That's why I want you to be careful."

He walked across and put his knee on the bed beside her. The mattress dipped and creaked under his weight. She reached for him, and they held each other, held tightly. Her body smelled familiar to him. Her hair moved against his face when she turned her head, the fragrance of it, too, moving through his senses. Evoking memories.

He leaned back so he could see her face. He shaped her cheek with his palm and pressed a kiss on her forehead.

"Go back to sleep," he said.

"I wasn't asleep. I was thinking."

"What about?" he asked gently. His palm trailed down her neck and over her breast, cupping it as he had cupped her face.

"A baby," she said.

The word was so low that he wasn't sure for a moment what she had said. And when he was, the emotion was there as well. His baby. Suckling the small rose nipple, just as he had tonight. Growing beneath the breasts he had worshiped. His baby.

"Out of order," he said lightly.

"Rings, baby, mortgage," she suggested, apparently agreeing. "I know. But..."

"But what?" he asked. They were only delaying. Postponing the moment when he would have to leave. Past due now, and no easier to say goodbye than it would have been at the beginning. Maybe even harder.

"We didn't use anything this time," she said.

He hadn't thought about it. Not until now. Another indication of how different this was. He was as careful as he was controlled. That's how he stayed safe, despite his job.

"You worried?" he asked. His palm moved, drifting downward, unthinkingly smoothing over the slight convexity of her stomach.

"No," she said. "Not unless you are."

"I don't worry. You know that."

She took her arms from around his neck, freeing him, but she put her hand over his, pressing it against her belly. "I know."

He touched her hair again with his lips. He closed his eyes against the surge of desire. "Gotta go," he whispered.

He felt her nod. He stood up, halfway expecting her to say something else, but she didn't. She was still sitting in the disordered bed, watching him. Finally he turned and walked through the door to the hall and through the dark kitchen and into the blackness of the alley. The same way he'd entered.

Maybe his mind was still back in the shadowed bedroom, but he thought he was aware, alert. He was checking his surroundings as he moved through the maze of back streets to where he had left his car. His eyes surveyed the darkness ahead of him, checking as carefully as he always did.

And when the first bullet hit him, besides the heat and the force of the blow, the only thing he felt was a deep sense of surprise because this wasn't how it was supposed to happen.

Not at all what he had been anticipating.

Chapter One

"That's blackmail, Rob," Abby Sterling said, her voice low and tight with anger. "And you know it."

"You're the one who put in a request for a change of assignment. I'm willing to grant it," her boss said. "There's no blackmail involved."

"Not *that* assignment," she said sharply.

In frustration, Rob Andrews raised both hands and ran them across his fifties-style crew cut. He didn't have much hair left. What was there was gray and so close-cropped that his scalp showed pink through it. When he finished the familiar gesture, he put both palms flat on his desk.

"Something less stressful," he enunciated carefully. "Something that will keep you off your feet. That's what you and your doctor requested. This is what I've got, Abby. You can take it or leave it. I don't care. You don't want something this cushy, I got plenty of people who will."

Blackmail, she thought again, but this time she didn't say it aloud. Rob was right. There would be cops who would jump at the chance. Only she didn't think she could be one of them. For a world of very compelling reasons.

"Look," her supervisor said, adopting his reasoned, adult-to-child voice, "I know you and Deandro never got along—"

"Understatement," she broke in before he could finish.

"Maybe. And maybe you had your reasons. I know he

can be a little...abrasive at times.'' He ignored her soft snort of mock laughter, and went on. "But you weren't the easiest person to get along with either, Abby. You made some waves of your own."

"I objected to Deandro's attitude. His 'I'm going to show all you bumpkins how it's done' style."

"Except that's exactly what he was down here to do."

Abby took a breath. Rob was right, of course. The FBI had been working with the New Orleans Police Department to finish cleaning up the police corruption, the well-documented and apparently pervasive corruption, which everyone from the mayor on down admitted had existed in this city too long.

There had been numerous arrests after the change in administration, but too many of the powerful, so-called Old Guard in the department had simply gone underground, biding their time until the reform efforts waned. Then, they believed, it would be back to business as usual—drug-running, protection rackets, all their very profitable connections with organized crime.

Despite the efforts of the last five years, NOPD still had the reputation of being cops on the take. It tarred all of them, even the honest ones like Rob Andrews and Abby herself. So when they got lucky enough to get the goods on a wise guy who was suddenly willing to trade the introduction of an undercover agent into the inner circle of the New Orleans mob in exchange for an agreement not to prosecute him, they had jumped at the chance.

Only, there was no one local who could bring it off. That's why the FBI had been asked to come in again and set up a sting operation, targeted not only at the mob, but at the remaining rogues in the department who had ties to it.

Abby wanted, probably more than most, to see this department cleaned up. She just objected to the cocky way Nick Deandro had gone about his part of the job. She had been pretty vocal in those objections, at least within the extremely limited circle of the Organized Crime Special Unit, those very few, hand-picked individuals who knew who Deandro was and what he was doing down here.

Real vocal, she amended mentally. Abby was nothing if not honest. Especially with herself. Nick had only been doing exactly what he'd been brought in to do, and so, even at the time, she hadn't understood her reaction to him.

"I can't help it if he rubbed you the wrong way," Rob said. "He has the kind of personality that rubs a lot of people the wrong way, I guess."

"Apparently," Abby said.

"You didn't shoot him, did you?" her boss asked, reading her tone. His question was full of black humor, despite what had happened to Deandro.

"I won't deny there were a few times I thought about it," she said truthfully. "How's he doing?" she asked, holding her eyes on Rob's by sheer willpower.

"Not so good," he admitted. "I guess physically he's doing about as well as anybody ever expected, but..." Rob's brows lifted and then fell, and his mouth tightened. He looked down at his hands a moment before he looked back up, pinning her with dark, troubled eyes. "And I guess, given the circumstances, that shouldn't be surprising. He still doesn't remember a thing, Abby. None of what we need him to remember."

"I thought the doctors said that would be temporary," she said. *Temporary,* she repeated silently. It had been more than six months now, and apparently—

"I'm beginning to think they don't know what the hell they're talking about. None of them."

"What about the blindness?" she asked softly.

That question was more difficult to get out. She still couldn't quite make her memory of the brash New York agent fit the stereotypical images she supposed everyone, herself included, had about the blind. Perceptions gleaned from television or the movies. Images of people who touched things carefully, who moved hesitantly, guided by white canes or dogs wearing halters.

Those were all somewhere within her consciousness when anyone said "blind," even if they shouldn't be. And she could not make any of those images match the ones of Nick Deandro that lingered in her mind. She hadn't been able to do that since she had heard about his injury.

"There's no change," Rob said. "No change in any of it."

"You think he's not ever going to recover," she said. That wasn't a question. It sounded more like an accusation, but she hadn't realized that in time to soften the harshness of her tone.

"Maybe not," Rob agreed. "He wants to remember, just like he wants to be able to see again. But what he *wants* to happen, what we all need to happen, may not be what any of us get."

"But everybody said he would," Abby said. "As soon as everything healed. When the swelling went down, blood clots reabsorbed, all that medical mumbo jumbo."

"Except we're past all the deadlines they gave us."

"Still…" Abby said, reluctant, as she knew Andrews must be, to admit defeat. Rob had worked too hard on setting this up. As had she and the others in this special unit of the Public Integrity Division. Too damn hard to see everything fall apart.

Of course, they were lucky that Deandro wasn't dead. Luck and a thick skull had saved Nick Deandro's apparently charmed life. Somebody had certainly intended to kill him that night. And they had nearly succeeded, but for some pretty quixotic reasons the FBI agent had survived, blind from trauma to the optic nerve and suffering from amnesia about almost everything that had happened since he'd been in New Orleans.

"You haven't completely ruled out the possibility that he'll recover," she finished her hesitant sentence.

"I don't want to rule it out. That would put the police-corruption part of this in the toilet, Abby, and you know it.''

She nodded, thinking about what they did have. As soon as Deandro had been made, they had pulled the informant, the one who had made the introduction, knowing his life wouldn't be worth a plugged nickel. He was in witness protection now, and he was singing like a bird.

She hadn't heard that he'd accused anyone in the department of having ties to his former comrades. Even if he had, however, any accusations that guy might make against cops would be almost worthless. No grand jury was going to give credence to it. It would smack of vendetta or of trying to buy immunity, especially if the officers involved were highly placed and highly regarded. The D.A. wouldn't get any corruption indictments out of anything he said.

The only person who might be able to stand up and finger the rogues in the department was Deandro, who was not only blind but couldn't remember anything that had happened in the weeks before that bullet cracked his skull. Even the D.A.'s office seemed to be trying to back off the corruption angle, concentrating successfully on getting indictments against the Mafia instead.

''Deandro never gave you any names?'' she asked.

''He didn't want to accuse anyone without solid proof they're dirty. He was trying to get it. The kind you take to court. Maybe he had. But unless he recovers, we'll never know.''

''Look, I'm sorry that this isn't working out—''

''I need you, Abby. Forget blackmail. And I guess you were right about that. I know damn well how you felt about Deandro. We all knew. But you're a member of this team, an important member, and I need you to put your personal feelings aside.''

''If you think you're going to talk me into believing that my bodyguarding Nick Deandro is a good idea—'' Abby had begun, anger creeping back into her voice, before Andrews interrupted.

"You hated each other's guts. That was pretty obvious to everybody. But the point is..." Rob paused before he made whatever the point was. He rubbed his hands distractedly over his head again, and Abby waited, unwilling to give him any help.

"The point is," he said finally, "that you two reacted real strongly to each other. Personality conflict. Whatever."

"You were closer the first time," she acknowledged. "We hated each other's guts."

"One of the doctors thinks that maybe some kind of stimulation might jog Deandro's memory," Rob offered.

"And I'm supposed to be that stimulation? Give me a break."

"Why not. If he remembers you—"

"He doesn't. He doesn't remember anything about his assignment down here. You've said so yourself."

"But that's the whole point of this. Maybe we can do something to trigger that memory. You seemed to evoke the strongest reaction of anybody in the Organized Crime Unit. Maybe just seeing you again..." Rob's voice faded, as he apparently realized what he had said.

"Well, now, that *is* a problem, isn't it?" Abby reminded him softly, those stereotypical images again inside her head. So unwanted. "Whatever there was about me that set off Deandro's animosity may not work in this situation."

"Maybe not. But you're still the best shot we've got. I need you to try. You've got as much at stake as the rest of us."

Her laugh was bitter. "Too much at stake to undertake something this stupid," she vowed.

Rob let that lie a moment between them, letting her think about what she had said. That was, of course, the crux of the matter. The hold her boss had over her. One she couldn't deny.

"Is this it?" she asked when Andrews didn't say anything else. He just sat there watching her, letting the silence get tense. Although Abby knew the technique as well as

Rob did, she gave in to that tension. "Is that what you're saying? I take this assignment or else?"

"I'm *asking* you to take it. For the good of the department. I'm not threatening you, Abby."

"Because you couldn't get away with that and you know it."

"Because you're a good cop," Rob corrected. "You're too good a cop not to know I'm right about this."

The quietness stretched again. There was part of Abby that screamed for her to agree. And another part that fought fiercely against even admitting the thought of doing this into her brain. A very bad idea, she knew. Because she would be opening herself up to all kinds of pain.

"I can put you to work answering the phone somewhere, I guess," Rob said finally. "I owe you that. But if you're worried about doing what the doctors want you to do, then this is the best I can offer. You show up at the safe house, put your feet up, and relax. With nothing, literally, to do."

"Nothing except make sure nobody dirty gets to our witness."

"Nobody's going to find Deandro," Rob insisted, ignoring her sarcasm. "They haven't yet. I'm not sure they're even trying."

"They believe he's dead?" Abby asked.

"Maybe. God knows he ought to be."

Another silence while they both thought about the reality of that. The shooter had pumped two bullets into Deandro before one of the building's tenants, who had been sitting in the darkness on a balcony overlooking the narrow street, finally started yelling his head off.

And a foot patrolman, part of the department's apparently successful attempt to increase police presence in the embattled neighborhoods, arrived within seconds after the first shot. In the aftermath, the shooter disappeared, apparently believing his job complete, even if he hadn't been able to verify the kill.

Maybe whoever had set the ambush up *did* think Nick

was dead. That would be comforting to believe, Abby supposed. She just wasn't sure she was optimist enough to buy it.

"There's a lady who lives out on this place," Rob went on, apparently still trying to sell her. "She cooks and cleans and shops. There's surveillance equipment all over the grounds, motion sensors, alarms, the works. The parish sheriff is less than five minutes away."

"You trust him?" Abby found herself asking. She regretted the words as soon as they were out of her mouth. Rob would take them as a sign she was at least thinking about it.

Maybe she was, she admitted. She was certainly thinking about a lot of things—things she had been resolutely pushing to the back of her mind for the last six months.

"He doesn't know who we've got out there. But even if he figured it out… Yeah, I'd trust him. He's worked with us before. He's as straight as they come—old-time law enforcement. His daddy was sheriff before he was."

"Who's out there now?"

"Mickey Yates. He has been from the time Deandro was released from the hospital."

"I heard Mickey had gone up to Birmingham with the group advising in their crime-prevention program."

"And you believed it, too, didn't you?" Rob asked, smiling.

"I had no reason not to."

Her boss nodded. "Exactly. But Mickey's got a wife and four kids. Deandro's not eager to have somebody new out there, but this has gone on far longer than I promised Mickey it would. He wants to go home before his wife divorces him."

"And I, on the other hand…" Abby said, thinking of her lonely apartment. No ties. Not even a cat to keep her company. "How were you going to explain my disappearance?"

"Something close to the truth. That your doctor put you

on medical leave. Until after the baby's born. That gives us three months. Isn't that about right?''

''About that,'' she admitted. Rob's eyes fell, briefly examining the bulge of her pregnancy, and then they lifted to hers.

''So…?'' he said.

The word hung in the air between them. *So what?* Abby thought. *What do you want me to say?* But Rob was right. She was too good a cop to dismiss his request for help out of hand. Besides, it was always possible he was on to something.

''So unless something shakes Deandro's memory loose, we don't have anything on the corruption,'' Abby finished for him.

Rob nodded. Apparently he'd made all the arguments he intended to make. And of course, he had really said it all.

The O.C. unit needed her to do this. She was the one most likely to make Nick Deandro remember something about his time down here. She understood the reality of that far better than Rob did. And her reasons for wanting Nick to remember were far more personal than those involved in simply being a good cop.

She had already told her boss she needed an assignment as free from stress and physical exertion as she could manage and still stay employed, keeping both her medical benefits and her salary. It was going to be hard to explain why this one didn't fit the conditions she'd outlined in her official request.

She supposed she could really apply for the medical leave Rob had suggested as her cover, but the paperwork would take time and her obstetrician hadn't recommended such a drastic step.

The problems Abby was having weren't that serious. Not yet, at least. Probably just stress-related, her doctor had assured her comfortingly. And ironically she was probably right about that, Abby thought. Only wrong about the causes of that stress. No one really knew about those. But would taking this assignment lessen that stress or increase it dramatically?

She sighed, pushing her hair back behind her ears. The sides of the straight, chin-length bob had fallen forward when she lowered her head to try to think this through without the pressure of Rob's steady regard.

She didn't want anything to happen to this baby. That's why she had requested a less stressful assignment. She would do anything for this small, dear life she carried. *Anything?* she questioned. Always honest, at least with herself.

"Okay," she said softly.

She glanced up in time to catch Rob Andrews's reaction. Although he had controlled it quickly, his shock had touched his eyes. He hadn't expected her to agree, she realized. That was clear, and she guessed it was natural for him to feel that way.

Because she hadn't expected to agree, either. She was not aware that her decision to become Nick Deandro's bodyguard had been reached until exactly the same time Rob had been. Not until the soft capitulation came out of her mouth.

THE SAFE HOUSE was outside the city, really isolated, surrounded only by swampy marshes that fronted a bayou. The only access was a winding dirt road that snaked off from a black-topped parish two-lane.

Its location was the main reason for choosing the place, of course—to keep anyone from accidentally stumbling across where they were hiding Deandro. Despite her position within the department, Abby hadn't even known this place existed. Maybe that meant nobody else did either, she hoped.

Unconsciously she put her hand against her rounded belly. Despite the fact that Rob had assured her help was only a few minutes away, she felt isolated as well as unsure. She would be pretty far away from her doctor, if anything happened.

Nothing's going to happen, Abby told herself determinedly, fighting that frisson of unease. Nothing was going to go wrong. That was one reason she had accepted this assignment. So she could put her feet up and relax, just as Rob had advised. All she needed to do was relax, she told herself again.

But this second admonition had more to do with the realization that Rob was holding the door of the car open for her to climb out. She wondered briefly how long he'd been standing there, while she had tried to control the sinking sensation in the pit of her stomach, reminiscent of the brief periods of morning sickness she'd suffered. Those were long past now, and despite the anxiety her doctor's thoughtful cautions had created, she felt strong and very healthy.

Strong except, of course, for her feelings about this. She took a deep breath, climbing carefully out of the car. The small precautions Dr. Clarke had suggested had created within her an exaggerated sense that she must take very good care of herself in order to take care of this baby.

"You okay?" Rob asked, apparently sensing her apprehension.

"I'm fine. Just a little nervous, I guess."

"Look at it this way, Abby. If he doesn't remember you, you have a whole new chance to make a first impression. Maybe even a better one this time."

She laughed. At Nick's expense, she supposed, feeling slightly guilty about that, but at least Rob's teasing comment had lessened the tension. Despite Andrews's hopes, she knew in her gut that Nick Deandro wasn't going to remember her. After all, during the last six months he hadn't remembered her or anything else that had happened since he came to New Orleans. And she really didn't buy the theory that simply being confronted with her again was going to shock him into remembering now.

"Let's go," Rob suggested.

She followed him reluctantly up the walk that led to the house. The structure was shaded by towering oaks, their limbs heavily draped with Spanish moss. The overhanging branches, stretched over the roof, looked like Hollywood's idea of the storied past in this part of Louisiana. As did the house itself.

It was a bastardized version of the classic Louisiana raised cottage, fronted by a gallery whose roof was held up by decorative wrought-iron columns connected to one another by an iron railing. The second story was topped by dormer windows that looked out above the flat roof of the veranda and down the avenue of interlocking oaks. The weathered cypress that had been used in the house's construction was a soft silver-gray, which blended in a monochromatic sweep with the color of the moss.

Abby wondered briefly how the department had gotten access to a place like this, but she supposed that didn't matter. It was just something else to pretend to contemplate in order not to have to think about the man who was waiting inside.

Men, she amended, as the door opened and Mickey Yates stepped out onto the veranda. He watched them come up the walk. Rob was thoughtfully carrying her suitcase, and he cupped his right hand under her elbow as they began to mount the stairs.

Abby's knees were trembling, so she didn't resent his old-school approach. She had never resented good manners, and Rob was an old-fashioned Southern gentleman. He was always slightly courtly toward the women in the department. Despite that, there wasn't a sexist bone in his body. That was one reason, she admitted, that she enjoyed working for him.

"Abby Sterling," Mickey said, putting out his hand. "As I live and breathe."

She could tell Mickey was surprised she was the one who had been selected to replace him as Deandro's bodyguard. Normally, she might have questioned that, sensitive to being the only woman to reach the level she had attained within this very male-dominated department. And that had been a struggle. Through the years she had learned to bite her tongue and overlook comments about what women could and couldn't do in police work.

Just like Deandro's opening remark at their first meeting. She had heard the same thing said a hundred times and had ignored it as meaningless, but for some reason hearing it from him had set off the spark of animosity that had flared between them.

It hadn't been directed at her. It had been made in response to someone's comment about his consumption of most of the beignets Rob provided for the first O.C. Unit meeting where Nick had been introduced. If he were ever injured in a shoot-out, Nick had joked, patting his flat belly, he hoped it wasn't up to some female partner to have to drag him out of harm's way. Abby had uncharacteristically taken the laughing rejoinder personally and as anti-female.

She didn't react the same way today, however, to Mickey's obvious surprise. Maybe because she had always liked Yates. Maybe because in this case she thought he might have a point, even beyond the obvious contrast between his bearlike body and her slight build. Considering the fact that she was also six months pregnant.

"I hear you're glad to see me," she said easily, slipping her hand into his. It was swallowed up by the ex-linebacker's meaty fist. "Our friend been giving you a hard time?" she asked.

Mickey's eyes cut to Rob, but they came quickly back. "Giving himself a hard time," he corrected.

Abby nodded, feeling petty. Her animosity to a well and whole Nick Deandro was one thing, but in the present circumstances it seemed only cruel.

"I think that came out wrong," Abby said. "I'm just having a hard time imagining Deandro as anything but..." She hesitated, searching for a one-word description of how the confident FBI agent had struck her on his arrival down here.

"Yeah, I know," Mickey said softly. "So did I."

No one said anything for a moment, but even their lack of comment about Abby's attempted apology was awkward.

"Anything I need to know before we go inside?" Abby asked.

Mickey made a face, sucking in his round cheeks as he thought. Finally he shrugged. "You bring your flak jacket?" he asked, but at least his eyes were smiling again.

Apparently he was willing to cut her some slack. Mickey had been around some of the times her temper had gotten the better of her and he certainly understood her past relationship with Deandro.

"That bad, huh?" she asked, smiling at his attempt at humor.

"I don't guess you can blame the guy. It must be pretty hard accepting something like this. Especially when all along everybody's told you..." He shrugged, leaving the rest of it unsaid, but they all completed the sentence in their heads.

Especially when all along everybody's told you that it's temporary. The amnesia. The blindness. Especially when you, and everyone else, were now coming to the conclusion that it probably wasn't.

"How about the routine around here?" Abby asked. She was pleased that none of the emotions she felt were in her voice.

"I just go with the flow. Whatever he wants to do. Maggie cooks, makes the beds. I read. Watch TV. There's not much else to do out here, Abby. Even less for him, I guess."

"Okay," Abby said, fighting her reactions to hearing about Nick's situation with a determined nonchalance. She wondered if either one of them was buying the act. "You off?"

"I can stay a day or two if you want."

He would if she asked, Abby knew, but the need to get home was in his eyes. Mickey had four kids and a wife, and he'd been away for months, except maybe for the occasional weekend.

"I'll be fine," she said. "Does he know I'm coming?"

"I told him there was going to be a changing of the guard. I couldn't tell him who, of course, because I didn't know. Rob said it would be better to let you introduce yourself."

She glanced at Andrews, who met her eyes without flinching. This was part of his plan. Deandro had been given no warning that she was coming, in hopes that something—her voice or her name, maybe—would trigger a reaction. A memory. An emotion.

She nodded, turning back to smile at Mickey.

"You doing okay?" he asked, his eyes examining her waistline, unembarrassingly assessing its added girth. From experience, she supposed. Four-time-father experience.

"I'm fine. Looking forward to the peace and quiet."

"Well, you'll have plenty of that. You have any trouble of any kind, you just call Sheriff Blanchard. The alarms go off at his office, too. But they haven't since we've been out here."

"That's reassuring," she said.

"Quiet as a tomb," Mickey asserted and then grinned a little sheepishly. "Not such a good comparison."

"Don't worry. I'm not superstitious. Not unless we have the resident ghost all these old places seem to claim."

"If we do, I haven't seen him. Or her."

"Hopefully, we can keep it that way," she said.

"You'll be fine," Mickey said. "Don't let him get to you."

"I won't," she promised. *Not if I can possibly help it.*

"You got to feel sorry for the guy," Rob said.

Abby supposed that was directed at her. A warning, maybe, to temper her usual acidity with Deandro, but Mickey responded.

"Yeah?" he said. "Well, if you do, don't do it so he's

aware of it. My best advice, Abby. Learned from experience. I'll wait in the car, Rob.''

"Thanks," Abby said. "Kiss the kids for me."

Mickey stepped down the steps of the porch, lifting a beefy hand in response. Abby and Andrews watched his departure for a moment. Mickey was eager to get home, but neither of them, it seemed, was eager to walk into this house. *Not at all eager,* Abby thought.

"You ready?" Rob asked.

She pulled her eyes away from Yates's ambling figure. "As ready as I'll ever be. And I still think this is a bad idea."

"Piece of cake," Rob assured her. "If it works, it works. If not, you put your feet up and relax for a couple of months."

She laughed, the sound soft and unamused. "Always the optimist, Rob. Except you're not the one who's going to be stuck out here with a blind guy who's mad at the world and looking for someone to blame for what happened to him," she said.

"I'm not *looking* for someone to blame," a voice assured her from just inside the darkened doorway. "I know damn well who was to blame."

At the first word, the timbre and accent of it unmistakable, the bottom fell out of Abby's stomach, just as it always did when the roller coaster reached the top and started to fly downward. Just as it had the last time she had listened to Nick Deandro's deep voice coming at her from out of the darkness.

Chapter Two

"But there is a small matter of being able to prove it in court," Nick added more softly. There was an undertone of bitterness in his voice, but whatever had been there before, anger Abby believed, seemed to have disappeared.

"It'll happen," Rob said reassuringly. "Just give yourself some more time."

Despite the kindness of the words, Abby read Andrews's tone as the same one he'd used when he first broached this idea to her. Adult to child. It had made her bristle then. It still did. She wondered what effect a meaningless platitude offered in that patronizing tone would have on someone like Nick Deandro.

Andrews went on, not waiting for a response to his assurance. "You remember Abby." It wasn't a question. It was framed in the familiar format of introduction, and that, too, seemed wrong, maybe even cruel in this instance.

"We've met before?" Nick questioned.

He had finally stepped forward into the filtered light, standing now in the open doorway where they could see him. He was barefoot, wearing worn Levi's and a pale blue cotton shirt, so faded as to be almost colorless. In spite his injuries and the long recuperation, the muscles revealed under the stretch of thin, aged fabric seemed as firm as they had always been.

He had lost a little weight, Abby decided, evaluating the

familiarity of his big body without really being conscious of doing it. Despite what had happened to him, Nick didn't look all that different. Not as she had expected—maybe even had hoped—he might. Nick Deandro didn't look nearly different enough to prevent the jolt of reaction deep inside her body.

His hair was longer than it had been the last time she had seen him. There was even a trace of curl now in the gleaming blue-blackness. That tendency had obviously been ruthlessly and deliberately controlled by the close-cut style he'd worn before.

Now it was as if he didn't care. Or maybe he simply hadn't noticed it, she acknowledged, her heart squeezing painfully in her chest at that realization. Because that was the other thing that was drastically different about Nick Deandro's appearance. The thing she'd been trying to avoid having to look at since he'd confronted them—the mirrored, opaque glasses that hid his eyes.

"I'm with PID," Abby said softly, fighting emotion. "Part of the Organized Crime Special Unit."

Control, she thought. She had demanded that of herself through these endless months, and she was determined not to give in now, just because she was finally faced with the reality of what had happened to Nick.

"Then you're saying we *have* met?" he asked.

"Yes."

"It seemed a simple enough question," Nick said, his words clipped, the tone caustic. "I like straight answers. The *first* time I ask a question."

"I guess we all do," Abby said evenly. If he thought he was going to intimidate her, he could damn well think again.

"How'd you get stuck?"

For a moment Abby wasn't sure he was still talking to her. The dark lenses weren't directed her way. Of course, neither were they focused on Rob. And she found that enormously disconcerting, as was not being able to read his eyes.

All of this was proving to be far more difficult than she could ever have imagined it would be, even in her worst nightmares, and she hadn't made it inside the house yet. She eased in a breath before she answered him, keeping the inhalation soft enough, she hoped, that he wouldn't be able to hear it.

"It's an assignment," she said.

"Did Yates ask to be relieved?"

Directed to her or to Rob? Again she wasn't sure, but thankfully, her boss fielded the question before she had to decide how to answer it.

"He's been away from his kids too long. I just thought it was time to assign someone else."

"Yeah?" Nick said. The single inquiring word was indicative of his disbelief. "He warn you I can be a bastard?"

The question was meant for her, Abby knew, despite the fact that the glasses were still focused at a point somewhere between the two of them. "He asked if I'd worn my flak jacket," she said. Straight answer. Just like he'd asked for.

"Did you?" There was a trace of something else in his voice now. Something besides bitterness. Maybe amusement.

"I can send for it," she said. "But you'll find my skin's pretty thick."

"Good," Deandro said. "It'll need to be."

He turned and disappeared as silently into the darkness behind him as he had appeared out of it. Abby took another breath, aware only now that she had missed a few. She waited, wanting to be sure that Nick was out of earshot before she spoke.

"Not exactly an auspicious beginning. And he doesn't remember me," she said. "It looks like all your maneuvering has been for nothing."

"I don't know," Rob said. "There was something there."

"Something called bad temper," Abby said. She bent and picked up the suitcase Andrews had put down as they stood talking and took a couple of steps toward the door.

"You let me carry that, Abby. You're supposed to be here to rest, remember. Nothing strenuous."

"There's nothing strenuous about carrying a suitcase. As much as I appreciate your concern, Rob, I can manage my own bag."

By that time, however, his hand had closed around the handle and was trying to manhandle it out of hers. She could either try to wrench it back or let it go. *And what the hell does it matter?* she wondered, finally releasing her hold. She wasn't going to fight Rob over a suitcase.

So she didn't bother to protest again, but simply continued past him into the dark interior. Her eyes gradually adjusted to the gloom, and for the first time she was able to distinguish some of the features of the house she would be living in for the next couple of months.

The cypress-floored entry hall was wide and spacious but dim, the outside light blocked by the overhang of the front gallery and the trees. On one side, more than halfway down the hall, a set of uncarpeted stairs led up to the second floor. A long parlor centered by a fireplace and a gilt mirror that dominated the room lay on the left. On the other side was a dining room with a table that could easily seat a dozen people.

The kitchen, which would have been added after the house was built, would be in the back, she knew, and the bedrooms upstairs. She wondered if the woman who cooked and cleaned lived in the main house. She couldn't remember Rob's exact words, but now that she thought about it, her impression was that wasn't the case. Which meant, she realized suddenly, that she and Deandro would be the only ones sleeping in the house at night.

"I want to show you the alarms before I leave," Rob said, interrupting that uncomfortable realization. "Don't be fooled by the age of the house. The security's pretty so-phisticated.''

She nodded, following him toward the back. The kitchen he took her to was modern and included most of the ap-pliances she was accustomed to, all the conveniences. There wasn't a dish out of place. And no sign of lunch being prepared either. No sign of the woman who was sup-posed to be working here.

Abby followed her boss across the beige tile to the se-curity-system control station on the wall. She strained to keep her mind on his explanation of how it worked, al-though she had seen systems like this before. She was aware of a prickling sensation on the back of her neck. As if someone were watching them.

That was something she'd have to get over pretty quickly, she decided. She couldn't afford to let this old house and its isolation spook her. She wouldn't be able to forgive herself for giving in to some primitive, intuitive feeling that might make her react in a way the department's good old boys would delight in characterizing as "just like a woman."

"And that's pretty much it," Rob said finally. "Got it?"

She nodded. "Where's the lady who cooks and cleans? Maggie? Isn't that what Mickey said?"

"Maggie Thibodeaux. She lives out in the old servants' quarters. This may be her day to go in for supplies. At our request, she drives to a little town more than thirty miles away to do the shopping. We don't want anybody to ques-tion why a woman who lives alone buys enough to feed three people."

"I assume she's been checked out?" Abby asked.

"She came with the property. She's kind of the caretaker out here when the house isn't in use. But she's had a thor-ough background check. The previous owners verified both her honesty and her ability to keep her mouth shut. That's part of the deal we made with her to allow her to keep living here."

"Seems like you're taking a chance, all the same."

"Maggie's got no interest in any of this. She doesn't care who uses the house as long as she gets to stay where she is. She's lived here all her life. She wanted to stay. And she's proven to be trustworthy on operations like this in the past."

"On ones that were this important?" Abby prodded. She didn't much like Rob's casual dismissal of her question.

"She doesn't have a clue who any of you are. You're just tenants, as far as she's concerned. Don't worry about Maggie. As a matter of fact, don't worry about anything at all. Deandro's been out here for months already, and nothing's happened. There's not been any sign anyone's still interested in him. No reason to believe they'll start being interested now."

The department's attitude toward that possibility seemed to her to be almost too casual, as if they had given up hope. And the arrangements they'd made to protect Deandro seemed pretty loose, too. Even given the location of this house and its security devices, for a witness as important as Nick Deandro might be, for a witness someone had already tried to kill, the Public Integrity Division seemed to be taking the dangers very lightly.

"Either they think he's dead or...maybe they know," Rob suggested softly.

"Know what?" Abby asked.

"That's he's not any danger to them. At least, not until— or *unless,* I guess I should say—he starts to remember."

ROB HAD INSISTED on carrying her bag upstairs. He walked down the hall beside her, peering into each of the bedrooms in turn. It was obvious which one was occupied, both by the set of freestanding weights and by Deandro's personal belongings on the dresser top, so neat as to be almost militarily organized.

Everything carefully in its place. Abby believed she understood the reasons for that. Or maybe that was simply one more of those stereotypical ideas she had about the blind.

She refused to move into the bedroom nearest to Nick's, the one Rob said Yates had been using. Her boss didn't make the logical objection to her rejection of that room, the one about security that she had expected. Instead he took her bag to the one she directed him toward, the bedroom at the other end of the hall. As far away from Nick's as she could manage.

"There's only one bathroom, I'm afraid," Rob explained. "Whoever did the modernizing downstairs apparently ran out of money before they did much upstairs."

"That's okay," she said. It wasn't, of course. That was the last thing she wanted. To share a bath with Nick. Suddenly her head was filled with images that were just as disturbing, maybe more so, than the ones she had experienced standing in the doorway of Nick's obsessively neat bedroom.

He doesn't remember me, she told herself. Not anything. Not the animosity. And certainly not the other. But she didn't analyze why that thought should be reassuring when she had come here with the express purpose of trying to make him remember.

She had researched this kind of traumatic amnesia in the endless months while she had waited for Nick to remember. Had waited for him to call. Had waited for him to be able to do something about what had been going on between them.

No matter what she had hoped, however, all the experts she read had agreed. The closer to the trauma lost events had occurred, the less likely it was that the memories of them would ever come back.

And after all, those few weeks they'd been involved, the time right before the shooting, weren't what Rob needed Nick to remember. They weren't the important part of what he had lost, as far as he or the department or the FBI was concerned. Those days—and nights—weren't important, she supposed, to anyone but her.

"You okay?" Rob asked again. She glanced up and realized that she had been standing with her hand on her stomach. Unconsciously touching the baby she carried.

"I'm fine. Maybe just a little tired," she lied.

She wasn't tired, except emotionally. After the upheavals of the last six months, she was emotionally exhausted. That was something else her obstetrician had been right about.

And instead of stepping back and forgetting all the things she couldn't do anything about, could not change, no matter how much she might want them to change, here she was— in the one place guaranteed to bring all those useless emotions roaring back. Along with a whole hell of a lot of new ones, she acknowledged. She realized that from the moment she had faced those dark, unfocused lenses downstairs.

Just put your feet up and relax, Rob had instructed. Only, there was nothing at all relaxing about this, and in her heart Abby knew it was going to get much, much worse before it got any better. If it ever got better. And everyone's hopes were riding on what happened out here. Including, she supposed, her own.

SHE JUMPED when the phone rang. Rob had thoughtfully moved it from Mickey's old room into hers before he left. Abby had been unpacking her clothes, hanging things in the tiny closet and folding her underwear to lay it in the lined drawers of the big East Lake chest. She grabbed the receiver on the third ring, expecting to hear Rob's voice, calling to check up on them.

But this wasn't a voice she had ever heard before, she realized quickly. It was female, and it was heavily accented. A distinct accent Abby was very familiar with, however, having heard it all her life.

"You the new one?" the voice had asked in response to Abby's hello, but the article had been pronounced "da." *Da new one.*

Abby's mind raced through the possibilities, but there was only one rather obvious conclusion to be drawn. "Maggie?"

"You switch off them alarms. I been out making groceries, and I'm coming in now. Don't want to meet up with the sheriff while I'm doing it." Except, of course, the words came out as "dem" alarms and "da" sheriff.

No one had mentioned to Abby if there was a code or a signal so she could verify this was really Maggie Thibodeaux. Again, the arrangements seemed too damn casual. Dangerous even.

But as Rob said, this watch had been going on for several months and nothing had happened. Maybe Mickey Yates had relaxed all those normal procedures with the slow, uneventful passage of that time. And this woman did know someone new was supposed to be arriving. That was a pretty good argument that she was exactly who she claimed to be.

"Okay," Abby said, giving in to that logic. "You come around to the kitchen door. I'll let you in there."

"I wasn't planning on unloading on the stoop. And I got my own key. But you come on down anyways. I'm looking forward to meeting the charmer they think is up to handling that man."

Abby could hear the rich chuckle that accompanied that comment in the few seconds before the car phone disconnected.

"LORD HAVE MERCY," Maggie Thibodeaux said softly when Abby opened the door, her .38 out but, as she held her arm straight down at her side, partially concealed behind her right leg. "And you pregnant, too."

"Too?" Abby questioned, but she knew what the woman meant.

Maggie shook her head in disbelief, her obviously dyed, too-red hair moving against the brown-freckled cheeks. She was very tall and thin, her almost skeletal frame swallowed by a cotton print dress gathered around her middle by a matching fabric belt that sported an enormous pearl buckle. That belt was the only thing that gave shape to her scarecrow figure.

"A woman *and* pregnant. Dawlin', that man's gonna eat you up for breakfast and be picking the little bitty chewed-up pieces of you outta his teeth all day long."

Abby laughed. She couldn't help it.

Surprise shone briefly in Maggie's dark eyes. "That's good," she said. "You got you a sense of humor anyways."

"He can't eat me. And I promise you if he tried, I'm too tough to chew," Abby said. She reached for one of the paper grocery sacks, but the caretaker pulled it away.

"Uh-uh," she said. "I carried babies. You don't need no backache to go along with the heartache."

For a moment, Abby wondered how she could possibly know, and then she realized that Maggie Thibodeaux could be talking about a hundred other things. Including Nick Deandro's uncertain temper.

"Heartache?" she asked, but she moved back out of the doorway, to let the woman enter and carry the bags over to the table.

Maggie put them down, and then she turned, putting her hands on angular, mannish hips that didn't look as if they were capable of expanding enough to carry a child. She surveyed Abby up and down. "How far along you?" she asked.

"Six months," Abby said. There was no way Maggie could make the connection. At least, no one else had.

Maggie nodded. "Be borned about Christmastime then."

"Close," Abby acknowledged.

"You all gonna be here until then?"

"I'm not sure," Abby said.

Her caution was both instinctive and protective. She supposed there was little danger of Maggie or anyone else connecting their presence out here with the D.A.'s ongoing indictments against the mob, which unfortunately were getting some play in the New Orleans paper, which had reliable inside sources. Those indictments, based on the source's information, had an excellent chance of getting results.

Nick's name had not been mentioned, of course, but still, the less said about police business, the better. Abby didn't believe there was such a thing as being too careful. Not with Nick's life. Not when she was charged with protecting it.

"You hungry?" Maggie asked suddenly. "I can make you a sandwich after I get the other stuff out of the trunk."

"I can do that. And I can help you with the groceries."

Maggie considered the offer a moment. "You put that gun down. Guns make me nervous. I don't like them things in my kitchen. I'll unload the groceries. You put them away. Cans go in the pantry. Most everything else goes in there."

She pointed to a side-by-side refrigerator-freezer and then headed back to the outside door. She didn't look back to see if Abby had obeyed her injunction against weapons in her kitchen.

Abby looked down at the gun she held. Waving it around at Maggie did seem a little ridiculous. The woman didn't seem to be a threat to anyone. Maybe this was why they all had gotten so complacent out here. It felt so normal. An old country house. And a lady who cooked and cleaned—familiar Southern terminology.

And whatever tinge of apprehension Abby had felt standing in this kitchen with Rob earlier this morning had disappeared. So normal, she thought again. She put the .38 down on the counter and began putting the groceries Maggie had brought in away.

They ate lunch sitting together at the kitchen table. Dreading her answer, Abby had asked about the possibility of Nick joining them, but Maggie shook her head.

"He don't like eating 'round other people," she said, the

sharp blade of her knife cutting in three parts the loaf of crusty bread she had unwrapped and put on the counter. "Makes him uncomfortable. Me, I always take a tray up to his room."

Abby nodded, trying not to think about that either, as she went back to pouring the tea that had been made sometime earlier and placed to cool in the refrigerator.

The roast beef po-boys Maggie fixed were wonderful, as was the potato salad that she piled high on one side of their plates. As they ate, Abby discovered that Maggie baked her own bread. And that she liked Nick Deandro.

"Didn't care much for that fat one. Messing around my house like a big ol' pig. Didn't ever pick up a thing he put down," Maggie said. "Make hisself a snack and leave everything out, all over my counters. The other one, now, that one's a gentleman."

Abby fought a smile, wondering if that distinction was based strictly on neatness. She, too, had a bad habit of leaving things out. The smile faded as she realized that doing so here might have consequences she preferred not to think about.

"This is the same guy who's going to chew me up and spit out the pieces?" Abby asked, injecting a lightness she didn't feel into her question.

"Oh, he's got hisself a temper, for sure. I ain't denying that. But when he loses it, it's for good reason."

"Such as?" Abby asked. She felt a little guilty about picking Maggie's brain, but the woman seemed more than willing to talk. And Abby was, she found, more than willing to listen.

"'Bout things he can't do no more. You know?" Maggie's brown eyes examined her face.

Abby nodded, not trusting her voice. This was something else she was going to have to get over—her emotional response to anything connected to Nick's blindness. Mickey had warned her.

"I guess that's not hard to understand," she said.

She picked up her sandwich again, but despite the home-made bread and the slices of roast and the thick, succulent gravy, she found she didn't want any more. She laid it back on the plate and noticed as she did so that her hand was trembling.

"Don't you worry," Maggie said softly, apparently having noticed the same thing. "He ain't really gonna hurt you. He ain't a woman-hurting kind of man. He's just all messed up inside right now."

Abby's eyes lifted from the sandwich. She suddenly felt an almost overwhelming need to confide in Maggie Thibodeaux. To tell her the secrets she had told no one else. To unburden on a perfect stranger the feelings she had kept to herself through these long months. Somehow, she felt Maggie would understand.

But she couldn't, of course. Nick Deandro didn't remember her. It was extremely unlikely now that he ever would. And no one else had ever known about their relationship or the guilt she had felt when Nick had been shot. Had he been found out because of their secret meetings? Because of his association with her?

She had been so surprised at herself when she had given him permission to come over the first time he'd called. And more surprised by her reaction when she'd opened the kitchen door, and he'd stepped inside, out of the protective darkness. It had been totally unexpected, even to her. Her response had been automatic and spontaneous, had seemed so natural. When she had moved into his embrace, her mouth opening eagerly for his first kiss, she had known that it was right she was there. So right.

But in the few weeks they had been involved, they had made no real commitments. She had willingly made love to Nick without them, the last time taking no precautions against exactly what had happened. That was so unlike her as to be an aberration of character. But she wasn't denying responsibility. Besides, she had always heard there were no accidental pregnancies.

Which meant that she must have intended to have Nick Deandro's baby. No one who knew either of them would ever believe that. And there was no reason to think Nick would believe it either. Not now. Not even if she told him.

Besides, Abby admitted, everything had changed. Nick had changed. *All messed up inside,* Maggie had said about him, but it was more than that, of course. Nick had physically changed.

And after months of brutal self-examination, Abby still didn't know how she felt about that. Maybe Maggie's phrase fit her as well, because she couldn't imagine the man she had loved being any other way than how he had been when she had fallen in love with him. And that hadn't included not being able to see.

She had secured the house, checking both the alarm system and the doors and windows before she went upstairs. Maggie had left after supper, as soon as she had finished cleaning up the kitchen. Suddenly, the house felt too big and too empty.

It wasn't, of course. But she hadn't seen Nick Deandro since he had appeared briefly this morning at the front door. She hadn't heard him either, so she had asked, just to make sure he was inside, before she locked the door behind the caretaker.

"He's here," Maggie had said. She had patted Abby's arm. "You go on and lock up the doors. He ain't gonna set off your alarms."

Abby had smiled, unoffended by Maggie's comforting gesture. It felt good to have somebody reassure her, even about such a small worry as that. She had worried alone for such a long time.

Millions of other women raised children by themselves, she had reminded herself over and over. She was as capable as they were. It was just not the way she had ever intended to do this.

Rings, mortgages and babies. Nick's words echoed in

her head, almost mocking. That was what she had always intended. And what Nick had suggested he wanted, too, but instead...

She flicked off the light at the bottom of the stairs, plunging the house into darkness. There should be a way to turn on the lights at the top from down here, she thought, but although her fingers examined the wall carefully, there seemed to be only the one switch.

She didn't turn it on again. There was a railing and as she stood there, eyes slowly adjusting to the darkness, the stairs seemed to materialize before her. As did a soft glow, building from the top down. Moonlight, she realized. Strong enough to penetrate the moss-festooned branches and drift into the upper level of the house.

She started up the steps, aware for the first time of a low ache at the base of her spine. She felt a splinter of unease push into her mind, and she firmly rejected it. The rational side of her brain reminded her of the car ride out here over some pretty crummy roads, of bending over the low bed to unpack her suitcase, and of the number of times she had reached up to put the cans Maggie had bought onto their proper shelf.

"What did he mean?" Nick asked.

His voice had been soft, but the words had come unexpectedly out of the moon-touched black at the top of the stairs, and her heart almost leaped out of her throat.

"God, Nick," she said, when she realized who had spoken. She hadn't been looking upward as she climbed, but now that she was, she could see him, silhouetted against the moonlight.

"Do you always have to hide in the damn darkness?" she said angrily. Her pulse had slowed, but the same sensation that she had felt on the porch was churning inside her again.

"Is it dark?" he asked, his voice velvet with feigned surprise. "Sorry. I hadn't noticed."

Abby's lips tightened, fighting nausea. Overreaction. Overreacting to him. To the whole situation.

"Is that supposed to be funny?" she asked angrily.

"Not to me," he said. "It's not a damn bit funny to me."

It took the wind out of her indignation, leaving it flat and limp and lifeless. Leaving her ashamed.

"What do you want?" she said, trying to control the tremor in her voice. She thought she could still hear the quiver, but she prayed that he could not.

It was like dealing with a strange animal. She knew that she couldn't afford to let Nick Deandro sense her fear. He was too bright, too astute not to figure out just from her tone that there had been more to their previous relationship than Rob had let on. Especially if she allowed the emotions she felt whenever she was around him to invade her voice and influence her behavior.

Only belatedly did she remember that the whole purpose of Andrews sending her out here was exactly that—to remind Nick of their previous relationship. She just wasn't sure that was her own agenda right now. Or whether she could deal with it.

"What did Andrews mean about you needing to rest?" he asked.

The question caught her off guard. It meant that Nick had been listening to what they were saying even before he'd appeared in the doorway. She tried to remember exactly what *had* been said, but her mind had been in such turmoil then—as it was now—that she couldn't be sure.

"Are you sick?" he asked, probing the dark silence. "Injured? Or maybe just emotionally distraught, Sterling?"

She read ridicule into the final words, and suddenly all the initial feelings Deandro's natural arrogance had once aroused in her reared their heads again, overcoming her pity.

"Are *you?*" she countered bitingly.

"I'm just trying to figure out why they would send you,"

he said. There had been no reaction to the mockery in her question. Apparently he still had better control of his emotions than she.

"Because I'm a good cop?" she suggested. There had been a thread of challenge in her voice. "Could that possibly be the answer to your question?"

"How many women are in the Organized Crime Unit?" he asked.

She hesitated before she answered, knowing he was right. "One," she admitted.

"So Andrews sends the one woman in the unit out here to play bodyguard. Would you like to explain the logic in that?"

"I'm as good a cop as any of the others," she suggested.

He laughed, the sound as dark as the staircase they were standing on. She could see as little as he could. Not expressions or body language. That was so hard, Abby thought again, just as she had when first confronted with those opaque glasses. So hard to know what was really going on in another person's head when you couldn't see him. Only a disembodied voice coming at you out of the darkness. So damn hard.

"Or do you suppose that, out of the kindness of his heart, your captain sent you here for recreational purposes?" Nick asked. "Or maybe you even volunteered for that assignment, Sterling. I *thought* there was something else in your voice..." He let the suggestion fade.

She waited too long to react, she knew. Too busy fighting memories. And when she managed the laugh, even to her it sounded forced, artificial. "Only in your dreams, Deandro," she said. "I'm a cop. This is an assignment to protect a witness. Whatever else you're *imagining*—"

"Tell me what you look like," Nick's voice interrupted. The timbre of it had changed, deepened perhaps. It sounded as it sometimes had in the familiar darkness of her small bedroom. Soft and very intimate.

"I don't think your having a physical description of me is pertinent to my ability to do this job," she said stiffly.

He laughed again at her awkward denial. "You're pretty small, I know. I could tell that much downstairs. From the sound of your voice."

"You think I'm too *small* to keep you safe? Because I'm a woman?"

He didn't say anything for a moment, and the silly comment hung in the air between them. "That bothered you for some reason," he said finally.

"I don't like sexism."

He laughed again. "That wasn't supposed to be sexist. I must be slipping."

"Slipping?"

"Here I am trying to proposition you, Sterling, and you're yelling discrimination."

"Proposition me?" She supposed her shock was clear.

"Or don't you sleep with blind guys? Blind guys who are 'mad at the world.' I think that was the phrase," he said.

Her words. The ones she had said to Rob at the front door. And anything she said in response to them would be wrong. It was almost like the old question about whether you were still beating your wife.

I don't sleep with blind guys. I don't sleep with any guys. But she had. She had slept with this one.

Something about your voice, he had said. Whatever would be in it now would be even more revealing. Because again she was remembering that small dark bedroom. And again she was hungry for his touch in the darkness. Such a long, empty hungriness.

"You think being blind gives you the right to eavesdrop on people?" she asked, fighting memory.

"Maybe. Especially if they're talking about me," he said reasonably.

"Don't flatter yourself. You're an assignment. That's all you are. I always discuss assignments with my supervisor."

Again the silence drifted between them before he broke it. "You don't like me," he said, his tone almost puzzled, as if she represented some problem he was determined to solve. "It's in your voice. But I swear there's something else there as well. I can hear it. I just can't quite figure it out."

"Guess that business about the other senses becoming more acute must be an old wives' tale," Abby said. Cruel, but not pitying. And hopefully not revealing.

"I don't know. Senses are…deceiving sometimes. Or revealing. Like whatever that is you're wearing…"

Her hand moved to her waist, spreading almost protectively over the stretched denim of the loose jumper she wore over a white cotton turtleneck top. And then, considering the circumstances, she realized what he meant. Not what she was actually *wearing*. Not her clothing. But the other very common meaning of that phrase. What she was wearing. Her scent. Her perfume.

She couldn't smell it. Her own senses were too familiar with the fragrance. Now it was almost like the natural aroma of her skin or her hair. But Nick had liked it. She knew because he had told her so. And foolishly she had worn it here.

"I'm tired," she said softly because she couldn't think of anything else to say. She realized that the whispered non sequitur sounded plaintive. Weary. But suddenly that was exactly what she felt. Weary of defending herself. Weary of being alone.

Now that she had seen him again, she was far more alone than before. Alone, even standing here again in the darkness with him. So damnably alone, considering all there had once been between them. "I'd really like to go up to bed now."

She almost added please, defeated by the aching emptiness. He didn't remember her. He didn't remember any of it, and she could never forget. She looked up, raising her eyes slowly to the head of the staircase. To the moonlight.

And found it empty. There was no one there in the shadowed darkness. On legs that trembled Abby climbed the rest of the steps, and when she reached the top, she looked down the long hallway. But the door to his room was closed.

It was a long time before she moved to the other end of the hall to hers. And an even longer time before she finally slept.

Chapter Three

Nick Deandro opened his eyes. *Still night,* he thought, preparing as he had on tens of thousands of other predawns to turn over, punch his pillow into shape, and go back to sleep.

Other times he had been pulled out of sleep by some subliminal sound, by a troubling dream, or maybe by the uneasy suspicion that he had been missing something in whatever case he was working on. The unconscious mind is a strange thing. Nick Deandro had always understood that. It keeps sorting through problems even during sleep, prodding the conscious mind to act, to think, to remember.

And this morning, when he finally did remember, he reached out to find by touch the bedside table and to read, also by touch, the hands of the glassless clock that rested there. Now oriented, he rolled over, facing the direction where he knew the windows were. Where the light should be.

He was testing, just as he had every morning that he had awakened in this bed. Testing to see if what they had all told him from the beginning was true.

It was no truer this day than it had been on any of the others. The blackness was still there, pervasive and unmitigated. He took a breath, fighting his despair, which was always worse in the mornings. That was another empty blackness, and one he couldn't afford.

He despised the soft sympathy he sometimes heard in voices, and he always overreacted to it. He wouldn't tolerate pity from those around him. He had decided months ago that neither was he going to tolerate it in himself. If this was what his life was going to be from now on, then he would damn well learn to cope.

Awake and listening now, he could hear the familiar sounds from the floor below. Maggie, cheerfully rattling pots and pans in the kitchen. That was routine. Morning ritual. And the other sound, unfamiliar for this time of day, took him a second longer to identify.

Someone was running water in the upstairs bath. Maybe that had been what awakened him. The sound of the water filling the tub. Mickey Yates had taken showers, usually at night, before he went to bed. And this noise wasn't exactly the same.

For a moment Nick thought that there might be something important about the sound of water running into a tub. The significance teased at the back of his mind, tantalizing, taunting him to remember what it meant. But he couldn't. Just as he hadn't been able to remember any of the other. Nothing of what had happened since he'd been in New Orleans.

There were the dreams, of course. Sometimes they, too, woke him. They drifted at him out of the darkness, visible, vivid with color, his vision unimpaired when he was dreaming. But despite that, they always reminded him somehow of another darkness. Reminded him of a lot of things. He awoke from them, his body trembling with need, his groin hard and aching.

He could never remember what—or whom—he had been dreaming about. But the incredible sense of loss was always the same. As desolate and as lonely as this other blackness he now lived in.

There was a woman involved in what had happened to him. He and the department knew that from more reliable evidence than the troubling dreams and his usually dependable gut instinct about cases. There had been the physical evidence that had been recovered from his clothing and his body after he'd been shot.

And of course, there was the woman who kept calling the hospital. Rob Andrews had been determined to find her, but she hadn't screwed up—not even once—to give them a chance at her.

She always used pay phones, booths in busy locations where no one paid any attention to anyone else. Places where the person using a particular phone might have changed ten times before the cops sent out to check on the call arrived.

"Our mystery woman," Rob called her. A little like the one he had sent out here to play bodyguard, Nick thought. A little like Abby Sterling, who was both distant and mysterious. And who, for some reason, didn't like him. That had been pretty obvious yesterday. She didn't like him worth a damn.

They had some background, he knew. He had put that together from the things she said. *He doesn't remember me,* she had told Andrews after Nick stepped back into the house. He had stopped in the hall before he went upstairs, wanting to hear what they would say to each other when they thought he was gone.

"He doesn't remember me" was exactly what Abby Sterling had said. And "all your maneuvering has been for nothing." Which meant that she or Andrews had thought that he might remember her. And even more telling, she had called him Nick on the stairs last night. His name—his first name—had slipped out of her mouth as naturally as breathing when he'd surprised her.

There had been something else in her voice last night. He had been trying to provoke a reaction when he'd confronted her, but the one he had gotten had been unexpected. Not the anger or her dislike of him. Those were understandable, given what he had said to her—his mocking suggestion that she might be Andrews's idea of a little recreation for a blind man.

Her reaction to that deliberate provocation was understandable. It was the other admission she made that had bothered him, long after he retreated to his own room. Her softly acknowledged tiredness and the defeat he had heard in her voice as they stood together in the darkness, separated by the rise of the stairs.

He still couldn't understand why Andrews had sent Abby Sterling out here, especially if she really needed some kind of rest cure. Not unless they had decided nobody was interested in him anymore.

And if that was the decision the NOPD had come to, Nick supposed he couldn't really blame them. He wasn't going to do them much good if he couldn't finger the people they needed him to finger. And so far...

He became aware that the sound of the running water had stopped. He tried to imagine Abby Sterling stepping nude into that tub, but he didn't have any frame of reference for that image. No idea of what she looked like. Except that she was small. That's what he had told her on the stairs, those simple words which had resulted in the accusation that he was sexist.

He didn't like women who played on that. Women who cried harassment when some idiot hung up a cheesecake calendar or told an off-color joke. To be fair, almost all the women he had worked with through the years cared a lot more about whether a guy could be trusted to do his job. Whether he was going to be there when things went wrong. They very rationally considered that far more important than whether someone guarded against every unthinking word that came out of his mouth.

If you wanted to, you could make something out of anything. Or out of nothing. He found himself hoping Abby Sterling wasn't that kind of woman.

And what the hell does it matter if she is? he wondered bitterly. *He* wasn't going to have to depend on her in a dangerous situation. Because he probably wasn't ever going to go back to work. At least not in law enforcement.

Angry with the negative direction of his thinking, a pessimism he'd fought for months, he pushed the cover off his body and stood up carefully beside the bed. He put his hand down, fingers groping to locate the edge of the bedside table again. Making sure he was exactly where he thought he was.

That was a lesson he had learned the hard way. He waited a moment before he moved, trying to picture the room and the exact location of the objects in it, mapping it out inside his head.

There were places he could go for this kind of training. They would teach him skills that would make it easier to navigate in this endless darkness. He was eventually going to have to think about that, he supposed. About a lot of other things as well. Like what the hell he was going to do with the rest of his life.

He heard the bathroom door open down the hall. He realized he was still standing beside the bed. Still nude. He hoped Sterling wasn't the kind who like to keep close tabs on her witness. In that case, she might be in for a hell of a surprise.

Unbelieving, he felt the undeniable response to the thought of his new bodyguard walking in on him right now begin to move through his body. And for the first time in a long while, Nick Deandro's lips tilted in amusement.

Then, remembering, they straightened back into a flat, cold line, jaw muscles clenched, as tight and hard as his aching body had been last night when her fragrance had floated up the stairs.

Familiar and evocative. He had made love to a woman once who had smelled like that. He knew it. He hadn't exactly known it last night, but for some strange reason he knew now that it was true. But there wasn't much doubt that that woman hadn't been the cold and disdainful Abby Sterling.

You don't sleep with blind guys? he had taunted her. She hadn't answered him, he remembered. But then, he supposed, she hadn't really needed to.

ABBY WAS SURPRISED to find Maggie already working in the kitchen when she came downstairs. To find the smells of the breakfast she was cooking invading the lower floor. She stood in the kitchen doorway for a moment before she spoke.

"How did you get in past the sensors?" Abby asked.

Maggie turned just her head, glancing up from the grits she was stirring. Her dark eyes examined Abby's face before she set the pan off the stove eye, the white-coated wooden spoon she had been using still held in her hand.

"There's no sensors in the back. I thought they would have told you that."

"And into the house?" Abby asked, thinking again that these arrangements were all a little too casual for her to be comfortable with. Even the fact that Maggie seemed to know exactly how the security system worked bothered her.

"Used my key. There's a delay before the alarm goes off. Time to reset the thing before it wakes up the sheriffs. You get any sleep, shug?"

The question was filled with concern, and Abby knew then that she did look as bad as the bathroom mirror had suggested. Her reflection had highlighted the bruised-looking darkness under her eyes and the tiredness within them. It had also pointed out the unnatural tension at the corners of her mouth.

The truth was she had spent a lot of hours last night tossing and turning. And then, when she had finally managed to go to sleep, she had spent more hours dreaming about the same things she had spent the last six months trying to forget. The confrontation on the stairs had brought all those buried emotions to the surface. Emotions she had *thought* were buried, anyway.

"Obviously not enough," she said. "What can I do to help?"

"You can just set yourself down at the table," Maggie said encouragingly. "You want it black or white?"

Coffee. Abby realized that was one of the aromas that had lured her from the hallway. The rich, fragrant smell of Louisiana coffee. She usually avoided caffeine but surely this late in her pregnancy one cup wouldn't matter.

"Black," she said. She pulled out one of the chairs, feeling as she had yesterday about the suitcase. It was just not worth struggling over. Maggie put a mug in front of her and poured a stream of black, chicory-enhanced coffee into it.

"A little sweetness?" she said.

Abby shook her head, picking up the cup and savoring the warmth against her fingers. Enjoying the smell of the coffee. And the first sip was almost as good as those preliminaries.

"You got to get over it," Maggie said softly. She was still standing by the table, holding the handle of the coffeepot with a folded pot holder, her left hand touching the glass knob on its top. "Whatever happened to you, you can't be thinking about it now. You got a baby coming. The time for grieving is past."

"I know," Abby said, looking up to smile at her.

"My mama used to say if you can't change it, there ain't no use worrying over it. That's still true as preaching."

"I guess you're right," Abby said.

Whatever was going on in her life was none of this woman's business, but Abby didn't feel even a glimmer of resentment over the unsought advice. It was almost a relief to have someone notice that she wasn't doing all that well. No one else in her life seemed to be aware of it.

"You not grieving over getting that baby, are you?"

Abby looked down into her mug, thinking about that. She had been grieving about the situation, maybe. About the loss of Nick. Worried about rearing a child by herself.

But not grieving about carrying the baby. There was no grief in that. And no regret. She didn't believe either of those things had ever had a place in her turbulent feelings these last few months.

"No," she said truthfully.

"Well, that's good," Maggie said, sounding relieved. "Babies come when they will. When the good Lord wants them to."

Or when you don't do anything to prevent them, Abby thought, almost amused by the fatalistic comfort the woman offered.

"I'm gonna take his plate on up. You want me to fix yours before I go? Or maybe you just want to drink your coffee in peace."

"Just the coffee, thanks," Abby said, lifting her head from her pretended concentration on her mug to smile her thanks. "Just for now anyway, Maggie."

"Don't you let him mess with your head," Maggie warned.

Abby's question must have been reflected in her eyes.

"That one's not an easy man, for sure," Maggie went on. "He don't let things rest. Always thinking about stuff. That's half of what's wrong with him. I done told him that."

She turned back to the stove and began dipping eggs and sausage and grits onto a thick stoneware plate.

Or maybe what's wrong with him is that suddenly he's blind and has forgotten a big chunk of his life, Abby thought. A part of his life which, good agent that he was, Nick Deandro would probably give anything to remember. All that was surely enough, she decided, to justify a little ill temper. Maybe even enough to explain what he had said on the stairs last night.

Maggie was right. Nick thought things through carefully. Abby had been aware of that even in the short time she had known him before he was shot. Always thinking everything through. Like what he had been trying to find out

when he confronted her last night—the real reason Rob
Andrews had sent her here.

That's what had kept her awake last night. Knowing that
she'd better get prepared, because eventually Nick was going to figure that part out. And she needed to decide what
she was going to tell him when he did.

WHEN THE GROUNDS alarm went off a few minutes later,
Abby was truly surprised, despite her previous concerns
about loose security. She eased herself up out of the kitchen
chair, easing her gun out at the same time. She had been
hiding out in the kitchen, she supposed, drinking coffee
while Nick Deandro ate his breakfast upstairs.

But if the alternative to hiding was another meeting like
the one last night, then she had decided that she preferred
being a coward. After her bath this morning she had left
off the customary and unthinking dabs of perfume. No
more memory triggers until she was ready to deal with their
possible effects.

Maggie, who had just returned from her trip upstairs,
looked over at the alarm box. "Front walk," she said non-
chalantly. "We got us some company." Her eyes returned
to the plate she was dishing up for Abby, leaving Abby to
walk over to kill the alarm. Apparently feeding her was
more important to Maggie than the fact that someone had
come calling.

But the caretaker might not realize the implications of
this unannounced visitor, Abby thought. The implications
of any visitor who had shown up at what was supposed to
be a safe house without phoning ahead. Abby hurried
through the dim entry hall and slipped into the dining room.
She twitched the damask draperies aside a fraction of an
inch to look out.

A marked police car, topped with the unmistakable bar
of multicolored lights, was sitting where Rob had parked
his car yesterday. And the man coming up the walk wore
a khaki uniform, his narrow hips circled by a thick black

gun belt holding all the necessary implements of his pro-
fession. *The local law,* Abby thought. Sheriff whatever-the-
hell-his-name-was.

He was above medium height, but not as tall as Nick,
she decided, watching him walk, and he was far more wiry
in build. His hair was brown, threaded with streaks of blond
or gray that caught the dots of sunlight that were being
diffused through the avenue of oaks.

Abby tried to remember the name Mickey Yates had
said. Broussard? She shook her head, knowing that wasn't
right, but she dropped the curtain she'd been holding and
started to the front door. The bell rang before she reached
it.

When she opened the door, the .38 still in her hand but
again concealed behind her leg, she watched the sheriff's
eyes widen. They were blue, darker and richer in color than
Nick's. His skin had been darkly weathered, but the lines
in it were interesting, especially the minute white ones that
fanned out from the corners of his eyes, marks put there
by constantly squinting into the strong glare of the Southern
sun.

His cheeks were lean enough that the slow smile he gave
her creased them. He had taken off his hat, and he dangled
it now in the fingers of his left hand, right in front of the
buckle of the belt that held his own gun.

"Can I help you, Sheriff?" Abby said.

His eyes held hers another moment, but he couldn't resist. She watched the blue gaze slide downward to her
waistline, examine it quickly, and then come back up to
meet hers again.

"Captain Andrews gave me a call yesterday afternoon.
Said someone new was coming out. I thought I'd drop by
to introduce myself. Let you know we're around if you
have any trouble."

"Then I guess I don't have to call your office and report
that the alarm you just set off doesn't mean anything,"
Abby said.

It was a rebuke, and the blue eyes indicated that he had gotten her message: He should have called. According to Rob, this guy was aware of what was going on out here, even if he didn't know who it was they had in protection.

"Sorry about that," he said. "Didn't mean to worry you."

She nodded. And then she let the silence build. He was the one who had come out here unannounced and uninvited. He must have had some reason. Maybe just curiosity. Maybe boredom. But she hadn't called him and asked him to show up, so conversation should be his responsibility.

"Everything going okay?" he asked finally.

"Everything seems to be fine," she agreed.

"Do I smell Maggie's coffee?" He cocked his head a little, raising his nose like a hunting dog. He shifted his weight at the same time, the boards of the old veranda creaking under his polished boots.

Local law, she thought again, trying to decide. Local law whose goodwill she just might need. There was no harm, she supposed, in giving the man a cup of coffee. Rob had vouched for him, and judging from Nick's behavior in the last twenty-four hours, there was little danger of the sheriff running into their reclusive witness.

"And you probably can smell Maggie's breakfast as well," she said. *Cops and doughnut shops,* Abby thought in amusement. But she had eaten more than a couple of complimentary beignets in her career. "Have you had your breakfast, Sheriff?"

His lips didn't move, but his eyes were suddenly filled with an answering amusement. It lightened the blue. He was really a very attractive man, Abby thought. Not handsome, but rugged-looking. A Marlboro-Man type, especially in the khaki uniform.

"Not that kind," he said. "Not Maggie's kind of breakfast."

"Then why don't you come in," she invited. "I'm Abby Sterling, by the way."

She stepped back from the door and slipped her gun back into its holster. She supposed it looked ridiculous worn over the long pink sweater, which was cut full enough to cover the bulge of the baby. She had given in and bought a few pairs of maternity slacks and some jeans, but she had refused to even consider the tentlike tops that she had fingered and then rejected at Wal-Mart.

For some reason, she was very aware of the sheriff behind her as she walked, leading the way through the dimness of the hall and into the brighter kitchen. Maggie turned as they entered. She had already set two plates on the kitchen table, and she was again holding the metal coffeepot, ready to add coffee to the two mugs that sat beside them.

"Maggie," the sheriff said. "How you doing this morning?"

"Doing fine, Sheriff Blanchard," Maggie said, directing a stream of dark liquid expertly into the mug Abby had been using before the alarm went off. "How you doing?" she asked without lifting her eyes.

At least now she had his name, Abby thought. That might be convenient since it appeared she was going to be having breakfast with him. And she was hungry, she realized, even if breakfast was not one of her favorite meals. Even if this one might be more appropriate for a stevedore down at the docks than for a woman her size. What Maggie had put on the two plates while she answered the door looked very good.

"Y'all sit down," Maggie urged, "'fore it all gets too cold to be fit to eat."

Blanchard moved before Abby could, politely pulling out her chair. She glanced at him, but his face was innocent of any expression. As she sat down, she thought she saw movement at the corner of his mouth, but she couldn't be sure.

When he took his place at the table across from her, sitting down with a creak of leather, an almost pleasant noise Abby was certainly accustomed to, his face and his eyes were as guileless as a schoolboy's. After a few minutes, amused by her realization, she decided that he had an appetite to match.

Maggie waited on them with careful but unobtrusive attention, keeping the coffee hot and the buttered biscuits in the basket replenished. Abby lost count, but she thought Sheriff Blanchard had eaten six of those.

"How do you manage to do that?" Abby asked finally as he began to spread pear preserves on another. Judging by the mason jar the preserves were in and the paper label that included nothing but a date, Abby guessed Maggie had made those, too.

The sheriff's blue eyes lifted from the biscuit to question hers. "Manage what?" he asked.

"To eat like that and still stay...in shape?"

"My daddy never put on weight either. Ate like a horse and never gained an ounce. Good metabolism, I guess. Or the fact that taking care of this parish keeps you plenty busy."

"I understand your daddy was sheriff here before you?" Abby picked up her coffee, looking at him over the rim of the mug, politely waiting for his answer before she took the next sip.

"Captain Andrews tell you that?"

She nodded. His eyes had moved to Maggie, who was standing at the sink, her back to them as she washed the pots and pans she had used to cook breakfast.

"He was sheriff here for more than thirty years," Blanchard said, his gaze shifting back to hers after a few seconds. "I grew up in that office. Felt like Opie most all my life."

She laughed aloud, the sound quick and spontaneous, and after a moment he joined her. "And that's not such a bad life, either, I guess," he added softly.

"I wouldn't think so," Abby agreed. "It must be pretty quiet around here."

"Most of the time. A few fights. Drunks. Some domestic violence, usually as a result of too much beer. No gangs. No drugs. Not that I know of, anyways. It's easier to keep all that out of here. Easier than someplace like New Orleans."

She nodded agreement, taking another sip of her coffee.

"So how'd you end up being a cop?" he asked. "Somebody like you."

"Somebody like me?" she repeated, her eyes lifting to his.

"Refined, I guess I mean. Probably college-educated. And I know what cops make in New Orleans. What y'all do for that little bit of money doesn't seem to me like it's worth the risk."

"You're a cop," she said, smiling at him. She had heard this or a variation of it a hundred times. She still didn't have an answer. Not one that made much sense to most people.

"Not there. I go home at night, and I sleep real good. Most nights, anyways. Not a call. Not a problem. And there's not any of the real meanness you all got to deal with. Crazy folks cutting each other up for a dollar or a dime bag. Drug dealers. Mafia. And I got respect in this parish. Nobody looks at me like I'm not fit to sweep trash off the sidewalks."

Abby couldn't deny that was the attitude of most citizens of the Crescent City toward their police force, especially given the corruption that had come to light in the last few years. But she had grown tired of trying to defend the cops in her city, so she decided to answer his original question instead.

"We all get in law enforcement for the same reasons, I think," she said. "Ultimately the same reasons. Trying to do good. To make a difference. Fight the bad guys."

"Protect the women and the children," he added with a touch of mockery, but his smile had reached his eyes again.

Hers was a familiar litany, she supposed. Even she had

wondered, especially since she had been involved in the corruption investigation, if there was anyone else left who still believed in all that.

She couldn't really explain why she was a cop. Not, apparently, in any way that made sense. Not even to another law-enforcement officer.

"I got to go," he said, pushing up from the table, gun belt creaking again. "Nice to meet you, Ms. Sterling. Maggie, you did yourself proud this morning."

"Thank you, Sheriff," Maggie said without turning around.

"I'll walk you out to the front," Abby offered, sliding her chair back. He was there before she could get up, pulling it out for her and putting his hand under her elbow, much as Rob had done yesterday.

She didn't pull away, but she met his eyes, letting hers reflect the tinge of coolness that was appropriate. He removed his hand, but he didn't hurry over the process.

Because he was a man who was very secure about just exactly who he was, Abby thought. About his masculinity. And secure in his position down here. His power. Opie Taylor all grown up and right at home.

MAGGIE HAD ALREADY cleaned off the table when Abby got back to the kitchen. She was scrubbing the dishes they had used in fresh dishwater, the bubbles foaming around the sunburned darkness of her freckled hands as she worked.

"I think he liked your biscuits," Abby offered. She walked over to the alarm box, intending to give the sheriff time to get out of the range of the sensors before she turned it back on.

The sound Maggie made in response was part harrumph and part something else. Surprised, Abby turned to look at her. Her back was stiff under the starched cotton of the housedress she wore.

"Should I not have invited him in?" Abby asked.

No answer beyond the soft clink of the dishes Maggie was handling. She turned on the hot water, letting it push the soap off the plate she held under its stream. Then she put the dish into the drain tray, and shut off the water with her elbow.

"Maggie?" Abby questioned.

"It don't matter," she said. Her voice was as stiff as her shoulders, thin and tight beneath the faded cotton print.

"I won't ask him in again if you don't want me to."

There was something going on here that Abby didn't understand, but it was obvious Maggie was annoyed. Or upset. And the only thing that had happened that might have brought that about, that might have changed the relationship that had been growing between them, was Sheriff Blanchard's visit.

"It don't make no never mind to me what y'all do. Food was here. He might as well eat as not."

Abby hesitated, still unsure what had provoked this reaction. Finally she nodded, and then felt foolish because Maggie still had not looked at her. She armed the system and waited a second to make sure that all was well.

When she turned around, Maggie was watching her over her shoulder. The caretaker's head turned quickly, the dark eyes dropped, and her attention seemingly returned to the dishes in the drain tray.

"Is there something I should know about Sheriff Blanchard, Maggie? Something I don't know that you need to tell me?" Abby asked softly. Woman to woman. There had been an element of trust in their short friendship. She'd hate for something to happen that would destroy that.

"I don't know nothing about that man. Nothing that everybody else in this parish don't know, too."

Unconsciously, Abby nodded. This was turning out to be a hell of an assignment, she thought. Nick Deandro was hiding out upstairs. She was avoiding him by hiding down here. In the meantime, she had invited into this supposed safe house someone that Maggie, who had lived in this parish all her life, didn't like. Obviously didn't like. Or didn't trust.

Opie Taylor, indeed.

Chapter Four

By the end of her first week at the safe house, Abby realized that Mickey Yates had been exactly right in what he'd told her. There was really nothing to do out here.

And if it hadn't been for seeing the occasional light out on the bayou, her periodic phone conversations with Rob, and Sheriff Blanchard's visits, she might have been forced to wonder if there was a world still functioning beyond that quiet avenue of oaks.

At first she had been amused when Blanchard arrived every morning, just in time for breakfast, almost as if he could smell Maggie's cooking all the way to his office. Maggie had begun setting two places at the table, although she still treated the sheriff as if he weren't welcome. Abby had never solved the puzzle of Maggie's attitude, and it hadn't gotten any better.

However, the more Abby was around the sheriff, the more she liked his quiet humor and easy manner. Apparently he felt the same way about her. The last two days he'd shown up in the late afternoon, on his way home, he said, and tonight he'd accepted her invitation to stay for supper. She welcomed the company, and after all, he presented her with no cause for anxiety. Indeed his frequent presence out here was reassuring.

After that first morning, Blanchard was careful to phone ahead so she could cut off the alarms. He was still friendly, and he hadn't again stepped over the line of being familiar. He was a fellow law-enforcement officer, so they had a lot of things in common, a lot to talk about.

And as the slow days had passed, Abby found herself looking forward to his arrival. Another voice. Just someone to talk to. And if this existence was lonely and boring for her, she often wondered, what must these last few months out here have been like for a man who had once been as vital and active as Nick Deandro?

Nick, she thought again, always coming back to the same problem. Surprisingly, there had been no further confrontations with the man she had been sent out here to protect. Indeed, she had seldom seen him in the last seven days. Given what had happened on the stairs that first night, she supposed she should be grateful for that, as she began to slip out of her clothes at the end of another long, uneventful day.

As she did every night, she laid the .38 down on the bedside table, right beside the book she had brought up with her. Her choices from the small bookshelf she had found in the parlor were pretty limited.

At least this one was a novel. Maybe a mystery, she thought, going strictly by the sound of its title. The dust jacket that might have confirmed her guess had disappeared, a long time ago to judge by the faded binding.

It felt good to get out of her clothes and into her long and roomy flannel nightgown. Its warmth and softness were comforting. It was a little bit of home. Something that was familiar.

She turned back the covers and crawled into bed, stretching out gratefully. She lay there a moment, deliberately letting the tightness in her back and shoulders relax against the mattress. Deliberately letting her guard down.

All week she had thought about why she had really come out here. Had thought about Nick. Because she had expected every moment to look up and find him standing in a doorway, the glint of his glasses trained somewhere near her face, ready to question her motives again. But she hadn't, and despite her anxiety over the possibility, she admitted that had been a disappointment.

As far as she could tell, Nick Deandro seldom left his room. And when Maggie went up and down the stairs to carry or retrieve his tray, she had volunteered no information about him. So it had been a damn long week, Abby thought again.

Trying to put Nick out of her head, something that was almost impossible to do now that she was living in the same house with him, she reached for the book she had found. It smelled faintly of mildew when she opened it, leafing through the preface pages to find the beginning of the first chapter.

WHEN SHE WAS JERKED awake by the noise, the low light on the table beside her bed was still on. The book lay across the hump of her belly, spread-eagled and mostly unread. Apparently she had been sleeping too soundly, like the drunks who stretched out on the benches along the river or curled in the sheltered doorways of the Quarter when the rain turned cold.

She was disoriented for a moment, trying to remember where she was and what she was doing in this strange bedroom. And when she did, a more important consideration moved into her consciousness. What had awakened her?

She had some memory of the sound, something that had been loud enough to wake her—an unfamiliar noise in this normally quiet environment. What *kind* of noise it had been, however, she couldn't have said if her life depended on it.

She lay perfectly still a moment, holding her breath and listening to the still night around her. There was nothing else. No other sound except her own too-strong inhalation when she finally allowed herself to draw another breath.

Her eyes shifted to the windows, but there was only darkness beyond the sheer curtains, gathered in folds across the black glass. She remembered finally to look at her watch. It was almost 3:00 a.m. Not Maggie, then, coming in to start breakfast. And the only other person in the house was…

Nick. Who was blind. Could Nick have been responsible for the noise she had heard? Was it possible that he had gotten up in the night for some reason and then bumped into something? Or fallen over something?

The unwanted image of that flight of steep stairs and of a sprawled, broken body at the foot of it tightened her throat. Her first instinct was to rush out into the hall. To call to Nick. To verify that he wasn't injured.

But she fought against that highly emotional response. She couldn't take the chance that was what she had heard. Because, of course, this might be something very different. And her job, the reason she had been sent here, was to protect Nick Deandro from whoever had tried to kill him before and might try again. Despite the fact that the bad guys didn't *seem* to be very interested in Nick Deandro anymore, she couldn't afford to take the chance that they weren't.

Worse case scenario, she reasoned, fighting her panic over just the thought of Nick falling, was that there was an intruder in the house. And that whoever it was had come to finish what they had started six months ago. To permanently silence Nick.

Anything less than that—a fall or accident of some kind—would be far better. And she had no choice about what she should do. No matter what her heart told her about getting to Nick as quickly as she could, she was here to play cop. To do her job and do it exactly as she had been trained.

She could feel the adrenaline now, moving into her bloodstream, and she welcomed it. It seemed to have cleared the last of the cobwebs, because those thoughts and decisions had been shooting through her brain with light-ninglike rapidity.

She threw the covers back, pushing them the rest of the way down with her feet, and clambered out of bed. She hesitated, only for a second, again listening. Ears straining to hear movement. Straining to hear anything.

She realized she was shivering, although the house wasn't cold. Maybe that was just the abruptness of the change from deep sleep to waking. Or the sudden shift from being covered warmly by the sheet and a couple of quilts to standing here clad only in her nightgown, substantial though it was. Or maybe, she admitted, it was fear. Not for herself, of course, but for the man she was supposed to be guarding.

She reached over and turned off the bedside lamp. Her hand unerringly dropped from the switch to the .38, finding the patterned grip even in the sudden plunge into darkness. She stood a few seconds more, still listening, as she allowed her eyes time to adjust. As it had last night, moonlight touched the house, fingering in through the curtained windows of her room.

She tiptoed across the wooden floor and pushed aside the sheers that covered the glass to look out on the grounds. Below, she could see the walkway that led up to the front door and, beyond it, the drive.

The trees cast wavering shadows on the pale dirt of the path. Nothing moved but the branches, stirring in the breeze she could see but couldn't feel. But still, watching the shifting pattern the leaves made on the dirt, she shivered again.

Whatever had made the noise hadn't been in this room. Nor had it been outside the house, she realized. It had been too loud for that. It had come from somewhere beyond the door she was hiding behind.

She crossed the room and then paused beside the closed door. There was no sound from the hall beyond. She reached out and caught the knob, turning it soundlessly with her left hand, pulling the door slowly inward. Her right hand was occupied with the gun, trained on the widening opening.

Nothing happened. And there had not been a repeat of whatever she had heard initially. Quiet as a tomb out here, Mickey Yates had said. And now it really seemed to be.

She slipped through the narrow opening, her eyes examining the hall that stretched silently before her, almost ghostly in the dim moonlight. Shadows aligned themselves out of the darkness into familiar shapes. The newel post. The linen press at the end of the hall. Nothing here that shouldn't be.

The head of the stairs was at the opposite end, right outside Nick's door. Which was open, she suddenly realized. The rectangle where the closed door should show, pale and regular as those of the rooms between them, was black instead. Nick's door was open, but she couldn't be sure what that meant.

She was moving now, hurrying to get to him. However, all her senses were alert, with both hands fastened around the grip of her gun, one supporting the other, as she hugged the wall. Her first stop was the bathroom, the most logical place Nick might be in the middle of the night.

It was across the hall from her room. Its door was open as well, and she stood in the frame, sweeping the gun before her in a semicircle, muzzle following the careful survey of her eyes. Nothing. There was no one here. One possibility eliminated.

She moved down the hall, hurrying to the door of the next bedroom. It was closed, so she turned the knob and pushed the door slowly inward, her eyes examining the interior. The unoccupied room was dark except for the silent presence of the cold, silvered moonlight. And it was empty.

She didn't bother to close the door behind her, and she increased her speed now, moving purposefully on bare feet across the hall to the next. But there was nothing there either, and she wasn't sure whether to be relieved or more apprehensive.

All that was left to check was Nick's room. She stopped

beside his open doorway, listening to the darkness. Listening for his breathing. For what would be the reassuring, yet unfamiliar sound of Nick's snoring. Listening for anything that would give her a clue as to what was going on. And she heard nothing.

The door was only partially open, and she couldn't see the whole room as she had been able to with the others. She put her left palm flat against the wood and pushed gently. The door moved noiselessly, the opening slowly widening. She stepped inside, her eyes seeking the bed, trying to find its occupant.

"Deandro." The whisper was right at her ear. Nick had stepped out of the shadows behind her, leaning over her shoulder to speak. "Downstairs," he added, just as softly.

So softly both words had been almost soundless. Her breathing had frozen at the first whisper, but by the time he had spoken again, her brain had accepted that this was Nick and not a threat.

She didn't flinch when he put his hand on her shoulder. It tightened briefly, and she questioned what that pressure was supposed to mean—reassurance or identification. But he had already spoken to her, and in doing so had revealed his hiding place. She wondered how he had known who was entering his room.

He hadn't released his grip on her shoulder. Had he touched her because he intended to go downstairs with her? Using his hand there to guide him as he followed her through the darkness?

If that *was* what he was planning, she thought in panic, then he could damn well think again. The logistics of that nightmare journey invaded her head when she should have been thinking about the intruder. About whoever was downstairs.

She turned her head to the side, putting her mouth nearer his ear. "You stay right here," she ordered, trying to keep her whisper as low as his had been.

She began to turn, but his fingers tightened over her col-

larbone, digging strongly enough into her flesh to prevent
her from stepping back out into the hall. Strongly enough
to elicit a small gasp of response.

"I'm going with you," he whispered.

She shook her head, furious with him. If she allowed
him to go downstairs, she wasn't sure she could keep him
safe. She needed him up here. She needed him to be where
he couldn't get hurt. Out of harm's way.

He didn't react, and she finally realized that he couldn't
see what she was doing. "No," she breathed. She raised
her hand and pushed angrily at his fingers. They didn't
respond, except to tighten again, painfully. "Stay here,"
she demanded.

"Listen," he ordered.

Despite the softness of the command, she automatically
obeyed. The noise from below was almost as quiet as their
voices, indistinct and distant, whispering up the stairs from
the darkness as her perfume must have floated to him that
night.

"You call the sheriff?" Nick asked.

"No," she admitted. "Not yet."

"Do it," Nick ordered.

"By the time he gets here—" she began, trying to con-
vey her frustration and at the same time keep her voice
quiet enough not to endanger him.

"You don't know how many of them are down there,"
he interrupted. "Call for back up, Sterling."

"I'm armed, and—"

"Your room. We both go. You make the call. Do it now,
damn it."

His hand was still controlling her. She probably could
have broken away from him, but he was right, of course.
By now, she had realized they were safer here. For the time
being, at least.

And no matter what was happening below, her job was
to keep Nick Deandro safe. *Not* to go rushing into a situation she didn't have enough information about, maybe get-

ting herself shot in the process. Calling the sheriff made a whole lot more sense. It's what she should have done in the first place, and she was sure Nick was thinking that.

"Okay," she said finally, giving in to his logic.

She took a step, half expecting the punishing grip to tighten again over her shoulder. She would have a bruise there tomorrow, she knew. Maybe she even deserved one.

She should have made that call before she left her bedroom. It would have been the smart thing to do, but she hadn't done it. Instead she had rushed out into the darkness, despite her attempt at rationality, because the image of Nick lying injured at the bottom of those stairs had been too compelling. Too frightening.

His fingers rested lightly now on the top of her shoulder, and he followed as she walked, careful to stay in the center of the narrow hall because she was aware she was his guide. Back down the route she had just traversed and into her room. When she reached the phone, she picked it up and punched in the single digit Rob had told her would put her in touch with the sheriff.

She was surprised, however, when he answered. "Blanchard," he said, his voice fogged with sleep, but still official.

"This is Sterling," she whispered. "We have an intruder."

"On my way," he said. "Front door." And then the connection was broken.

A man of few words, Abby thought, carefully putting the receiver back in its cradle. She was suddenly aware that Nick had removed his hand. He was still standing beside her, but he was no longer touching her.

"Five minutes," she said, repeating what Rob had told her.

He nodded. There was enough light in the room that she could see the movement of his dark head. If she had been alone, she would have gone over to those windows, where she had earlier looked out on the moonlit drive, and watched for the sheriff.

Instead, she moved to stand in front of Nick, putting herself and the .38 she was still cradling in both hands, between him and the door. And they waited together until the siren destroyed the stillness.

"WELL, WE DIDN'T find your intruder," the sheriff said, "but we think we pretty much know what happened."

Abby was standing in the entry hall, her arms crossed over her breasts, rubbing her left hand unthinkingly against the soft flannel of her right sleeve. Her right hand still held the .38, but her grip on it had relaxed.

She had waited here after she opened the front door, letting Blanchard and his sleepy-eyed deputy make the search of the downstairs without her.

"What *happened?*" she repeated, questioning the wording he had used.

"Raccoon. Maybe a possum. You got a pretty big mess in the kitchen, but at least you don't have a human prowler."

A raccoon, Abby thought, feeling the hot blood sweep upward into her throat. She had called the parish sheriff out in the middle of the night because of a raccoon?

"How could a raccoon get in?" Nick asked from behind her.

She hadn't even realized he had come downstairs, but then she had followed the sheriff down the hall toward the kitchen, away from the foot of the stairs Nick had just silently descended.

"Window left open, maybe. Loose screen. They're pretty ingenious."

"And the alarms?" Abby asked. "Why didn't the alarm go off?"

The sheriff shook his head, but his eyes hadn't moved back to her face. They were examining Nick's instead. And when they finally did, he had no answer for her.

"I can't tell you exactly *how* it happened, Abby. How something wild got in. But based on the look of the kitchen, that's our best guess as to what you heard. The garbage can's turned over. Stuff is scattered all over the floor like he was prowling through it. That doesn't look to us to be the work of an intruder. Leastways not the kind you folks are worried about." There was a touch of amusement in that, and Abby resented the implication.

"I don't understand how a window could be open and the alarm not go off," Abby said stubbornly, trying to think about any way that might have happened. If Maggie had left a window open, then the alarm should have sounded when Abby switched the system back on after she left. That was the way it was supposed to work.

"Sometimes…" the sheriff began, and then he hesitated. He shifted his feet a little, and the leather belt creaked with the movement of his body. "Sometimes these things just happen. You think you've got the thing turned on, and…" He shrugged, seeming uncomfortable for the first time since she'd known him.

"I turned it on," Abby said softly. She had. She knew she had. She had a very clear memory of arming the system after she had locked the door. "So it *should* have gone off."

"Well…" the sheriff said again. He shrugged, holding his hands out from his body. "Maybe there's a short," he said finally. "Who knows? You should get somebody to check it out in the morning, I guess."

"You talk to Maggie?" Nick asked.

Maggie, Abby thought. Where *was* Maggie? Was it possible she had slept through the arrival of the patrol car, its siren splitting the night?

"Maggie sleeps sound, I guess," the sheriff said. At the question, his eyes had shifted again to Nick, assessing. He put out his hand. "Sheriff Lannie Blanchard."

Abby didn't move, and she couldn't think of anything to say that might help. After a moment of having it ignored, the sheriff lowered his hand, and his gaze came back to hers. Questioning. She shook her head mutely, feeling the flush that had begun when he said ''raccoon'' spread into her cheeks. Except now she was embarrassed for them. For the two men.

''Well, thank you for coming, Sheriff Blanchard,'' she finally said into the awkward silence. ''I'm sorry I got you both out of bed on a wild-goose chase.''

Blanchard grinned, apparently recovering his customary poise. ''Wild something chase, anyway,'' he said easily. ''That's what we're here for. Don't you hesitate to call on me any time, Abby. Any time at all.''

The last invitation had been softer. A little too personal. A little out of place.

''I won't,'' she promised, despite the discomfort she felt. Her response had been automatic and unthinking, because she liked him. ''I'll see you to the front.''

She turned and walked past Nick. He was wearing jeans, she realized, getting her first good look at him, and nothing else. She could see, despite the darkness of the hallway, a scar high on his chest, left by one of the bullets he'd taken in the New Orleans ambush six months ago.

Her eyes lifted from it to his face. There were no glasses tonight. Even in the shadows under the stairs where he was standing, she could see the clear blue of his eyes. And then she was past him, leading the way to the front door. She could hear the sheriff and the deputy following her, their booted feet echoing on the wooden floor.

'''Night, now,'' Blanchard said to Nick as he passed. ''Y'all get some sleep. Everything's gonna be fine.''

When she had let them out, Abby turned to find Nick still standing in the hall, exactly where he had been before.

''I armed the system,'' she said into the silence. She didn't know why it was so important that she convince him of that. Maybe because she felt like a fool. Maybe because of the disbelief she had heard in Sheriff Blanchard's voice.

Nick nodded, but he said nothing. She walked down the

hall toward him, her bare feet making no sound. When she walked by him, he still didn't move, so she wasn't sure he knew she was there. She walked on toward the light of the kitchen.

What she found there was exactly what the sheriff had described. There was garbage scattered over the tile floor and the sugar canister had been overturned on the counter. Her eyes circled the room. Nothing else appeared to be out of place.

She looked at the windows, but they, too, seemed to be secured. Then why the hell hadn't the alarm gone off? She walked over to the box and realized, even before she reached it, that the light wasn't blinking. Which meant, of course, it was not armed. Not operating. Because it hadn't been turned on. Was it possible that she had forgotten?

"Tell me exactly what it looks like," Nick said.

She turned and found that he had moved into the kitchen. The fluorescent light the sheriff had turned on over the sink put blue-black lights in the darkness of his hair. His chest was still powerful, dark and broad, the scar an ugly red star, high on the smooth bronze of his shoulder.

And there was another one at his temple, the more critical one, of course, although it was less visible because of its location. Maybe that's why his hair was longer, Abby thought. To hide that mark. And it almost did. That and the glasses had made it far less obvious yesterday than it was tonight.

"Sterling?" he questioned, and she tried to pull her mind away from the memory of her hands moving against his strong body, which had been unmarred then. Away from that and back to the job at hand. Protecting Nick.

"The garbage can is turned over. And the sugar canister on the counter. The contents of both are scattered. Nothing else seems out of place. I guess the can falling over is what we heard. It's metal."

"And the windows?" he asked.

"They're...I haven't checked, but they appear to be closed."

"Blanchard could have done that," he suggested.

That was true. Maybe one of them had been open and she hadn't noticed. But that still didn't explain the alarms.

"The system isn't on," she said. She wasn't sure why she had told him that, other than the fact that it only seemed fair. She was aware he would never have known if she hadn't told him.

But that would be cheating. She was supposed to be protecting him, and if she had gone up without making sure the house's security systems were all activated, then she hadn't done her job. And he had a right to know that. Maybe he'd complain to Rob and get her replaced. Maybe she needed to be replaced.

"You said you armed it." His voice wasn't accusing, but she was doing enough of that for both of them.

"I did," she said softly. And then a little more desperately, trying to remember. "I swear I did. I let Maggie out, and then I walked over to the box."

"And turned on the system?"

She nodded and then realized her mistake. "I did. I promise you I did."

"Okay," he said calmly, perhaps hearing the increased agitation in her voice. "Then something or somebody turned it off later on."

"The raccoon?" she asked sarcastically.

"Power outage," he suggested.

"But it should come back up when the power did."

"A short. Break in the line."

"Cut?"

"Maybe," he said.

She flicked the switch to test that hypothesis, and the arming light immediately winked at her. Mockingly. "It's back up," she said softly. Not cut. Which meant, she supposed...

"I turned it on," she said again, trying to sound convincing. For his benefit or her own? "After Maggie left," she said, replaying the scene in her head.

This time he said nothing in response. There was nothing to say. The system hadn't been armed, and if their intruder had been someone other than the wildlife Sheriff Blanchard had suggested, then she and Nick might both be dead right now. He certainly understood that as well as she did.

"I'll call Rob in the morning," she said. Her job. She was the one who was responsible for the situation out here. Responsible for seeing that everything possible was done to protect Nick Deandro. Tonight it hadn't been.

"He can send someone to check it out," Nick said.

She nodded again, her eyes watching the slow blink of the arming light. There was nothing wrong with the system now. Nothing wrong with the wiring. Maybe it was possible that she only thought she had tripped the switch.

"Sterling?" Nick said.

Her lips tightened, fighting the unforgivable urge to cry. *Damned hormones,* she thought. This reaction was ridiculous. So she had screwed up. There was no real harm done. Only to her pride. Her reputation.

"You still there?" Nick asked quietly.

"I'm here." The words were too soft, maybe even touched with what she had been feeling. She would hate it if he heard despair in her voice, the threat of tears, too near the surface.

"You better get some sleep," he said.

The concern in the quiet sentence was almost out of context. Almost, until she put it together with what he had said that night on the stairs. Something about her being sick. Or emotionally distraught. He apparently thought she was about to fall apart. And maybe, she admitted a little ruefully, she was.

"If you're ready to go back upstairs…" she offered, strengthening her voice and turning away from the mocking blink of the light to face him.

Despite the scarring, Nick looked more like himself tonight than he had before. Maybe it was that he wasn't wearing the glasses. Maybe it was the fact that he was asking questions. Police-type questions. And giving her orders—at least he had been, upstairs. Giving them in that familiar tone of confidence.

Cocky, she had thought at the beginning. That wasn't exactly what she was hearing tonight. But whatever was in his voice was infinitely better than the dark bitterness that had been there the first day she'd arrived out here.

"If I'm ready?" he repeated, his tone questioning.

"I'll take you up," she said, remembering the feeling of his hand on her shoulder tonight, following her through the darkness of the upstairs hall.

"I can find my way upstairs, if that's what you're offering," he said, his voice now hard and very cold. "I've lived in this house for more than five months. I don't need or want your help, Sterling. Or your guidance."

More humiliation. For him as well as for her, with her unthinking stupidity. But despite that, the sharpness of his tone sparked something defensive inside her. It always had.

He probably believed, as did Lannie Blanchard, that she had forgotten to set the alarms. Now, it seemed, he had also decided she was insulting and inept in dealing with his blindness. And none of it was fair.

"You needed me earlier. Upstairs," she argued. She regretted reminding him of that as soon as the words were out of her mouth. But she couldn't take them back. After all, they were the truth.

He laughed. "Hell, Sterling, I just didn't want to get shot. I wanted to make damn sure you knew exactly where I was at all times. Touching you seemed to be the simplest way to accomplish that."

"Are you saying—"

"I'm saying that when people with guns play hide-and-seek in a dark house, I don't intend to be the one who gets blown away. It's not a pleasant experience, I can tell you from experience."

He turned, moving confidently across the kitchen floor on broad, bare feet. His hand reached for the door frame and touched it just before he stepped through into the hall.

"How did you know?" she asked. She couldn't resist asking. How did he know that she was the one who had entered his room and not whoever had created the noise they had both heard down here? "How did you know it was me in your bedroom?"

He didn't turn around to look at her, and of course, there was no need. But he told her. She couldn't see his face, but his deep voice, coming to her out of the darkness, was again familiar. So damned evocative.

"Because you still smell the same," Nick Deandro said softly.

Shock held her motionless, an incredible tightness ballooning in her chest, crowding her breathing. And as she watched, eyes widened in disbelief, Nick disappeared into the shadows.

Chapter Five

Nick had been trying to decide what he should do since he'd come back upstairs. He knew he wouldn't sleep again. Too many things were happening. Things he didn't understand.

And, locked in this endless nightmare of darkness, there wasn't much he could do about any of them. The information he needed to sort them all out was probably inside his head. He just couldn't get to it. Couldn't break through the wall of amnesia, as black as the world that stretched before him now.

But he thought he understood the way Rob Andrews's mind worked, because Andrews was supposed to be a good cop. Which meant there was more going on here than met the eye.

The soft snort of amusement when he thought about the wording of that phrase was as bitter as his comments to Abby Sterling had been. He hated hearing embarrassment in someone's voice because they had used some perfectly innocent phrase referring to sight. Almost as much as he hated hearing pity. But he hated self-pity even more, he thought in disgust. Yet he had reacted with that very emotion tonight when Sterling had made her offer.

Why the hell shouldn't she think he needed her guidance? How was she supposed to know that holding on to her shoulder had been his way of keeping them in contact in the face of an outside danger? Good cops always tried to stay in contact. Usually it was done by radio or visually, but in his case…

Good cops. The phrase echoed suddenly, bringing him back to the problem. Identifying the good guys. Figuring out if Abby Sterling was one of them. Was that why Andrews had sent her out here?

Or was it possible the police captain believed she was the woman who had been so interested in his condition after the shooting? Whoever it was who kept calling the hospital had known the name they had hidden him under, information that had been available to only a few highly trusted individuals. People who were members of the elite Organized Crime Special Unit within the department's Public Integrity Division, for example. People like Abby Sterling.

Nick had already determined to his own satisfaction that they had some kind of shared background. He just couldn't be sure what kind. And he wasn't sure what the rest of it meant, either.

Like Andrews's cryptic reference to Sterling's need for rest. The fact that she had come to his room tonight before she had called the sheriff. And the fact that she had apparently forgotten to arm the security system, leaving the way open for whoever wanted to enter this house unannounced.

All of those meant something, he knew. He sensed that those things were important, even beyond their obvious implications. Except he wasn't sure exactly why.

Maybe if he could remember something about Abby Sterling, he could figure it all out. There was something he should be remembering, he knew instinctively. Something beyond the fragrance of her skin. Beyond the disturbing weariness he had heard in her voice. He knew there was something.

Only he just couldn't remember what the hell it was.

"I ARMED THE SYSTEM," Abby said again. She wondered how many times she was going to feel the need to reiterate that. And however many it was, she knew her avowals weren't going to change what had happened last night.

"I believe you," Rob said calmly. Reassuringly, even. Until he added, "That's what bothers me the most, Abby."

She read the truth of that in his voice, even over the phone line. Maybe it was good they had had this scare. Abby had thought that everyone was a little too relaxed about protecting Nick. Rob included. He didn't sound relaxed now.

Maggie had shown up around 6:00 a.m., letting herself into the house, apparently without creating any problems with the alarm. She hadn't mentioned hearing the sirens or being aware of the sheriff's visit, so Abby had asked.

"I heard the sheriffs," Maggie said, not meeting her eyes. "That don't mean I'm gonna rush out to see what's happening. That ain't necessarily a healthy thing to do in the middle of the night 'round about here."

"Why not?" Abby asked, curious again about that seeming distrust of the local law.

"You live as long as I have in this parish, you learn to mind your own business. If you know what's good for you," Maggie added cryptically.

If Maggie had not been aware of the excitement here last night, there was, by the time she arrived, certainly nothing in the appearance of the kitchen that would have given away the fact that they had had an intruder.

That's what Abby had done during the long hours before daybreak. Those hours she had spent alone down here after Nick had made his enigmatic pronouncement and disappeared. She had cleaned up the mess and then made herself a pot of coffee.

Of which she had been drinking entirely too much, she realized, deliberately putting her mug back on the table and pushing it away. This was a habit she had broken early in her pregnancy, and she didn't need to get re-addicted now.

But somehow it had helped last night, she acknowledged, as she had sat there waiting for the sun to replace the moonlight filtering through the draping moss. Something about the familiar feel of a cup in her hand had helped her get through those long dark hours of thinking. Of remembering.

"Look," she said to Rob, and she found that she was the one trying to be reassuring now, "the sheriff is satisfied that no one was out here. That nobody got into the house. Deandro doesn't seem to be worried about it. So maybe…"

Her voice faltered as her mind again replayed the scene when Maggie had left yesterday. The actions she had taken were as clear in her mind as they had been before. Crystal clear.

Abby wondered if she had thought about this so much that she had now created the clarity of the memory she so desperately wanted to be inside her head. The memory of her hand throwing the switch and the arming light blinking in response.

"What did Deandro say about what happened?" Rob asked.

…you still smell the same. That's what Nick had said. At least that's what she remembered. She knew, however, that wasn't what Rob meant. So she tried again to wipe those disturbing words out of her head, just as she had been trying to do all night.

"He suggested that maybe it was a short. A break in the line." She waited for a response to that, but Rob didn't articulate whatever he was thinking. "But it wasn't," Abby went on, trying to be fair in her assessment. "As soon as I flicked the switch, the thing came back on."

"So what do you want to do?" Rob asked.

Run and hide suggested itself. Only, not just from the incident last night, she realized. She was beginning to accept that she was going to have to take the blame for that glitch in security, whatever had happened. What she wanted to run from now were the emotions that had been stirred up by Nick's words, but she resisted the impulse to cowardice.

"First of all, I want you to send someone to check out the system," she suggested.

"You got it," Rob said. "That's probably not a bad idea anyway. I don't know when it was last done." There was another small silence before he asked, "You think I ought to talk to Nick? Get his take on things?"

"Why not?" Abby agreed, keeping her voice calm.

After all, she had nothing to hide. She had done what she was supposed to do. She had reported the incident to her supervisor, including all the possibilities as she saw them. At the same time she had asserted her surety that she'd turned on the alarm. An assertion that she had mentally questioned each time she'd made it.

"He's in his room. I can take the phone up to him," she offered. She hoped Rob wouldn't push this. That he would suggest that taking the phone upstairs was too much trouble for her. He didn't.

"If you don't mind," he said instead.

"Of course. Hold on."

She pushed up again from the kitchen table, its top a familiar landscape after a week in this house, and began the journey upstairs.

She hadn't seen Nick since last night. Not since he had told her she still smelled the same. She found she wasn't eager to see him now. That didn't mean, however, that she hadn't thought about what he had said. About what it had meant. And especially about whether or not she should mention the comment to Rob. She still hadn't decided on the answer to that, despite how important she knew it might be.

The door at the top of the stairs was closed, and she knocked softly, ridiculously hoping she wouldn't get an answer. Maybe Nick was making up for the sleep he'd lost last night. He responded immediately, however, his deep voice inviting her in.

When she opened the door, it was obvious he hadn't been asleep. He was sitting at a desk that had been placed in front of the bedroom's two windows. He was dressed, wearing the same pair of worn jeans he had thrown on last night and a white polo shirt that made his skin appear even darker, very tanned and healthy. Not at all like the invalid she had been imagining him to be before she'd come out here.

But the dark glasses were back in place, as if protecting his eyes from the glare of the morning sun. For some unfathomable reason, Abby was relieved to see them. She recognized how contradictory her relief was. Their black opaqueness had bothered her before, but last night, without them, he had once more been Nick. He had seemed far too much like the totally confident man she had fallen in love with.

"Maggie?" he questioned, his head turning toward the door.

Reflex action, Abby supposed, since the glasses were focused not on her, but a little to the left. That hurt. The pain of it ached in a place where she didn't want to hurt. Somewhere within her memories of his strength. His masculine surety. Of the cockiness she had once claimed to despise.

She realized that she didn't want that sightless uncertainty to find a place within her memories of Nick. Of what they had briefly had together. She didn't want it there for his sake, and selfishly, not for hers either. Yet she despised the part of her that felt that way about his blindness.

"It's Abby Sterling," she said, forcing her reluctant feet to move across the room to where he was sitting. He rose at once, still facing the door. He was turned toward her advance, but his head didn't follow her movement. It did lift slightly when she spoke again, standing next to him now, beside the desk.

"Rob wants to talk to you. On the phone," she said.

While she waited for his response, she reexamined the scar at his temple, made more prominent by the glare of the light from the tall windows, and she realized that she had been right before. The temple piece of the glasses bisected it, serving to camouflage some of the damage.

"About last night?" he asked.

She nodded and then mentally kicked herself. How many times was she going to do that before she remembered? "Yes."

He held out his left hand, palm up, and she laid the phone in it. "I'll wait downstairs," she said. "Just yell when you're through. There are a couple of things I need to mention to him before you hang up. Things I forgot to tell him."

She was babbling. Nervous at being this close to him. She could hear the tension in her own voice, in the too-rapid stream of words. She assumed he could hear it, too.

"Tell him now. Then you won't have to come back up," he suggested, holding the receiver out to her.

"I'll have to come back to get the phone anyway."

"Something you don't want me to hear, Sterling?" he asked. He sounded amused.

"No," she denied.

She began to turn away, fully intending to go downstairs while he talked to her supervisor, despite his demand that she say whatever she needed to say to Rob in front of him. Before she could make her escape, however, Nick grabbed her.

The movement was sudden and totally unexpected. His fingers brushed quickly over her shoulder, then down her arm to fasten like a vise around her wrist. At the same time, he brought the phone he held in his other hand up to his ear.

She twisted, struggling to free her arm from his hold. Her efforts had no effect on those iron fingers.

"Deandro," he said into the mouthpiece, ignoring her.

Abby could hear Rob's voice, like an insect hum through the wires, but she couldn't distinguish words.

"That's about it," Nick said after he had listened to the captain's low voice for a few seconds.

Was he agreeing with what she'd told Rob? Abby wondered suddenly. A little of the guilty tightness eased in her chest. She looked down at Nick's hand while he continued to listen.

Her wrist looked incredibly thin, fragile almost, under the controlling pressure of his strong, dark fingers. She had stopped struggling against his grip, but he hadn't loosened it. She knew she would have another bruise to match the one that had already formed on her shoulder.

She had examined that in the bathroom mirror this morning. She stood in front of the glass after her bath, watching as her forefinger carefully touched the blue discolorations his hand had made. She thought she could trace the outline of each individual finger, clearly marked on her skin. And she knew that eventually, after this, she would also be able to see those same marks on her wrist.

That was surprising, because what she remembered most from before was Nick's gentleness. Big hands that were incredibly tender, drifting knowingly over her body. Touching. Caressing. Never leaving a sign of their undeniable power on her skin. Leaving nothing behind except the passion they had aroused.

"Sounds good to me," Nick said to Rob.

Her eyes lifted again to his face. He was still turned toward her, and now the dark lenses were fixed on her eyes. Her heart skipped a beat before she realized that was simply a trick of her imagination. Or an accident.

"Nothing's surfaced. Some recurring dreams. Things I know I should remember," Nick went on. "But everything's gone when I wake up. Almost everything," he amended.

The black lenses hadn't released her. Neither had his fingers. She realized suddenly that Nick had wanted her to hear this. He didn't care about what she had to say to Rob. He had stopped her because he wanted her to hear what he was saying right now. *Everything's gone when I wake up. Almost everything.*

"Sterling wants to talk to you again," he said.

She wasn't prepared, because she had been lost in her memories. For so long they had been all she had. Now Nick was touching her again. Not the way he had before. Not anything like it had been before.

But then, Nick Deandro wasn't the man he had been before, of course. That was one of the things that had made her afraid to come out here, she now understood. She had been afraid of her inability to love the man Nick had become.

He held the phone out to her, and slowly her hand closed over it. His fingers loosened abruptly from around her wrist at the same time hers fastened over the receiver.

Permission to leave? If so, she didn't take it. Nick's hand fell to his side, seemingly relaxed, but still she didn't move. Except to lift the phone to her ear.

"Rob," she said softly.

"You got something to tell me?" he asked.

"Yes," she said. Nothing else. The silence stretched, seeming to reverberate with tension along the line.

"But you can't do it now?" Rob guessed.

"That's right," Abby agreed.

"He remember something, Abby?"

She hesitated. Thinking about what Nick had said last night…. *You still smell the same.* And what he had just said about almost everything disappearing after the dreams. *Almost* everything.

"I think maybe you're correct," she said finally.

"About you?"

"That's about it. The other thing wasn't important."

"Good work," Rob said softly, but she could hear the elation in his voice.

"Not much," she warned.

Rob was very bright. Apparently he was reading her cryptic messages easily. She hoped Nick wasn't having as much success. His attention was still focused on her, however, and she realized that she hadn't said anything to Rob that might be construed as the additional information she had claimed she needed to give him. She had to come up with something fast, and she settled on making a suggestion.

"I think," she said hesitantly, "if it's okay with you, I'll ask the sheriff to come out here when you send the guys to check the alarms. We want to be sure there's nothing wrong with our connection to his office."

"Sounds good to me," Rob said. "You're still in charge, Abby. I want you to know that I have every confidence in you. In the job you're doing."

She wasn't sure whether she was relieved by that or not. She wasn't even sure she agreed with it. "Thanks, Rob," she said softly. "I'll be in touch later on," she added, and then she lowered the phone and clicked the off button on the receiver.

"Is that all you wanted to tell him?" Nick asked. His gaze still seemed to be unerringly directed at her face.

"Yes," she said. Nodding again. Another bad habit. Like remembering everything that had ever happened between them each time she was around him. "I said it wasn't anything important."

"Just an opportunity to call on the friendly local law."

There was something in his voice that didn't fit the situation, but he didn't elaborate. Maybe the comment was simply a gibe at her failure to call the sheriff last night until Nick had reminded her that was what she should be doing. The smartest thing to do in the situation.

"I just thought we needed his cooperation in seeing that the alarms work," she said. "Besides, you're the one who wanted me to call him last night."

"It made sense at the time."

"I guess more sense than what I wanted to do," she acknowledged softly. Guilt again. Nothing she had done since she'd been on this assignment had been handled with the professionalism she expected from herself. And she knew why.

"I'm not criticizing, Sterling," Nick said. "You wanted to know who was in the house. You wanted to go downstairs and find out. I probably would have wanted to do the same thing."

"But that wasn't my job." Her tone was flat. She had made the wrong decision about how to handle the threat last night. And maybe, she admitted for the first time, maybe she had even forgotten to turn on the alarm.

All of which made her appear pretty damned incompetent, she supposed. So she made the offer she had thought about making to her superior. "You want me to ask Rob to send somebody else out here in my place?"

She had to push the question out. Had to make herself offer to be replaced on an assignment, something she'd never done in her professional life. But in all fairness, it was Nick's right to decide who he wanted protecting him. It was his life at stake. As he had reminded her, he had ample cause to know that getting shot wasn't a whole hell of a lot of fun.

She knew, however, that she could do this. She could keep him safe. She would never have accepted this assignment, despite her need to see him again, the need to sort out all her feelings about what had happened to him, if she hadn't felt she could protect Nick Deandro as well as any other cop in the unit.

But after what had happened, he had every right to have lost confidence in her abilities. So did Rob. She had expected them to and had been surprised when neither of them had mentioned having her relieved.

"I didn't ask for a replacement, Sterling," he said.

"Because I was standing here?" she suggested.

"You were standing here because I wanted you to be. If I had intended to get you thrown off this assignment, I wouldn't have wanted you around while I talked to Rob."

"I thought that was because of...something else."

"Like what?" He sounded genuinely puzzled.

"Maybe that you wanted me to know you remember things."

He laughed, nothing but a breath of sound. "Not *things*. Sometimes I remember…images, I guess. Just from the dreams, maybe. They're there for a few seconds, still in my head when I wake up. I never know what they mean. And they're nothing important. Nothing that's helpful to the department."

"Is that what you meant last night?" she asked.

He didn't pretend not to understand. "About identifying you by the way you smell?" he asked.

"I wasn't wearing any perfume last night."

"Its scent was there all the same. In your hair. Maybe in your clothing. Still the same."

The last phrase had been added after a pause, after she thought he was through with the explanation. And that was the crux of it, of course. The same as when?

"The same?" she whispered.

"I keep thinking I should remember you," Nick said instead of clarifying. "That there's something…"

She waited, wanting him to remember. As she had wanted him to remember all along. Somewhere deep inside she had always thought that he *should* have remembered her. Even if he had forgotten the rest. All these months she had fought the urge to think that if he had really cared about her, he would remember.

It was illogical. Irrational even, given what the doctors had told Rob and what she had read. As if she thought Nick could pick and choose what he would recall. As if she believed he didn't want desperately to remember everything so he could help put away the people who had done this to him.

But still, she acknowledged, somewhere inside she had always thought that if he had truly loved her, he would eventually remember. As if it was a test of some kind. That expectation was totally and completely unfair. And it was born, she also understood, of loss. And of loneliness.

"Something I ought to remember," he finished, his voice, like the laughter, now only a breath of sound.

She could see the small furrow that had formed between his dark brows. It creased the area above the bridge of his nose, above the glasses.

"It'll come," she said softly. The same stupid comfort Rob had offered him. The patronizing assurance she had belittled.

Nick laughed again, louder this time, but his tone was dark and still without amusement. "That's what they keep telling me, Sterling. About all of it."

"You don't believe them anymore."

She shouldn't have spoken the sudden realization aloud. It was too much like admitting to him that no one else believed it either. She should be comforting. Reassuring. And instead she was probably making things worse.

"Would you?" he asked. "After all this time?"

"I don't know," she admitted.

He nodded, the movement slow, as if he were thinking about it. Deciding. He didn't say anything else, and finally he turned his face to the windows, looking into the light that should have been too bright to be comfortable. *Should* have been, and for him was not.

Her eyes fell, determinedly fighting the emotions that aroused. Fighting pity for him. Fighting rage that so much had changed for the man he had been. Fighting her own loneliness.

For the first time she noticed what covered the surface of the desk he had been sitting in front of when she entered the room. "What's all this?" she asked softly.

The top of the desk was empty expect for hundreds of pieces of a jigsaw puzzle, which lay in small piles around the corners of its surface. Some of those pieces had been fitted together. Most were the straight-edged ones. The perimeter of the puzzle's picture had almost been completed, and nearly every piece of the open square formed by the outer, edged pieces had been filled in. Of course, there were hundreds of other pieces from the uncompleted middle of the puzzle that still remained unconnected. Those were the ones piled around the corners of the desk.

"*This* is almost two months' work," Nick said, his voice amused. His fingers had found one of the scattered pieces and were carefully tracing around its small curves and protrusions.

"It took you two months to do this?" she asked, shocked.

Again he nodded, and his lips tilted. His fingers were still moving over the small bit of cardboard. "But I didn't have much else to do. Mickey mentioned that there were several of these in a closet downstairs. He did a couple, working on them at night. I hadn't done one in years. Couldn't imagine wanting to, but finally, out of boredom, I guess, I asked him to lay this one out on the desk. And to put the pieces face up for me."

Abby looked down at the puzzle again. Her eyes burned, hot tears stinging behind her determined examination of the pieces. She blinked them away by pretending to herself that she needed to see the colors. The finished picture would be flowers of some kind, she thought. It was hard to tell because the box these scattered pieces had come out of was nowhere in sight.

"I can do that now," Nick said. "The surface of the front is smoother than the other. I can distinguish between them."

Unbelievably, there was a hint of pride in that small claim. She didn't know what to say to him. Or why he had told her. "That's nice," she said softly.

Then, in the sudden frozen silence that followed that inane comment, she wished she had bitten out her tongue instead. God, why hadn't she just kept her mouth shut? Saying nothing would have been far better than that. Rob's stupid platitudes again.

Suddenly Nick's hand was on her arm. She raised her

eyes from the puzzle to find he was looking at her. Except… Except she knew that he wasn't. He couldn't be.

He had turned slightly so he was facing her, his fingers wrapped around her upper arm. There was no pressure this time. Not an unpleasant one, anyway. His thumb caressed. Moving up and then down against the softness of her sweater. She wanted it moving over her skin. As it had done before. Before all this.

"Abby," he said softly.

It was the first time he'd called her by her first name since she had been here, and when he said it, all the memories imploded. All the times he had whispered her name, his lips moving then against her hair. Or against her forehead or her throat. Her breast. Her name gasped into the heated darkness as his hips arched into and then retreated above hers.

The pressure of his fingers increased minutely. No force, but there was no doubt that they were drawing her toward him. His head lowered, and the light from the windows they were standing beside suddenly glinted off the dark glasses. Interrupting the spell. Allowing her to think again.

Nick was going to kiss her. She knew that was his intent. And maybe, if he did, it might be the catalyst that would break through whatever barriers were preventing him from remembering. She wanted him to remember. To remember her. She had wanted it for months. Had even dreamed about it. Dreamed about him.

I know all about the treachery of dreams, Nick, she thought. *About the things you remember in them. All about those memories, and I know how much they hurt.*

She was still watching his mouth lower inexorably to hers. Moving in slow motion, it seemed. Time had stopped, but her mind was racing.

Because if he kissed her…if she leaned toward him, allowing his lips to fasten over hers, he would also embrace her. She knew that. It was a progression as natural as breathing. As natural as it had been the first time she had moved into his arms. Surprised that she wanted to. Surprised by how right they had felt closing around her body.

As they would now. Except now... Except now he would know...

She stepped back, away from him. His fingers tightened involuntarily on her arm, but he didn't exert enough pressure to pull her back to him. Instead, his head lifted, and again it seemed he was looking directly at her.

They stood like that for what seemed like an eternity. Separated by the length of his arm, his fingers still around her upper arm.

"I guess I was wrong," Nick said softly. His fingers uncurled, freeing her.

Run and hide. It was what she had wanted to do before. Then she had bravely resisted the impulse to cowardice. This time she didn't even try.

NICK WAITED until he heard the door close behind her. And despite what had just happened, he didn't believe Abby Sterling would be cruel enough to stay in the room, watching him. Tricking him with the sound of the closing door.

Behind the safety of the glasses, he closed his eyes. He made himself breathe. Deeply. Once. And then again. He turned, and leaning forward, put his hands on the top of the desk, palms flat. And he felt beneath the sensitive surface of his fingertips the puzzle he had worked on so long.

Therapy, maybe. More likely just something to pass the long hours. It was a puzzle. Nothing else. No great accomplishment. But he had shown it to her as if the fact that he could put a few bits and pieces of cardboard together was some kind of big deal.

He was a cop. An agent. And he had been a good one. Good at working undercover. Good enough that nothing he had done would have given away the role he had been playing. He really believed that. He had done this same job too many times, in too many different locations. Slipping into the role he had been sent to play down here was like slipping into a second skin.

One that was familiar. One that fit. He wasn't the kind who made careless mistakes. Even Andrews didn't suggest that he had this time. But still, something had gone terribly wrong.

And that something, he knew instinctively, had to do with Abby Sterling. It had to do somehow with the relationship between them. Only he didn't know what, because he couldn't remember her.

Nothing other than how it felt to have that scent all over his clothes. All over his skin. That had been one thing that had come back to him last night. And the reason he had allowed himself to touch her today.

That and the fact that she had sounded so damn vulnerable last night. Blaming herself for what had happened. He had wanted to comfort her. He had wanted to take her in his arms and hold her hard and tight against the protection of his body. And the urge to do that was not unfamiliar.

She was so damn small. Almost too thin. He had worried about that. Worried about her. And he wasn't a guy who ever worried. It was counterproductive.

Suddenly his fingers tightened against the wood of the desk. They curled inward, pulling a piece of the jigsaw puzzle into his palm. Curling tightly around it because of what he had just thought.

He had been remembering, he realized. Remembering a woman. Who was small and blond. Long blond hair. Very slender. Fragile. And he had worried about her.

He didn't know where the memories had come from, but suddenly they had floated up to the surface of the dark pool that had been his mind, like something that had finally broken free from the reeking, mud-clogged bottom of a stagnant lake.

He tried to force it now. Tried desperately to see her face, but there was only an impression. An image. A brief memory. Of a woman he had cared about.

Of a woman who didn't now even want his hand on her arm? Of Abby Sterling? Who certainly didn't want his mouth over hers, he acknowledged. In spite of whatever might have happened between them in the past, she had made her feelings about that abundantly clear today. And he knew why, of course.

She just didn't get quite as big a thrill as he did, he guessed, out of the fact that he could *almost* put together a jigsaw puzzle. Almost. Given an endless amount of time.

Suddenly the rage and self-pity Nick Deandro had fought for months boiled over. As black and as cold as the despair he fought every morning. As black as his whole world.

And there was only one clear memory of the time he'd been in the South shining through that darkness. The memory of a woman who had wanted him to kiss her.

With both hands, palms flattened again, Nick Deandro swept the pieces of the puzzle he had worked on for two months off the desk. He heard the soft impacts as they struck the windows and the walls. He didn't stop until he was certain that there was nothing left on the surface of the desk for his groping, destructive hands to find.

Chapter Six

"Everything checks out," Blanchard assured Abby. He had insisted on being the one to follow the technicians around the grounds and the outside of the house, and after a couple of fruitless protests, Abby had given in and let him.

Again she reminded herself that her job was to protect Nick. The sheriff was perfectly capable of overseeing the search for an apparently nonexistent glitch in the system. Finally, when the repair crew had completed the job and he had escorted them off the property, Blanchard had come into the house to report that all was well. He was standing again in the kitchen doorway.

Abby nodded in response to his report, knowing that she should be relieved, but also knowing that what the technicians had failed to find put the blame for what happened last night squarely back on her shoulders.

"You never did see our intruder, did you?" the sheriff asked, hitching the leather gun belt up a little to a more comfortable position on his narrow hips.

"Neither hide nor hair," Abby acknowledged. "And I was in here most of the rest of last night."

"We probably scared whatever it was off when we arrived. It must have gotten out the same way it got in. You leave a window open last night, Maggie?" Blanchard asked suddenly. The blue eyes had left their contemplation of

Abby to focus on the caretaker, who was in the process of peeling potatoes for supper.

"No, sir," Maggie said without turning around. "I don't leave no windows open around here. Me, I know better than that."

The sheriff nodded, but his mouth pursed and his eyes followed the movements of her thin hands as they chopped up the firm white flesh of the potato she had just peeled. The snick of her knife against the wood of the chopping board was the only sound in the room for a few seconds.

"I hope so," the sheriff said finally. "I hope you know how important security is around here."

His questioning made Abby uneasy. Whatever had happened last night hadn't been Maggie's fault. It also seemed to her that in emphasizing the seriousness of a breach in security the sheriff might be giving too much away.

Rob had said that they were only tenants to Maggie. But given Blanchard's comments and the invasion of the technicians, it must surely be obvious that they were something more.

"I know," Maggie said. She didn't look up from her work. The same response she always had to Blanchard's presence.

"This wasn't Maggie's fault," she said.

Maggie surely didn't need her defense. The caretaker hadn't struck Abby as someone who was reticent about speaking her mind. But she had to admit there was something peculiar about Maggie's reactions to the sheriff. Almost out of character.

"If anyone was careless about security," Abby added, "I suppose it must have been me. Considering the fact that they found nothing wrong with the system."

"Well," the sheriff said, drawling out the syllable as his sympathetic gaze came back to her. "Don't beat yourself up too much about it, Abby. We all make mistakes. I expect you've got other things on your mind these days."

His eyes dropped to her thickened waistline and stayed

there a moment before they came back up to smile into hers. "When's the happy event?" he asked. This was the first time he'd openly referred to her pregnancy, although his eyes had made this same examination the first day he'd shown up out here.

"The end of December," Abby said. This wasn't something she wanted to discuss. Not here. Not now.

"I'm surprised your husband was willing to let you come way out here by yourself." There was a question implicit in the comment, and his eyes found her left hand, the one that was wrapped around a glass of iced tea, the empty ring finger in plain sight.

His gaze, lifting quickly to hers, openly questioned that. He had probably noticed it before, Abby figured. She didn't think much of what happened in his parish escaped Lannie Blanchard's notice. That was only an impression, of course, but a pretty strong one.

"I'm not married," Abby acknowledged. "But despite the preconceptions, pregnancy really isn't an illness, you know. Or a disability. It doesn't prevent me from doing my job. I don't know what happened to the alarm last night, but whatever it was had nothing to do with the fact that I'm pregnant," she declared. "I can assure you of that."

He smiled, amused, it seemed, by her quiet passion. "I'm sure it didn't," he said, a little condescendingly. Abby felt her temper rise. "Sorry I can't stay and eat, Maggie."

His gaze had shifted again to the caretaker, who still did not look up from her preparations, not even to remind the sheriff that he hadn't been invited for supper tonight. Seemingly unperturbed by Maggie's lack of response, Blanchard went on.

"Whatever you're fixing smells mighty good. However, duty calls. I'm sure y'all understand." His blue eyes had come back to Abby's with the last comment. He nodded to her and then stepped back into the hall that led to the front door.

Which she would need to close and lock after him, Abby

realized. She'd be damned if she'd give anyone further grounds to doubt her ability to do her job. She put the glass of tea down on the kitchen counter and followed the sheriff. He had stopped at the foot of the stairs and was looking up them.

"I think I've seen him before," he said, softly enough that there was no danger of his voice reaching the upper level of the old house. "Can't remember where that was, though."

He turned to her as if he expected Abby to supply the information. She said nothing, leaving the expectation lying unacknowledged between them. His lips lifted in amusement, his smile again creasing the lean, tanned cheeks.

"And I don't suppose you're going to tell me where it might have been," he said.

"I don't suppose I am," she agreed.

She walked over to the door, opening it to the twilight. There was a breeze blowing across the marsh, and it was filled with the scent of backwater and the soft noises of the night creatures who had already started their serenade of welcome to the falling darkness.

He obligingly stepped through it, out onto the veranda. Once there, he carefully set his hat on his head, adjusting it to the perfect angle to flatter his lean features. It shaded his eyes, but she could still read the intensity in them when he turned back to face her.

"You may not have a husband, Abby. But that baby you're carrying's got itself a daddy. That's a conclusion it doesn't take a law degree to come to. I don't understand what any man's doing letting you come out here on this kind of assignment."

"This kind of assignment?" she repeated, a hint of challenge in the question. She found that she was really interested in exactly what Blanchard thought they were doing out here.

"Don't you make the mistake the rest of the country makes about us," he warned softly. "Don't you believe just because we talk slow that it means we aren't too smart. Brains have got nothing to do with living in the sticks. You should know that as well as I do."

He waited, but she didn't say anything. Neither denial nor affirmation, although she was as Southern as he, both by birth and experience.

"That man upstairs is somebody," he said finally, breaking the uncomfortable silence he'd created. "Somebody real important. Somebody NOPD needs to keep safe. And if you've read the New Orleans papers lately, it doesn't take much of a brain to figure out why. Just like it doesn't take much of one to figure out who would be most interested in finding out where he is."

"I don't know what you're talking about, Sheriff Blanchard," Abby said calmly. "I'm not sure you do either."

He smiled at her again, but the smile didn't quite light the shadowed blue eyes as it had the first day he'd come out here.

"That's okay. I don't expect you to tell me anything else. But you be careful, Abby. You hear me? Don't you take any chances. And you call me if you hear anything. *Anything.* I'd rather come out here to find another raccoon in that kitchen than to find the two of you…"

He bit off the rest. He didn't need to say it. She knew what he meant. And what he was warning her about. And he was right, of course. The people who were after Nick Deandro weren't the kind who played games. Or the kind who cared about babies or pregnant women.

Protecting the women and children. It was Blanchard who had said that to her. Something about getting into law enforcement to protect the women and children. Maybe that's all he was trying to do now. At least he seemed to be taking the situation out here more seriously than anyone else had been. He nodded, touching the brim of his hat in a silent, old-fashioned gesture of farewell.

"I'll call," she promised, grateful for his concern. As Maggie's had been, it was welcome, if unexpected. She waited until he had crossed the veranda before she decided to tell him that.

"Lannie," she said. He turned in response, blue eyes questioning. "Thank you," Abby said. "Thank you for being concerned. Thanks for everything."

He smiled at her, and then he turned and stepped off the porch, moving quickly down the broad steps, the tap of his boots against the wood brisk and confident, and then onto the path. She watched in the gathering dusk until the taillights of the patrol car had disappeared into the darkness at the end of the tree-shadowed drive. Then she closed and locked the front door against the approaching night, double-checking the lock before she went back to the kitchen.

And the whole time, she was remembering his warning. *If you read the papers it doesn't take much to figure out why. Just like it doesn't take much to figure out who would be most interested in finding out where he is.*

It was a little ironic that Blanchard thought Nick was their Mafia informant. He had put the right two and two together, but he had come up with five. Still, the fact that the sheriff had connected Nick in anyway with what the D.A. was doing in New Orleans was troubling. Because he was right, of course, about Nick's importance to that investigation. And apparently it *hadn't* taken much at all for him to have figured that out.

"I GOT TO GO," Maggie said earnestly. "You got to understand that. I don't have no choice 'cause this here is *my baby* we're talking about."

This on top of everything else, Abby thought. And it had come totally out of the blue. "He called you?" Abby probed.

She supposed that was possible. She had been out of the house a few minutes with the technicians, before Sheriff Blanchard arrived to take charge. It was possible someone had called Maggie in that short window of opportunity, but it also seemed pretty unlikely.

"Called today," Maggie said, nodding vigorously. "I hate to leave you in the lurch out here, shug, but I got to go."

Abby took a breath, trying to think. She'd have to call Rob. He would have to get someone else out here. She could handle the cooking for a few days, although she was no great shakes at that. There wasn't much else that Maggie did around the house that was vital.

But Abby couldn't leave to do the shopping. And besides, there was the much larger issue of security. Maggie Thibodeaux knew a lot about them, and she might have figured out even more, after the sheriff's pointed questions tonight. She knew all about the alarm setup. Way too much, as far as Abby was concerned, despite the fact that she didn't really distrust the caretaker.

"I'll have to make some arrangements," Abby said. "About supplies and things. Get someone in to clean. Can you give me a few days, Maggie?"

"I wish I could. I wish I could, for true. But I gotta go. You know how it is when your baby needs you."

Not exactly, Abby thought, but she didn't see how she could refuse. She didn't have any control over Maggie. That had been part of this flawed setup to begin with. She had thought that from the first. Now it was coming back to haunt them. But at least it was Rob's problem and not her own. Except immediately.

"Until tomorrow?" she said.

"Dawlin', I swear I can't. I would if I could, but I can't. They coming for me. Be here in 'bout half an hour. They gonna blow, and you need to turn off them sensors till we get gone."

Abby didn't like this at all. She didn't like that Maggie had planned it without telling her. Had given someone—her son, she supposed—information about how security worked around here.

"But don't you worry," Maggie continued reassuringly. "You and that baby be all right out here. You got the alarms. Y'all be all right tonight, and then tomorrow you can do something else. Go somewhere else.''

Abby nodded. She supposed she didn't really have a choice. Maggie Thibodeaux was not a prisoner. She was not even an employee of the NOPD. And Maggie had waited until the supper dishes had been washed and the kitchen made spotless before she had dropped her bombshell. Too late, Abby supposed, for her to do anything about it tonight. Other than to inform Rob. She'd have to call him at home, but that was all right. This was his headache. One of the perks of being the man in charge.

"I'm sure sorry," Maggie said softly, probably reading Abby's face. "But it's for the best. You'll see."

Whose best? Abby wondered, but given what had happened with Nick upstairs this morning, maybe Maggie was right. Maybe moving somewhere else *would* be for the best. It might give her an opportunity to evaluate her feelings about Nick, and to do it in a situation that wasn't rife, as this one now was, with far too many emotions. And far too many memories.

"SOMETHING ABOUT her son needing her," Abby explained to her boss when she reached him. "Supposedly he called her today."

"Supposedly?" Rob repeated, hearing the doubt in her voice.

Abby hesitated. She had no basis for doubting Maggie's story. Other than the timing of this. And the woman's strange behavior whenever Sheriff Blanchard was around.

That in itself, she admitted, might mean nothing. There were plenty of people who didn't like their local law-enforcement officers. They didn't even have to have a reason for that dislike, other than the badge they wore.

"I didn't hear the phone," Abby clarified. "I wasn't outside with the tech people long. Blanchard saw to most of it."

"They find anything?"

"Not even the raccoon," she said.

"Come again?" Rob requested, his voice puzzled.

"Nothing. A not-very-funny joke. On me, I guess."

The silence occupied the line for a moment. But she supposed it was best not to give Rob too long to worry about that strange comment. "So what do we do?" she prompted.

"Just what we've been doing," he said.

Which was not exactly what she had wanted to hear.

"For the time being, anyway," Rob added. "You seem to be having some results with our primary objective. Besides, I don't have a place I can bring you all right now. I'll need a few days to make those arrangements. Think you can manage for a while?"

"Until the food runs out. If Deandro's not choosy about what he eats," she said. One part of her was relieved that they were staying put for a while. The other half was...frightened? Maybe that wasn't the word, but it worked.

In spite of Blanchard's warning tonight, she was not afraid of what might happen out here. No one in the department really seemed to believe anyone was coming after Nick. She was afraid of something else. The feelings that had been stirred up. Except, of course, they had really been there from the beginning.

She supposed she could blame them on raging hormones. But she knew the real reason this assignment was proving to be so difficult. She had understood that when she agreed to come out here. Despite seeing Nick again, none of that confusion had lessened. If anything it had increased. Because nothing had changed but Nick. And to her deep shame, Abby honestly didn't know how she felt about that.

She made Maggie alter her plans. Nobody she didn't know was coming on this property tonight, Abby decided. Rob had told her she was in charge. Maybe she couldn't prevent Maggie from leaving, but she could make her do it in the most risk-free manner possible. Maggie could wait at the end of the drive for whoever was coming out to pick her up, Abby decided. That car would not be allowed to enter the grounds.

Although she hadn't protested, the caretaker hadn't been happy about the change in plans. Or maybe she didn't like the fact that Abby had called the sheriff and asked him to come back out and make sure that whoever came for Maggie left right away.

"And, Maggie. I'll need your key to the house," Abby said.

"I've had a key to this house since before you was born."

"I understand that, but Sheriff Blanchard told you that we're very security-conscious right now. With what happened here last night, I'll feel better knowing that no one else has a key."

"I ain't gonna give it to nobody," Maggie said, her face tight with offense.

"I'll still need your key before you leave, Maggie. I'm sorry if you're insulted," Abby said. She wasn't sure what she would do if Maggie didn't comply. Ask the sheriff to step in, she supposed. She would hate to do that, since Maggie obviously didn't like Blanchard. But she would. She would have to.

Luckily, it didn't come to that. Maggie fished in the opening at the top of her cotton dress and produced an old-fashioned cloth change purse. From that she took out the house key and placed it grudgingly on Abby's outstretched palm.

"How long will you be away?" Abby asked.

"Don't know exactly," Maggie acknowledged.

"If we leave before you get back, I'll leave this for you with Sheriff Blanchard."

Maggie's lips tightened. The harrumph was softer this time, but the cold disdain was in her brown eyes.

"What'd he do to you, Maggie?" Abby asked. "What'd he do to make you dislike him so much?"

Stubbornly, the caretaker shook her head, eyes falling to the change purse, which she closed with deliberation and replaced in its hiding place. "I'll go get my suitcase," she said.

ABBY WAS WATCHING from the front windows when the sheriff's car arrived. He had touched the siren, probably to let her know he was here. In the flare of headlights, she could see Maggie's figure silhouetted at the end of the drive, her thin body looking lost and forlorn in the darkness under the big trees. The lights cast her shadow, highly elongated, onto the drive behind her.

The sheriff immediately got out of the patrol car and walked around in front of it, briefly interrupting the twin beams of the headlights. He seemed to be talking to Maggie, and Abby found herself wondering about their conversation. And about everything else between those two. Like Nick's jigsaw puzzle, there were too many pieces missing for her to be able to figure out Maggie and the sheriff's relationship, which had apparently been formed long before she and Nick had shown up out here.

The sheriff had gotten back into the patrol car, again passing between Abby and the headlights, several minutes before the second car appeared. Abby watched as Maggie traced the same path, moving in front of the patrol car to climb into the other. She was still watching when both sets of red taillights finally disappeared into the darkness.

She checked the lock on the front door and then started down the hall, intending to go back to the kitchen to do the same with the back entry. And to verify that the alarm system's light was blinking. She found Nick sitting on the stairs.

"Your friend decide not to come in?" he asked.

His elbows were propped on his knees, big hands relaxed and hanging loosely between his legs. The dark glasses seemed to be focused on her face, just as they had been this morning.

"Sheriff Blanchard, you mean?"

"You have any other friends out this way?"

She debated arguing the point with him—whether the sheriff was her friend or not. But, given their last exchange, she decided Nick might be right. Right enough that she didn't want to be challenged on her feelings about the local law.

"He was just out here to make sure that Maggie got off the property," she explained.

"Maggie?" The crease had reformed between the wings of his dark brows.

"Some kind of family emergency," Abby explained.

"Is Andrews sending someone else out?"

"I think the plans are for us to survive on our own until he can make some other arrangements."

"What kind of arrangements?" Nick asked carefully.

Abby hesitated before she answered, but then she decided that he certainly had a right to know about the decisions the department was making about keeping him safe.

"To move you to another location," she said.

"Because of Maggie? Or because of last night?" She wondered if he could be right.

"He didn't mention it until I told him Maggie was leaving."

"What kind of emergency?" Nick asked.

"I don't know. She wouldn't tell me. Something about her baby needing her."

Nick laughed. He put his hands together, fingers interlocking. One thumb rubbed over the other, and Abby couldn't resist watching its movement. Just as it had moved against her arm this morning. Slow and unhurried.

"Her baby," he said. "Maggie's son. The youngest one."

Apparently Maggie had confided a lot more information about herself to Nick Deandro than she had to Abby. Of course, Nick had been here for more than five months, Abby reminded herself.

"Why doesn't she like Blanchard?" Abby asked, wondering if Nick could shed some light on that mystery. She didn't really expect an answer, but he gave her one. One that explained a lot.

"He busted her kid. Drug charges."

"Possession?"

"Dealing," Nick said softly.

"In this parish?"

That information didn't fit with what the sheriff had suggested about the crime out here, but maybe he meant he hadn't had any trouble after that arrest. It was hard to imagine Maggie's child being a drug dealer, but then kids went bad all the time. Went against their upbringing. Especially with the temptation of drugs and the big money they offered.

And suddenly, this all made sense. Maggie would be one of those parents who didn't want to believe anything bad about her child. It was far easier to blame the law than the child. To blame whoever had made the arrest.

"This *is* his jurisdiction," Nick said.

"No wonder she can't stand him," Abby said.

"Kill the messenger," Nick agreed.

Abby nodded. And realized her mistake. "I guess so," she said. "Did you need something?" she asked, realizing that Nick's presence on the stairs was something very much out of the norm.

"I guess you could say that," he said.

"What is it?"

"I wanted to apologize for this morning. For touching you."

Whatever she had expected, it wasn't this. She didn't know how to deal with it. Or what to say to him. Even the word *touching* echoed, reviving memory. His hands on her body.

"Why don't we just forget it happened," she suggested.

He laughed again, the sound quiet and yet not as dark as his previous laughter. This was almost natural. Almost as it had been before. When she had known him before.

"That should be easy enough for me," Nick said. "Just one more thing I don't remember."

It was the most bitter of ironies, she supposed, that she was suggesting to Nick that he should forget something that had happened between them.

"It's just that you remind me of someone," he went on.

He lifted his hand, rubbing distractedly at the scar on his temple. She watched his fingers, hoping he wouldn't say any more. She wasn't ready to hear any more.

"She was a cop, too. Maybe. I don't really know that, but at least..." He hesitated, seeming to be thinking carefully about what he was saying. "At least, I used to worry because I thought she wasn't tough enough. She seemed too damn fragile."

Abby said nothing in response. She hadn't dreamed that Nick had worried about her. Or that he had seen her as fragile. She should have resented his concern, she supposed, but she couldn't, of course. Because she had done her share of worrying about him, and no one could argue that Nick Deandro wasn't tough enough for his job. Any job. And yet...

"She was small. Thin like you. She wore that same perfume." His face lifted as he inhaled. "She had long blond hair that used to tangle around us when we made love."

When we made love. The whispered words hung in the air between them. Hovering there like the too-familiar scent she couldn't smell. Like memory.

"And I thought..." He spoke again into the silence, and then his voice faded. "This morning I thought for a moment you might be that woman," he finished.

Shouldn't she whisper the words her heart was screaming? *I am that woman. I am.* Still she hesitated, not understanding her indecision. Surely what had been in his voice just now should be enough to overcome any doubts she had. Any question that they still belonged together, despite everything.

She was carrying this man's child. And she had loved him, more than she had ever loved anyone else in her entire life. But still she didn't say the simple words that would end this cruel charade she and Rob Andrews had conspired together to create. Conspired for different reasons, of course. But she was as guilty of having ulterior motives in coming out here as Rob was in sending her.

"I need to check the back," she said instead of telling Nick the truth. Instead of telling him anything. "We don't want a repeat of what happened last night."

He didn't respond in any way, his hands still locked together, but unmoving now. She walked past the foot of the stairs where he was sitting and toward the safe, beckoning light of the kitchen.

When she got there, she found that the back door was locked, just as she had known it would be. And the arming light was blinking, slow and steady as a heartbeat. That should have been reassuring, but it wasn't. It was mocking again.

She had known this was wrong. To come out here. To pretend to him that nothing had ever happened between them. But she had rationalized her decision by thinking that seeing Nick again might give her a chance to understand her feelings. To understand the terrible duality of them.

One part of her wanted desperately for Nick to remember. To remember her and what they had had. And another part held back from that because she was afraid it would never again be the same. That she wouldn't feel the same way about him. That she *couldn't* feel that way about him anymore. And if that were true, her rejection was something she knew Nick didn't deserve. Not on top of all the other.

She turned off the kitchen light and stood a moment in the darkness, trying to imagine being blind. Trying to think how she would have reacted to that awful change. She found that she couldn't even imagine what it must be like.

And she wasn't Nick Deandro. She was a woman. Women were expected to be vulnerable. They were allowed to be. Allowed some uncertainty and even fear. As men were not.

She had never wanted Nick to be uncertain or afraid. Those were things she had never associated with him. And she didn't want to now. Perhaps that was unfair, immoral, cowardly even, but she knew it was also true.

Shaking her head against the injustice of her feelings, she turned away from the blinking light and headed back to the stairs, hoping desperately that Nick wouldn't still be sitting in the darkness there. Hoping that they wouldn't have to talk about this any more tonight. Hoping she wouldn't have to think about the kind of person it seemed she really was.

When she reached the door to the hall, she turned around again, glancing back into the kitchen, at the red dot of light, still blinking steadily on the far wall. Double-checking because of last night. A little paranoid, she supposed.

She could never explain why she didn't scream when his forearm fastened across her throat, pulling her back against the hard wall of his chest. She hadn't made a sound. Because she had known instantly that it was Nick's arm. And that it was Nick's hand grabbing her left wrist.

She lifted her right hand, which was still free, and began to pry with trembling fingers at the muscled forearm that was across her neck. There was no loosening of the pressure. Nick wasn't hurting her, but he could. Maybe he was even trying to make her aware of how easily he could.

"What the hell do you think you're doing?" she demanded.

"Good question, Sterling. Why don't you answer it?"

"I don't know what you're talking about."

He laughed, the sound right beside her ear, so close she could feel his breath against her cheek. She could even smell him. Man-scent. Nick.

So familiar it made her knees weak. She wanted to lean

back against his solid strength. To relax against it. To feel his arms close around her and lift her. She wanted him to carry her upstairs to one of the beds and make love to her in the mindless, forgiving darkness. Just as he had before.

"What the hell do you have to do with all this?" he said instead, his voice harsh. "Why don't you tell me why Andrews sent you out here?"

"To protect you," she said. She was trying to think what he wanted to know. If she was the woman he had dreamed about? If so, this seemed a strange way of trying to get information.

"To protect me from the mob, I suppose."

"From the people who tried to kill you," she agreed.

"Except that's *not* who tried to kill me, Sterling. You and Rob Andrews and I all know that."

"I don't know what you're talking about," Abby said. She didn't. She didn't have any idea what he meant.

"They call in a mechanic, and I'm going to be dead. Very, very dead before he leaves the scene," Nick said.

She thought about that. A mechanic. A professional hit. That's what they had all thought. "He got interrupted," she suggested. That was what she had been told, anyway. "A cop showed up."

"A real pro would just kill the cop. You know that as well as I do. No mechanic is going to leave me bleeding on the street without making sure I'm dead. He does, and *he's* a dead man."

"What are you saying?" Abby asked.

"That it was somebody else that night. Somebody who wanted me, but wasn't quite cold-blooded enough about it to shoot two other people. Somebody who screwed up."

"Not a pro," she said. He was right. She didn't know why she hadn't thought of that possibility before. Why Rob hadn't. Or maybe, she thought suddenly, maybe he had.

"You got it, Sterling. Not a pro. Somebody local."

"Somebody local," she repeated, trying to figure out

what he was saying. And then it hit her. "Somebody in the department? You think one of us…"

She didn't complete the sentence. His forearm had tightened reflexively, and her fingers struggled again against the increased pressure. This time they had some effect.

It eased minutely, and in response she drew a breath. It was deep and uneven—from fear, shock or maybe lack of oxygen. She wasn't sure, but she was grateful for the reprieve.

"The woman I told you about," Nick said, his mouth against her ear, the words still soft in the darkness, nearly caressing. "I'd been with her that night."

"You remember that?"

"Not a memory. I just know that I was. And there was…some evidence of that. On my body."

Abby closed her eyes, the images of the last night they had spent together moving through her mind like the frames of a movie. Individual images, clear and vivid. Feeling the sensations, even. Reliving the emotions.

"And Rob knew that?" she asked finally.

He nodded, his chin moving up and down against her hair. And then he asked, "Are you that woman, Sterling? Are you the woman Andrews thinks set me up for the hit?"

Chapter Seven

The shock of that took her breath. She had had no idea where his questions had been leading. No idea that Rob believed a woman was mixed up in what had happened.

Maybe that's why he had sent her out here. Not to jar Nick Deandro's memory, as he had told her, but as a test of some kind. An attempt, if he believed she was involved, to entrap her.

If that were the case, then Nick wasn't the victim of this charade. She was. Victim. Suspect. Did they both think she had had something to do with the hit? Not professional, Nick had said. Not the usual mob mechanic.

She understood now that he was probably right about that. Only, he was terribly wrong about the rest of it. About her role in what had happened to him. "You're wrong," she said.

Suddenly his hand released her wrist. She didn't know what he intended, not even when she felt it touch her cheek. There was nothing about the movement that was the least bit uncertain.

His fingers tangled in her hair, tracing downward to the abrupt end of the chin-length strand he had captured. And only then did she understand...*long blond hair that used to tangle around me when we made love.*

Slowly his hand fell away. Not to grip her wrist again. Not to touch her in any other way. But his forearm was still around her neck and the familiar feel of his big body was pressed tightly behind hers.

"Are you that woman, Sterling?" he asked again. The import of the question had changed somehow with the difference in his tone. She knew that what he was asking now was not what he had asked before.

They weren't the same two people who had met on those nights in the darkness of her small apartment. Hiding because it was dangerous to do otherwise. Meeting only when Nick believed he could safely get away from his assignment for a few hours. When he could disappear without being missed.

Are you that woman? It seemed like such a simple question. It wasn't, of course, and it was one she still didn't have any answer for. All she had was another question. *Are you that man, Nick? That same strong man?*

Suddenly, his arm released her throat. It slid across her body, and his hand wrapped around her upper arm. His other hand found her left shoulder. Still standing behind her, gently holding her shoulders, Nick bent and pushed his mouth into the softness under her ear. His tongue traced over her skin, leaving a trail of heat and dampness behind.

Automatically, she tilted her head to rest her cheek against his hair, feeling the black silk of it brush her throat. His teeth teased the sensitive lobe of her ear. Finally his tongue slipped inside the small ivory channel, the feel of its movement hot and enticing. Then his breath touched the moisture it had left, soft coolness against the warmth. A shivering seduction.

So familiar she was unable to prevent reaction. Her knees trembled, almost giving way, and a small moan escaped, the sound originating from deep within her throat. Sensual. Needy.

In response to that clearly expressed need, Nick's hard fingers moved, biting suddenly into the top of her shoulder, forcing her to turn and face him. His left hand fastened on her right arm, and he lifted, pulling her body upward by his strong grip on her upper arms, even as he lowered his head.

His mouth settled over hers, and Abby's opened, responding to the feel of his lips as reflexively as a baby's hand will tighten over a finger placed within its palm. She stood on tiptoe, straining to increase the sweet contact with his tongue, which demanded response with the compelling surety it had always had.

Nothing had changed, it seemed. Not about this. And suddenly kissing him was not enough. It wasn't a conscious decision, because she had known what would happen if he ever held her.

But somehow she had forgotten to be careful. Her body had forgotten why it should maintain a distance. Overcome by a more powerful need, it reached for his, seeking the once-familiar contact. Needing it. Needing him. She had existed for too long with nothing but memories of this. And now...

She was aware of the enormity of her mistake as soon as he stiffened, but by then, of course, it was too late. Again, his hands on her shoulders tightened, this time pushing her away. Obeying, as she had always obeyed him, Abby took a step back.

His hands fell to the bulge of her pregnancy, the palms cupping over the unmistakable contour of it and then tracing the shape downward. "What the hell?" Nick said, the question so soft it was almost a whisper. "What the hell is going on?"

HE HAD THOUGHT he was so smart. Believed he had figured some of this out. At least why Abby seemed so damn familiar. He had even thought he understood what she was doing here. And now he knew he had been wrong about it all. Wrong about everything.

His hands fell away from her body, and he stood in shock, trying to think. Abby Sterling was pregnant. And although he was no expert, it seemed to him she was pretty far along.

He waited, but she didn't say anything in response to his question. He could hear her breathing, even the occasional soft shuddering catch in its rhythm. Breathing so unevenly it sounded as if she'd been running. Was she that disturbed by what had just happened between them? *Almost happened,* he amended.

But then he was pretty damn disturbed, too. It had been a hell of a long time since he'd been with a woman, and this had felt...right. Abby Sterling's mouth fitting under his. Perfect. Familiar. And he didn't understand how that could be.

Part of it was her size, he supposed. The feel of her wrist under the grip of his big fingers, the bones so incredibly delicate. And that damn perfume made it hard for him to think clearly when he was around it. Around her.

Then it was difficult to do anything but be aware of the screaming need of his body. The endless wanting that was just like the dreams that woke him and left him to lie alone in that bed, his body aching and trembling.

That was really why he had begun this fantasy, he supposed. Why he had begun to believe Abby Sterling was the woman he dreamed about. Because they wore the same perfume, he mocked himself. *Some cop, Deandro. Some real smart detective work.*

There must be at least a million women who wore that same popular scent. Would he want all of them? Would he go through life imagining that they, too, were someone he had once made love to? Someone he had once loved.

He had been reluctant to use those words before, especially after Andrews's suggestion about the woman's possible involvement in the hit. But they had been in his mind. In the back of it, anyway, because of the intensity of the dreams. Because of the terrible sense of loss that was always there when he woke up.

Obviously, he had transferred that need, that emotion, to

the first woman he'd come in contact with since he'd been shot. To Abby Sterling, who was some other man's wife. Who was carrying some other man's baby.

Apparently he was not only blind, he thought bitterly, but brain-dead as well. He used to pride himself at being good at what he did. Figuring things out. Thinking everything through.

This time he had done his thinking all right, but not with his brain. He had relied on another notoriously less reliable organ. And on his famous gut instincts. All because Abby Sterling had somehow "felt" familiar.

She even had tonight. When he had put his mouth over hers, his hands fastening around her upper arms to pull her up to him. It had felt so...right. How the hell could she feel this familiar and be a stranger?

All the while, his rational mind was still trying to deal with the shock of his discovery that Sterling was pregnant. The bodyguard Andrews had sent out here to protect him was pregnant, he repeated mentally, disbelieving. And that made no sense.

Unless.... The thought was sudden. And considering everything, it was also frightening. Given his situation, it was frightening as hell.

But he denied his urge to touch her again. To put his hands over the hard roundness of her belly. To try to judge with his fingers how advanced this pregnancy really was. And he fought against seriously considering the possibility that had just entered his mind.

Even as he did, the hard ache in his groin increased, the blood rushing there in response to the image he knew didn't belong in his head. The picture of a dark-haired infant suckling the small, perfect globe of her breast, blue-veined and rose-tipped. His baby? Could this possibly be his baby?

Without his conscious volition it seemed, his fingers moved, trembling as they began their upward journey. They hesitated, without touching, over the bulge they had explored before. He wanted to. God knew, he wanted to touch her again, but that would tell him nothing. Nothing he didn't already know.

Abby Sterling was pregnant. He knew that, but he sure wasn't familiar enough with women in that condition to be able to tell anything about the time frame. More than six months? To his shocked, searching hands she had certainly felt big enough for that. And if so...

He could still hear her breathing, but the inhalations were softer now, more even. She sounded less like she was running a race. Calmer. Maybe that was only because he no longer had his hands on her body.

Sexual harassment in anybody's book, he thought, almost amused by the realization. Running his fingers over her stomach as if he had some right to touch her. To touch the shape and incredible tautness of her pregnancy. To try to measure it.

But still, he needed to know. He needed to understand why his body had betrayed him. Why he had believed so strongly that he had known this woman before. Known her in the oldest sense of that word, the Biblical one.

His hand continued to rise as the thoughts circled inside his head. It had moved above waist level, however. Moved higher. Determined not to grope. Determined to find out, as he had asked her, just what the hell was going on here.

He stretched his arm forward a little, reaching for her face, and his fingers made contact. There was something soft under their tips. Fabric of some kind. Sweater?

He moved his hand slightly and knew by the texture that he was right. Under the sweater, he could feel bone, and he allowed his hand to trace along it. Collarbone. As delicate under his exploring fingers as her wrist had been this morning.

He had to fight the compulsion to move his hand downward a little, to cup his palm under her breast. To feel the weight and shape of it in his hand. Surely then he would know. Surely he would be able to tell...

Stupid. Infinitely stupid, some still-rational part of him jeered. She was a woman. Just as a million women wore this perfume, a million of them would feel the same to his groping, untrained fingers. And he could imagine how she would react to that particular attempt at identification.

He touched her neck instead, his fingers gliding upward. And then her cheek. She didn't move, didn't flinch from the contact, and he couldn't imagine why she was allowing this. His fingers traced lightly over the bones of her face. Jawline. Cheekbone. The incredible smoothness of her skin. Small, slender slope of nose.

But there had never been a picture in his head of the woman from the dreams. Even if he had any experience at "seeing" someone through his fingertips, he would have nothing to compare this experiment to when he finished. Nothing.

Finally he touched her hair again. That single memory had been so clear. Even now he could remember watching her gather the golden strands with both hands and hold them bunched high on her head. At some time he had done that. Had watched her hold her hair off the heat and dampness of her neck.

And he had felt it spread over his body, the spiderweb fineness of the strands caught against the dampness of his own skin. Against his face. Caught in his late-afternoon beard. He had tangled his fingers in the curling length of it. And now, instead...

"I'm sorry," he said.

His hands fell from the strand he had touched. He had known before, when he had felt her pregnancy, but he had wanted to be wrong. He took a step away from her. And he waited.

A long time. Standing alone in the darkness of his humiliation. His stupidity. His blindness.

"It's all right," Sterling said finally.

Her voice was different, but he couldn't tell what was in it. Apparently he couldn't tell a damn thing about what was going on around him. Stupid, mindless groping in the dark, trying to believe he could still figure things out.

"This is what Rob meant," he said. "About needing to rest."

"Yes," she agreed.

Which told him two things, he realized, his mind worrying at what had happened. Still working at the puzzle despite knowing how wrong he had been before. It meant Abby Sterling's pregnancy was pretty far along or her supervisor wouldn't have been so concerned about her. And it also meant, of course, that nobody was still trying to find Nick Deandro.

Which should have been comforting, he supposed. But it wasn't. Not a damn bit comforting. "They finally tell Andrews I'm not ever going to remember?" he asked.

She hesitated a fraction of a second too long before she answered him. Since he had been reduced to reading voices for information, the lack of an immediate denial was a pretty good clue to the reality of what was going on.

"No one's said that," she hedged.

"But that's what they think."

"Rob believes the mob thinks you're dead."

"Those guys don't buy the death of a witness until they touch the cold dead body with their own hands," he said. "Andrews knows that. So I can't figure why else he would send someone like you out here."

"Someone like me?" she repeated softly.

Nick laughed. "I forgot. Gender sensitive."

"What does that mean?" The same tightness that had been in her voice when he'd confronted her on the stairs was back. A little angry. A little insulted. But it was better than hearing what had been there before. That tinge of pity after she'd blown her denial by hesitating over it.

"It means that Mickey Yates wasn't about ready to drop a kid when he came out here. It means something sure as hell seems to have changed about my situation."

That sounded bitter. Self-pitying, even to him. And he

supposed she could read his voice as well as he could read hers. But that realization had really hurt.

It deepened the despair that had been there since the beginning. The fear. He kept hoping he'd get better because everyone had kept telling him he would.

Now he knew the truth. They weren't worried about protecting him because apparently everybody knew he was no longer a threat to anyone, despite their endless reassurances. And if they were wrong about the amnesia, then they were probably wrong about the rest of it, too. About the blindness. But he couldn't deal with the thought of that now. Not while Sterling was reading every nuance of his voice, as he was trying to read hers.

"They call off the indictments?" he asked instead, speaking around the knot of frustration that was building in his throat.

"They're still expecting you to be able to testify. Eventually. They're still counting on you," she added.

"Spare me, Sterling. At least spare me that load of crap. That all I've heard from Andrews and everybody else for months. At least admit what's going on here."

"What do you think is 'going on here'?" she asked angrily. "Why don't you explain what you think the fact that I'm pregnant means?"

"You know as well as I do what it means. Andrews sends you out here for a rest while you pretend to be playing bodyguard for somebody who apparently doesn't need a bodyguard anymore."

"Implying I'm the next best thing to no bodyguard."

"Implying that if Andrews was really worried about somebody coming for me, he sure as hell wouldn't put you in their path."

She took a breath, audible, and he waited, but the silence stretched. Apparently she was thinking about what he'd said.

"Because I couldn't protect you?" she asked finally.

"Because he's not going to put a pregnant woman in

jeopardy. You know that as well as I do. If I can read that good ol' Southern boy that well, then you sure understand how his mind works. He wouldn't do that. So that means—''

"Nothing," she interrupted. "It means nothing. I'm a cop. I'm part of O.C. Special Unit. I'm still on the payroll, Deandro, and I'm expected to earn my money. And for your information I'm pregnant, not disabled."

"Thanks for reminding me, Sterling. I guess I needed that little lesson in the distinction between me and you."

"That's not what I meant," she said hotly. "Damn it, you always—'' She stopped, the angry words cut off abruptly.

"I always what?" he asked. "What do I always do, Sterling? Rattle your damn feminist chain?"

She didn't answer. He heard her move instead. Preparing to go past him, to get out of the kitchen and go back upstairs, he thought. To avoid him and his unanswerable questions.

Suddenly, he was angry, too. Part of it was his frustration, or maybe fear, boiling over after months of trying so damn hard to keep it in check. Part of it was fury over her assumption, again, that he was just being a sexist bastard.

But part of it was also the knowledge that there were still a lot of things unresolved here. Things that he couldn't figure out. Maybe even things that she and Rob Andrews were keeping from him, which was pretty easy to do now. The truth of that made him even angrier.

He reached for her, intending to stop her escape, but his hand brushed against her body and slid off. Missing her, he realized, because she had sidestepped, avoiding him. At that, anger flooded his body, the hot white strength of rage overcoming everything rational. "Don't you dodge me, damn you," he said.

He lunged for her, but again she wasn't there. Not where his hand had just touched her. Where he had expected her still to be standing. He swung his arm in a wide arc in front of him, fingers reaching for her. And encountering emptiness.

Blindman's bluff. He remembered playing the game at some birthday party when he was a kid. He hadn't liked it then. Wearing that damn blindfold. The other kids laughing and dodging away. The feeling of helplessness. And he liked those things a whole lot less now.

"Sterling," he said. He knew his voice was too loud. He was almost shouting at her.

"You need to calm down," she said.

She didn't sound calm. She sounded like somebody who was upset and trying to pretend to be calm. He had turned toward the sound, estimating distance in his head. He reached for her again and heard movement. She was still avoiding his hand. And she could do that all night. Play blindman's bluff with him.

"Where's your womanly compassion, Sterling? I'm trying to find you and you're avoiding me. Not exactly playing fair."

"Whatever you're playing, Deandro, I'm not interested in signing up for the team."

"Blindman's bluff," he said bitterly, and as he spoke, he lunged toward her voice again. She wasn't there.

"Stop it, Nick," she demanded. "Stop it right now."

She sounded more upset than he was. Maybe she was. Maybe he was scaring her. He hadn't meant to do that. He hadn't meant to do anything to her, but when she had avoided his hand, leaving him groping in the dark like some damn blindfolded child...

"We both need to calm down," she said. "This isn't helping anything."

"I'm not going to hurt you."

"I know that," she whispered.

Suddenly there were tears in her voice, and the sound of them stopped him. Stopped whatever insanity had been driving him. He wasn't sure what he had intended when he'd begun. But he hadn't intended this. Not what it had turned into.

His hand fell. He had made a complete fool of himself. About everything. First by trying to kiss her because she reminded him of a dream. And then this. Groping for her like some sex-starved adolescent. Groping blindly.

"We can talk some more in the morning," she said softly. "We'll feel... We'll have had a chance to think it all over."

"One good reason, Sterling," he said, his voice as low as hers had been, working for calmness. He was begging, he supposed, reduced to that by this situation which had left him in the dark and groping for answers. "Give me one reason."

"A reason for what?"

"Tell me why Andrews sent you out here. The real reason. One good reason for it to be you he sent instead of somebody else. And spare me the crap about being a good cop. Everybody in that unit is a good cop. Why you, damn it?"

He waited, listening again to the sound of her breathing. Trying to decide what to tell him? What he would buy?

"He thought I might be the one of us you'd remember," she said finally.

"The one?"

"Of the unit. Rob thought meeting me again might... stimulate you to remember something."

He damn sure had been right about that, Nick thought. Only, Andrews hadn't had in mind exactly what she had stimulated.

"Why?" Nick asked. One good reason was all he had asked her for. He hadn't heard it yet.

"We had words a couple of times. A personality conflict."

"What kind of words?"

"I don't know," she said. "Just...words."

Her voice sounded as defeated as it had on the stairs that

night. Tired of this confrontation. Tired of his questions he supposed, but he was going to have some answers or he was going to call Andrews and get him out here. Tonight if he had to.

"Just…arguments," she went on hesitantly. "Nothing important. We just seemed to rub each other the wrong way. We struck sparks, Rob said. He thought… I think he was hoping maybe we would again. And that would make you remember me. Remember something."

That was what she had meant on the porch that day. *He doesn't remember me. It looks like all your maneuvering has been for nothing.* Andrews had probably had to do a hell of a lot of maneuvering to get the powers-that-be to agree to a very pregnant woman as bodyguard for a government witness. Even if everybody was ready to give that witness up as a lost cause.

"Is that the truth, Sterling? Are you telling me the absolute truth?"

"It's the truth," she said softly. "I swear that's really why Rob sent me out here. Because we didn't like each other worth a damn."

He nodded. He could imagine how he would have responded to her chip-on-the-shoulder feminism. Probably just the way he had reacted tonight. With sarcasm. Smartmouth bastard. He always had been.

"What about the resting business? What was that all about? If pregnancy shouldn't be considered a drawback to your doing this job," he asked, the touch of sarcasm creeping back into his voice, "then why all the stuff about doing nothing strenuous? Why does Andrews think you need some kind of rest cure?"

Again she hesitated. But she told him finally. And it was something else that made sense. Something else he could believe.

"I put in a request for a new assignment. My doctor thought I needed something less demanding. Not necessarily less strenuous. That's Rob's interpretation. Less stressful, I guess.''

His anger was fading. Maybe because her voice was so quiet. Maybe because he had begun to believe her.

''I've had some problems,'' she added. ''Nothing…serious, but enough that my doctor was a little concerned.''

''Concerned you might lose the baby?'' he asked and then wished he hadn't. He didn't need to know Sterling's secrets. She had explained all that he needed to understand. Her personal life, her health, this baby, weren't any of his business.

''Just…concerned. It's nothing serious,'' she said again.

He wondered if that was intended to convince him or her. Whichever, it changed how he felt. Maybe they had given up on him, but the decision to send Sterling out here apparently hadn't been made for any of the motives he'd been assigning to it.

''I didn't hurt you, did I?''

''Hurt me?'' she questioned, confusion in her voice.

''When I grabbed you?''

She laughed, and he realized it was the first time he had heard her laugh. The sound was unexpected. And for some reason it moved through his body in a physical wave of sensation.

''You didn't hurt me,'' she said. ''I'm not fragile, Nick. Or sick. Despite what you think.''

''I think…'' he began softly and then stopped the words. He had been a bastard. It seemed to come too easily to him. Especially these days. And what Abby had said made sense. More sense than what he'd been thinking these revelations might mean.

''I think I need to apologize, Sterling,'' he said softly. ''For touching you. For yelling at you.''

''It doesn't matter,'' she said. ''You deserved an explanation. It was wrong of us to pull this on you, but…''

He finished it for her when she hesitated. "But they need to make me remember. Any way they can get it to happen."

"They need you to remember," she agreed.

There had been a small emphasis on the first pronoun. Not deliberate, Nick thought, but there. It was something else to think about, to figure out.

"I'm going upstairs now," she said.

Asking his permission, maybe. And why not? He'd spent the last ten minutes chasing her around the kitchen like some kind of madman. She sounded tired again.

"You okay?" he asked.

He couldn't have stopped the question if his life had depended on it. He remembered how the hard, full contour of her belly had felt under his exploring hands. The reality was that that was a baby. A child who needed to be born and deserved a chance to grow up. She had already had some trouble. He didn't want to have done anything that might cause her more.

"I'm fine," she said. "Stop worrying."

"I don't worry, Sterling. It's counterproductive."

The quality of the silence between them suddenly changed again, and he listened to it, trying to decide why. He hadn't figured it out before he heard her footsteps on the wooden floor of the hall and listened to them fade away into the darkness.

ABBY'S KNEES were still trembling as she climbed the stairs. Overreaction, maybe, but she had not been prepared for any of this. Certainly not prepared for the feel of Nick's mouth over hers. Not prepared for his questions. Not prepared for the macabre game of blindman's bluff they had played.

She had told him the truth, and she supposed that meant she should be feeling a lot better about the encounter than she did. And a lot less guilty.

She knew, however, that what she had told Nick tonight had been Rob Andrews's truth and not her own. She had been sent out here to do exactly what she had said. That was not, however, why she had agreed to come.

She had come to find out if her feelings about Nick had changed. To find out if she was still in love with him. And after what had happened tonight, she was more confused than she had been before.

It was obvious that her body still wanted him. That his touch could still send shivers of need and anticipation coursing through her. And she now knew that despite the damage the bullet had done, the undeniable brilliance of the mind she had admired was still there. Still functioning. Nick Deandro was still a good cop.

And it hadn't bothered her when he had touched her face. The feel of his exploring fingers had been almost sensual. Almost the way his hands had touched her before—the same tenderness, the unexpected gentleness, given their size and his strength, that she had missed.

That was one reason she had instinctively avoided his hand tonight when he had reached for her. She didn't know the angry, frustrated man who left bruises on her skin. That wasn't the Nick who had made slow, almost endless love to her in the darkness.

What she had done in avoiding him had been worse than cruel, but it had also been unthinking. Now, however, the image of his hand moving gropingly before him in a wide sweeping gesture, seeking her in the darkness had been implanted in her mind.

And it fit, of course, with all the preconceived notions she had brought out here with her. That was the problem. It fit exactly with those stereotypical images of the blind she had struggled so hard to keep away from her precious memories of Nick Deandro.

Chapter Eight

There had been no unusual noises this time to interrupt the country quietness of the night. No disturbances other than those originating in Nick's brain as he tried to fit things together.

He had gone over and over what Abby had told him about Rob's motives in giving her this assignment. And they made more sense than Andrews sending someone out here that he suspected of having been involved with Nick before the shooting. That would be too dangerous, since they still didn't know how Nick had been made.

So obviously, imagining that Abby Sterling was the woman he'd dreamed about had been wishful thinking. Because of the intensity of those dreams, maybe. Because of the need they created in his body. The incredible longing. Or the sense of loss they always left behind.

He rolled to his side and reached out to touch the bedside clock. It was after seven. Later than he normally slept. Of course, Maggie's pot-banging was what usually woke him every morning, and Maggie was gone. It was very quiet. Maybe Sterling was still asleep. He closed his eyes again, thinking about that. And thinking, almost against his will, about what had happened between them last night. Reliving it.

Feeling her arms under the relentless, too-tight grip of his hands. Pulling her toward him for his kiss. Being aware of her response. Then Brailling her face, trying, like a fool, to imagine from the brush of his fingers what she looked like.

He tried to push his mind away from the other discovery. From the memory of his hands cupping around the baby she carried. The memory of them tracing over the tight swell of the child growing within her body. But he couldn't deny the effect that had had on him. The effect it still had, he acknowledged reluctantly, feeling his body's response to that unwanted image.

He still couldn't imagine why he was reacting to Sterling's pregnancy in that way, with this almost sexual excitement. He had never had a thing about pregnant women. Up until now, he had avoided examining that subject too closely. He wasn't the kind of guy who was interested in rings, mortgages and babies.

That phrase suddenly reverberated. It didn't drift through his head like the other thoughts had. It impacted instead, seeming strangely familiar. As if he had thought it before. Déjà vu, he guessed, dismissing the feeling.

He turned over, opening his eyes and facing the windows. Ritual. Meaningless ritual. At least, he realized suddenly, it had always been meaningless before. Because this morning there was a haze over the blackness. Not a light. It wasn't even a lighter blackness. It was too vague for that.

He closed his eyes and counted to twenty before he allowed himself to open them again. Whatever it was was still there. A milky, translucent…lesser black. That was the best description he could come up with.

And what the hell did he think that meant? he wondered, fighting the excitement that was clawing into his stomach. That sense of elation shouldn't be there, he knew, and so he denied it, just as he'd tried to deny his reaction to Sterling.

This was something that might not mean a damn thing, he told himself again, trying to get a grip on the building emotion. It wasn't a return of his vision. He couldn't even distinguish the two windows. Not their shape or form. There was nothing but a subtle difference in the quality of his ever-present darkness.

He closed his eyes, ordering himself not to hope, not to even think about what this could mean. He had been told that it would take a long time for all the effects of the head injury to go away. A long, slow process of healing, the doctor had said, and one that, frankly, might not result in any improvement in his vision, depending on the condition of the optic nerve itself.

But this, whatever it was, was the first encouraging sign he'd had in six months. And in spite of the doctor's caution, he couldn't completely contain the spurt of hope. He had been about as far down last night as he had gotten throughout this entire ordeal. Making a fool of himself in front of Sterling. Playing blindman's bluff. Trying to kiss her.

But she had responded to that, he remembered. Her mouth had opened under his, her tongue moving in answer. He might be blind, but he had kissed enough women that there was no doubt about what had been going on between them. It had been mutual. Until he had realized she was pregnant.

He didn't want to think about Sterling and last night. Instead, he pushed the covers off and stood up, deliberately turning his face away from the windows. The milkiness immediately disappeared. He turned around, facing the windows above the desk, and the haze was back. He closed his eyes, a sense of relief and elation again surging through his body.

A beginning, he prayed. At least, maybe, a beginning.

BREAKFAST WASN'T going to be up to Maggie's standards, of course. Abby had already decided that Nick would have to make do with whatever she could manage, which wasn't all that much.

She had poured cereal into a bowl and put a small pitcher of milk on the tray, along with a banana which she had left unpeeled. She had two slices of toast in the oven and had placed a small custard cup of pear preserves on the tray. And there was coffee, of course. At least he wouldn't starve.

She had started across the kitchen to check on the toast when she realized Nick was standing in the doorway leading from the hall. He was wearing jeans again and a navy knit shirt.

He looked fit, Abby thought in relief. Tough. Normal. Despite the glasses. He looked…good. He looked just like Nick, and her body reacted to that realization, almost exactly as it had when he had touched her last night. The quick lurch of desire in her lower body. The slow seep of moisture, hot and so incredibly sweet.

It was exactly the same effect he had had on her those steamy nights in New Orleans when she would open the back door of her apartment and find him standing there, nearly hidden by the darkness. He would be leaning against the railing, and as soon as he smiled at her, the same fevered faintness would move through her nerves and muscles, weakening her knees.

Then she couldn't wait for him to push past her into the apartment. Because she knew what would happen between them. She knew how he would make her feel. Like no one in her life had ever before made her feel.

Just exactly as she had felt last night when his lips had trailed against the sensitive skin of her throat. She had been so hungry for his touch. She had thought that was simply the feel of the familiar darkness around them. Or the length of time since Nick had kissed her. Since anyone had kissed her.

She knew now that it was more than that. It was Nick. Same effect. Exactly the same effect he had always had on her. Nothing had changed physically about the way he made her feel.

And for once she was almost glad he couldn't see her

face. Those emotions would all have been revealed there, and Nick was very good at reading her. Too damn good.

"Sterling?" he asked.

Maybe even good at reading the quality of her stillness.

"Not Maggie, I'm afraid," she said, trying for briskness, trying to banish the hungry need, if not from her body, at least from her voice. "Breakfast this morning may be a little skimpy. Not up to Maggie's standards."

"That's okay. I never could manage all that Maggie fixed."

"I thought men liked that kind of meal."

"Maybe if you're a lumberjack," he said.

She wondered if that were a reference to his enforced inactivity, but he was smiling. And then she realized this was the first time she had seen him smile since she'd been here. It was a real smile. Not bitter and not mocking.

"I thought the same thing, but Blanchard manages. Half a dozen biscuits along with everything else."

He made no response, and the smile faded. She just had time to wonder if that was because he didn't like the sheriff, before the scent of something burning began to permeate the kitchen.

"Damn," she said. She opened the oven door and black smoke billowed out. She shouldn't have turned it on broil, she supposed. Or maybe she just shouldn't have allowed herself to be distracted by Nick's unexpected appearance.

"Can I help?" he asked.

"You can tell me you like your toast burned."

"I like my toast burned," he repeated obligingly.

"Like hell you do," she said, taking the cookie sheet out of the oven with the help of one of Maggie's pot holders. She carried it with her to stab the alarm's deactivation button and then over to the door. Operating one-handed, she struggled with the lock before she managed to open it. She pushed the screen with her hip and threw the ruined toast out into the backyard.

She left the door open, and watched a moment as the

smoke began to eddy toward it. Disgusted with herself, she walked across the kitchen and put the baking sheet back on the top of the stove. Then she turned off the oven.

"You didn't really want toast," she advised, turning to look over her shoulder at Nick. Luckily, his lips were still, except for a minute twitch at one corner. His darkly rugged features were aligned, however, in a perfectly noncommittal arrangement.

"I guess not," he said.

"Good," Abby said. "There's cereal and a banana. Will that tide you over until lunch? I can make sandwiches then."

"That's fine, Sterling. I eat anything."

"How about take-out pizza for breakfast? That's the normal extent of my culinary endeavors, but we're probably too far out to get delivery. On second thought, I doubt Rob would approve."

He laughed, and for some reason her stomach reacted again.

"Cheap date, Sterling," he said.

That had been a standing joke between them. They couldn't go out. Not together. Their options were extremely limited as to entertainment. Not that they had ever had any problem entertaining themselves. Not any problems at all, she thought, and realized she was remembering again.

She pushed those images from her mind. But even as she did, she acknowledged that successfully doing so was becoming increasingly difficult. This was Nick. Still Nick. And despite her fears and uncertainty about dealing with his blindness, he still made her knees weak.

"I'll take your tray up," she offered. She walked across to the table and took the handles of the wooden tray Maggie used.

"No," Nick said. "Just…" He hesitated, and she could see the depth of the breath he took before he finished. "Just put whatever we're having out on the table, Sterling."

She waited a moment, eyes examining his face. What

she could see of it. His mouth was set, almost rigid with tension.

"I can carry the damn tray upstairs," she said. They had been over this last night. Pregnant, not disabled.

"I know," Nick said softly, his voice still calm. "But if you don't mind, I prefer to eat down here."

"Why the change of plans?" Abby asked, her fingers tightening around the wooden handles, ready to pounce on any you-need-to-take-it-easy spiel.

"Maggie gets paid to wait on me," Nick said. "You don't. You're a cop, Sterling, not a maid."

She thought about it. He was right, of course. She hadn't signed on to become chief cook and bottle washer. He was certainly capable of coming downstairs for his meals. It made sense in the circumstances, but somewhere in the back of her head Maggie's words echoed. *He don't like eating 'round other people.*

And he still wouldn't, of course, but she could manage to arrange that, even if he ate downstairs. "Okay," she said. She put the tray back down on the table and set the items she had put on it in front of the chair nearest to where Nick was standing.

He began to walk toward the table and when he was within a foot or so, he put his hand out, accurately finding the high top of the ladder-back chair. She looked down, concentrating on what she was doing instead of watching him. She heard the scrape of the chair being pulled out, but still she refused to look up.

Then she realized he was near enough that she could smell the fragrance of his body, just as she had last night. Apparently Nick had just showered, and the pleasantly fresh aroma of soap and shampoo predominated. But the other scent was there as well, sensuously underlying them. The warm masculine scent of his skin. The fragrance of his body. Achingly familiar.

She turned back to the stove and picked up the baking sheet she had left there, intending to put it into the dishwater. It was still too hot to handle, but in her confusion she hadn't even thought about using the pot holder this time. She dropped it to clatter with a metallic reverberation on the top of the stove.

"Damn it to hell," she said softly, putting her burned fingers into her mouth.

"It's probably time to clean up your language, Sterling."

"Am I offending your virgin ears, Deandro?" she asked sarcastically. She turned and watched his fingers moving over the few items she had set out. They touched each carefully, examining and orienting. And their movement was just like the pictures she had in her mind when she heard the word *blind*.

Only, even moving slowly from one item to the next, they were still Nick's fingers. Dark and hard and powerful. She had reason to know how powerful. The bruise she had known would be there had already formed along her wrist.

But there were, of course, all the other images of his hands. They, too, were evoked in her consciousness by the movement of his fingers. Once he had touched *her* just this carefully. Tenderly. Finding places on her body that responded with such joy to their caress. And it seemed, as she watched them now, she could almost feel them moving over her skin again. Eliciting sensations she had never felt before. Or since.

"Kids," Nick said.

"What?" she said, thankfully drawn back from that echoing sensuality by the prosaic quality of his tone.

"Once you've got kids, you have to clean up your act."

"My act's already pretty clean, thank you."

"Just trying to help. You're the one who'll get the ugly notes from the kindergarten teacher. Sugar?" he asked.

"Yes, dear," she retorted.

He laughed, dark head tilted a little to the side. "I thought I was the one who was supposed to have the smart mouth."

"You don't have a monopoly." She put the sugar bowl

down on the table beside his coffee. She wasn't sure whether he wanted it for that or for the cereal. She watched his hand move over it, checking to see that the lid was off.

"You want some help?" she asked.

She hadn't meant for it to happen, but her voice had softened. The banter was better, she knew, regretting her offer to help him as soon as the words left her mouth. They hung in the air between them.

"If I do, I'll ask," Nick said, but there was no anger. Just a simple statement of fact.

She nodded, and then realized again that was pointless. "Okay," she agreed. She went back to the stove and the baking sheet, picking it up with the pot holder this time.

"Sterling?"

She turned back to face him.

"Thanks for offering," he said softly.

She inhaled, deeply enough to ensure that there was no breathless emotion creeping into her voice this time. "You're welcome," she said, realizing suddenly that none of that exchange had been half as painful, knowing the old Nick as she did, as she would have expected it to be. And realizing, surprisingly, that asking if he needed any help had not been painful for her at all.

"WE'RE SURVIVING," Abby told Rob Andrews when he called that afternoon. He was checking up on the situation, of course. And calling to tell her that they didn't have a place in New Orleans ready to move them to yet.

"It won't be long," he reassured. "Having any problems?"

Not any she planned to discuss with her supervisor, she thought. "Not really," she said.

"Is Nick listening to this conversation right now?"

"He's upstairs."

"So what did he remember, Abby? You said it was nothing important."

She had never clarified what Nick had meant by the comment. Maybe it didn't mean anything. Only something he had dreamed about. A fragrance. Nothing that would help the case. She hadn't meant to mislead Rob or to get his hopes up.

"Abby?" he prodded.

"I may have been wrong about that, Rob," she admitted.

"About him remembering something?"

"He thought I was somebody else."

"Somebody else?"

"Some woman. He said you knew about her. Someone who was involved with what happened to him. Or at least involved with Deandro before it happened."

She was surprised Rob had kept that from her. He hadn't told her something that might be pertinent to the assignment she'd been given. She wondered if he'd had a reason not to tell her, or maybe just not had a good enough reason to tell her. Or maybe he didn't think this had anything to do with what they were trying to accomplish. After all, Rob had no way of knowing that she and Nick had once shared much more than animosity.

"I guess he means our mystery woman."

"Mystery woman?" Abby questioned.

"Somebody kept calling the hospital to get information on Nick's condition after he was shot."

Abby worked at controlling her voice. "A woman?"

"She even knew the name we were hiding Deandro under. Knew way too much as far as I was concerned."

"How could she have known that?" Abby asked.

She hadn't realized at the time exactly how the department would interpret those calls. Or maybe she simply hadn't cared. Her concerns had all been directed toward a very different objective. She needed to know how Nick was doing, but she had been reluctant to keep asking Rob for medical information. Maybe reluctant out of guilt, out of worry that she had somehow been responsible for what had happened to Nick, that their clandestine meetings had led to his cover being blown.

She knew that what they had done was a serious breach of security. Nick was critically injured, but she had hesitated to destroy his career, and maybe her own, when she couldn't know for sure that their affair had had anything to do with the shooting.

"I don't know," Rob said. "That's what we've been trying to figure out. You have any ideas, Abby?"

She examined his voice, trying to decide if there was any nuance of suspicion. "It's a leaky department," she suggested.

"That's what scares me," Rob agreed. "That's what scares the hell out of me."

"Nobody in the O.C. Unit is dirty, Rob. We were all too carefully screened. The commissioner himself picked us. Individually. Nobody who'd ever been on the take. No possible connection to the rackets or to the Old Guard."

She waited a moment, listening for his agreement.

"I guess you're right," he said, but she sensed that his affirmation was hesitant.

"You worried about somebody specific?" she asked softly.

"What I'm worried about is the two of you. I don't like what happened out there the other night."

"A glitch," she said. And it might have been. Or her mistake, caused by her distraction over being with Nick again.

"Maybe, but I want Deandro back in town. He needs to start working with the prosecutors. They're eager to see if they can get anything for a corruption indictment."

They both knew how unlikely that was now. "How soon?" she asked.

"A day or two. No more. That's a promise, Abby. Just hold on for a couple of days."

"You got it," she said easily.

It couldn't happen soon enough for her. The tension was building within her. The guilt. The need to confess the truth to Nick, and then to see where they would go from there.

After all, that was the right thing to do. This was Nick Deandro's baby she was carrying.

Even if he still didn't remember her, she now knew that he did remember being involved with someone in the weeks before the shooting. If his memory of those weeks they had been together came back, he would sure as hell resent the fact that she hadn't told him the truth. Her truth.

"You doing okay?" Rob asked. "Not having any trouble, are you? Baby-wise, I mean."

"Not baby-wise or any other. Everything's under control, Rob. Just get us a safe house with security that's dependable."

"I'm working on it. You want some backup?"

She thought about it. It might make sense, but she realized she didn't really want anyone else out here right now. And she decided she'd think about her reasons for that later.

"I guess not. Unless you're worried I can't do the job."

"That's not it, Abby, and you know it. I'd never have sent you out there if I hadn't thought you could handle anything that happens. No matter what."

"Okay," Abby said, grateful for his vote of confidence, since she wasn't sure she had handled everything as well as she thought it should be handled. "Let me know when you know something."

"You got it," Rob agreed, and the connection was broken.

Abby held the phone for a moment, thinking about what she'd done. Assured Rob that everything was fine, despite her internal certainty that she'd armed the system that night. Denied the need for another cop out here, despite what was building between her and Nick. And left herself open for a whole lot of pain.

Heartache, Maggie had said. That was exactly what she was courting, of course, but she couldn't leave now. Because Nick was here and because nothing that needed to be resolved between them had been. Including her own feelings.

"SIT DOWN and eat, Sterling," Nick said.

She glanced over at him, pulling her eyes from their studied contemplation of the shadows that were beginning to drift in over the expanse of the bayou that was visible through the kitchen windows. The dying sun was reflected in the dark waters.

"I haven't spilled anything during the two meals I've eaten down here," he added. "I don't plan on it tonight."

"What is that supposed to mean?" she asked.

"That I promise not to offend your delicate sensibilities."

"What the—" she began.

"That *is* why you're not eating with me, isn't it? Afraid I'm going to do something you don't want to see? Dribble food down my shirt or turn over my tea?"

"Maggie said you don't like to eat around other people," she defended. Damn him, he knew exactly how to get to her. How to make everything she did appear in the worst possible light.

"Sit down and eat," he said again. He had put down his fork, and both hands were on the table, one on either side of his plate, apparently waiting for her to comply. "And I'll wipe my mouth, I swear," he added. "No disgusting table manners from the blind guy."

"Damn you, Nick." She said it aloud this time, but it didn't matter because he'd succeeded. She had already been jerking out the ladder back opposite his.

"Food, Sterling," he suggested.

He was right, of course. It didn't take her long to dip a plate and pour a glass of tea and return to set them down, way too hard, on the table, making her point she hoped. When she sat down, she realized that the meal didn't look all that appetizing.

Most of what she'd fixed had come out of cans. The ham and the potato salad she'd found in the refrigerator. But she had also tried to think as she'd put the simple dinner together what would be easiest for Nick to handle. Although he was right, of course. He had had no trouble with breakfast or lunch.

"Satisfied?" she asked, when she was sitting across from him. She poked her fork into Maggie's leftover potato salad.

"You talk to Rob today?" Nick asked, ignoring her question.

"This afternoon," she said. Her voice was still tight with anger, a contrast to the calmness of his. She watched as he cut a piece of ham with his fork and carried it to his mouth.

"You gonna tell me what he said, or am I supposed to guess?" he asked after he'd chewed and swallowed it.

"He said it would be a couple of days before we could move."

Nick nodded. His fingers wrapped around his glass of iced tea, and he took a sip before he spoke again. "Is that all?"

"He asked if I wanted some backup out here."

His hand hesitated, the bottom of the glass hovering just above the surface of the table. "You accept?"

"No," she admitted. "Maybe I should have." It sounded like a question, and she hadn't meant it to.

The glass descended to the table. "Why?" he asked.

"Because of what happened the other night, I guess."

"I thought you and the sheriff had decided that was nothing. A glitch in the system."

"Maybe," she agreed. "But there's always the possibility, I guess, that someone was really out here."

"Someone looking for me?" he asked.

"Maybe," she said again.

"You worried, Sterling?"

"Are you?" she countered.

"I told you. I don't worry."

"Not even about…" Her voice faltered, the question she had been about to voice unspeakable.

"About this?" he asked, his hand lifting to touch the rim of the dark glasses that covered his eyes.

"Do you?" she said softly.

His lips moved, tightening fractionally. His hand fell to rest again beside his plate. "Sometimes," he said. "Ironically, mostly at night. I sometimes wonder what the hell I'm going to do with the rest of my life if they're wrong."

That was not something she had ever considered, not in all her agonizing over this situation. What a man like Nick Deandro would do for the next fifty years if this were permanent.

"Have you figured that out?" she asked.

"Not yet," he admitted. "But I'm working on it. Now that I'm at least forced to think about the possibility. And I'll tell you, Sterling, it scares the hell out of me."

"That must be a real novelty," she said. She looked up from her mindless prodding of the defenseless potato salad to smile at him, and then, faced with the opaque blackness of the lenses, realized the futility of that form of comfort.

"A novelty? Being afraid?" he asked.

"For you. Considering what you do."

"Working undercover?" His tone had lightened, and she was glad. It seemed they were back on less treacherous conversational territory.

"Always being that close," she said. "Living on the edge."

"I don't think about it much. I guess you couldn't do it if you did. I know the language, the attitude. It's a skin that fits. I grew up with those guys. Punks. Hoods. Mafia types."

"Wise guys," Abby said.

"Not very. Considering the level of intelligence, I always wonder where that term originated. A hell of an oxymoron."

She laughed.

"You laugh a lot, Sterling?" he asked softly. The glasses seemed to be focused on her face, and his own mouth was unmoving, the line of his lips almost set as he waited for her answer.

"What?" she asked, confused by the unexpected question.

"It just sounds so familiar. Hearing you laugh," he explained. "And yet, considering what you told me about our relationship, I just can't imagine you and me sharing a lot of jokes. Or am I wrong about that?"

They had shared a lot of things, of course. But he was right. It hadn't been that kind of relationship.

"Too long, Sterling. When you take that long to answer a simple question, then it's a sure indication you have something to hide. You know that as well as I do. So if you're not covering up the reason Rob Andrews sent you out here to play bodyguard, then I'm wondering just what the hell you *are* hiding?"

Chapter Nine

She was taking too long again to answer. Nick supposed she figured it didn't matter. She had already blown it, so she might as well think about what she was going to say before she said it. He waited, not rushing her.

"This is getting a little old, Nick."

"I agree," he said.

His mouth was dry, but he didn't reach for the tea. He'd been pushing his luck in inviting her to sit down at the table with him. He wasn't nearly as confident of his skills as he'd pretended.

"I'm not hiding anything," she said. "I told you why Rob sent me. I told you the truth."

"Now explain to me why *he* let you come."

"Rob?" she asked, her voice puzzled. "I told you that—"

"Screw Rob. I'm talking about the guy whose baby you're carrying. What the hell is he thinking about letting you take an assignment like this?"

Silence again, but he didn't remind her this time of how revealing those hesitations were.

"This is my job," she said finally. "He understands that."

"You can always refuse an assignment. Andrews wouldn't force you. In your situation he probably couldn't. Not legally. Not even if he was that kind of bastard."

"I want to make this case as much as any of you," she said.

That was probably true, as far as it went. "And your husband's willing to let you put your baby's life on the line to do that?"

The question was hitting below the belt, but he needed an answer. And if you have to play the game in the dark, he thought, you can't always follow the rules.

"There's no danger to my baby," she said sharply.

There had been no hesitation in *that* response. But there had been something. Maybe a tinge of fear. Or deception? Only, he couldn't figure out why she would lie to him about this.

"I don't know. It's seemed a little stressful out here the last couple of days to me," he said sarcastically. "*You've* seemed a little stressed. That doesn't worry you, Sterling?"

"Stop it, Nick," she ordered.

"So what did he say when you told him?" he prodded, ignoring her demand. Despite his previous decision, his hand had somehow found his glass, the outside of it slick, sweating with condensation. He had already closed his fingers around it, preparing to bring it to his mouth when she answered.

"I'm not married," she said.

His hand stopped in midair, but he controlled the reaction, forcing himself to continue the motion he'd begun. Then he made himself take a sip before he spoke again.

"I guess a lot of people do it that way these days," he said. His tone was carefully nonjudgmental, but he wouldn't have pegged Abby Sterling for one who did. "It's just not the usual order of things, I guess."

"Rings, mortgages and *then* babies," she said softly. "I do know the order, Deandro, but sometimes things just don't work out like they're supposed to."

It was the same phrase he had thought of this morning, and again it reverberated inside his head. He couldn't ever remember having heard it before, not in any context. But, of course, that was the problem. He couldn't remember a hell of a lot he should remember. That he needed desperately to remember.

"It's tough to raise a kid alone," he said.

"Millions of women do it. And most of them do a good job."

"If they have to," he agreed. "I just wonder how many of them would choose to do it alone if they had another option. If the father was around to do his part. Guys used to be better at that kind of commitment."

"A lot of things *used* to be different. Once the department would have fired me for getting pregnant, married or not."

"And instead here they are, giving you this plum assignment of playing bodyguard somewhere out in the wilds of south Louisiana. It seems to me, thanks to the women's movement, Sterling, you got really lucky."

His mockery was again apparent, but rather than getting angry, surprisingly she laughed. "Rob promised I could just come out here, put my feet up, and relax. Although it's been a little short of that, it's not been totally awful."

"Wildlife intruders and cooking duty. Doesn't sound too relaxing to me."

"I guess he thought the pleasure of your company would make up for those," she suggested.

This time Nick laughed. "Was he right?"

"I don't know. Maybe. After all, here we are having a civilized dinner together. No one who knew the two of us a few months ago would have thought that would ever be possible."

"Did everybody know about our 'personality conflict'?" Nick asked, cutting another bite of ham.

"In the O.C. unit? I guess so. It was pretty obvious that we weren't admirers of one another."

"Your guy know?"

"My guy?" she repeated, her voice puzzled.

"The kid's father. The one who's not around."

"I didn't say he's not around," she said stiffly.

"If he let you come out here, Sterling, then he's not around. Not in any way that matters."

"You don't know what you're talking about, Deandro. As usual."

In the silence that followed her comment, he could hear the sound of her fork clinking against the plate. Then ice tinkling in her glass.

"So, did he?" he prodded finally.

"Did he know that you and I didn't get along?"

Nick nodded.

"Why don't you just ask if it's someone in the unit?" she said. "What game are we playing now, Nick?"

"So is it somebody on the force?"

"What the hell business is it of yours?" she demanded angrily. "My private life doesn't have anything to do with this assignment. Rob Andrews didn't think so when he sent me out here. So why don't you just get off it, Nick."

"I'm just curious as to what he's doing while you're here."

"Minding his own business?" she suggested.

"Which I should be doing?" he asked, allowing his amusement to show.

"It would be nice for a change."

"Okay. Only, before I do, tell me one thing, Sterling. One thing that I just can't seem to remember."

"That's not funny, Nick."

"It wasn't meant to be. I'm serious."

"Something you think I can tell you?"

"Maybe."

"What is it?" she asked. Grudgingly.

"That phrase you used. Where'd you hear it?"

"What phrase?"

"The one about rings, mortgages and babies," Nick said softly. "I just wondered where you'd heard it."

More silence. A long one this time. And he knew what that meant. He had been on the right track all along, and then he had let himself get sidetracked. He had let Abby lead him astray. He had doubted, because of his blindness, what his instincts had been telling him about her all along.

Background. They had a *lot* of background. That's why she'd been so familiar. Why he'd reacted to the perfume she wore. Which meant, he realized suddenly, that it was possible—

"I don't know," she said, interrupting that realization. "Just...around, I guess. Why?"

"Yeah? The strange thing is I thought that this morning. Those very same words. They were right there in my head, just exactly like you said them. But I don't think they're a saying or anything. Do you?"

Another pause. Telltale delay. Abby really wasn't very good at deception.

"Maybe," she said. "It's just the way things are supposed to happen. The order. Everybody knows that."

"And sometimes, for one reason or another, they don't."

"Sometimes they don't," she agreed softly.

"You in love with him, Abby?" he asked. Suddenly, unexpectedly, his throat was thick, tight and aching, as he waited for her answer. Wondering what she'd tell him. If she'd tell him anything. If he would want to hear it.

"I was," she said finally.

The whispered words had come into his darkness after a long time. He knew from that she had really thought about what he'd asked her, trying to decide, maybe. And there was another question, of course, that he needed to ask. But somehow he couldn't.

He wasn't even sure that she understood that he now knew. Or sure that he *wanted* her to understand. And more importantly, he wasn't sure he really wanted to hear what she would say if he asked that second question. After all, she had already told him a lot. Maybe more than he had wanted to know.

I was, she had said. Very definitely past tense.

THE DREAM AGAIN, Nick thought, coming awake with a start. He must have been dreaming. But there were none of the now-familiar images in his head when he opened his eyes to the darkness. And his body wasn't hard, aching with need and desire.

It had been. Last night. He had done a lot of thinking up here last night. Thinking about Abby. About what she had said. There were too many clues that fit. Too much revealed by her responses. Revealed in both what she said and what she didn't say.

Even revealed in how she had responded when he'd pulled her to him. In her mouth's answering movement. In her voice. Her scent. In the way her body felt under his fingers. Too many clues. Too much circumstantial evidence piling up *not* to build the case he had built.

Abby Sterling was the woman from the dreams. The woman his subconscious mind had been trying for months to force him to remember. He just hadn't been exactly sure why remembering her was so important. More important, apparently, than anything else, even the case he'd been working. And now he knew why.

Abby Sterling was carrying his baby. With his strong sense of family, his sense of responsibility and duty, that alone would have been enough, of course. The guilt over letting her carry that particular burden by herself would be enormous. For someone like him, anyway.

And he had realized last night that that's exactly what she had been doing these last few months. Carrying all that responsibility alone. While he'd been hurt. While he couldn't even remember her.

It made sense out of the so-called mystery woman's calls to the hospital. Not someone involved in the hit, as Rob had believed, but someone involved with him. Judging by the intensity of the dreams and by his reactions to Abby since she'd come out here, his body's unthinking physical reactions, she was someone he had been *totally* involved with. Totally in love with.

Someone who shared with him the memory of that telling phrase. *Rings, mortgages and babies.* Had that been a plan they'd talked about? Or an invitation? Had he already asked Abby Sterling to marry him before he'd been shot?

His baby, he thought, the wonder of that interfering, as it had interfered over and over again last night, in the logical thought process he was trying to follow. When he put everything together, that was the undeniable conclusion he came back to again and again. Abby Sterling was carrying his baby.

Good Italian boy that he was, he should be celebrating. Breaking out the champagne. And he would have been, of course, if it hadn't been for one small thing. The doubt and uncertainty he had heard in Abby's voice.

And the undeniable reality of her answer last night. *You in love with him, Abby?* he had asked. *I was,* she had whispered finally. Definitely past tense.

He couldn't blame her for that. He wasn't the same man who had fathered this baby. There was no one who was *more* aware of that reality than he was. More aware of the changes. Changes even beyond the obvious one of his blindness.

He had always been so damn sure of everything. Sure of himself. Of his abilities, both physical and mental. Now that surety had been compromised. He'd been made. He'd let himself get shot, and as a result…

He took a breath, deep and hard, but he forced himself to complete the thought. As a result, he had been reduced to stumbling around in the darkness, both figuratively and literally, while this case and this relationship moved in new directions. Moved beyond him. *I was,* Abby had said.

Despite the frustration that was building, the same frustration that had kept him awake too long last night, Nick was aware that there was something that he should be concentrating on instead of this. Something that was even more…

Smoke, he thought suddenly. He took another breath,

drawing it deeply into his lungs. Something was burning, the smell as acrid as the toast Abby had thrown outside this morning.

His room was at the top of the stairs. If something were burning downstairs, then the smell would probably drift straight up that opening, just as the black wisps that had filled the kitchen at breakfast had eddied toward the opened door.

He was out of bed and pulling on his jeans almost before that thought had formed. *Abby.* The fear engendered by the image of Abby caught in the conflagration this wooden structure would become was almost paralyzing. Consuming.

He fought his panic, trying to remember everything he had ever heard about fires. About what to do if you were caught in one. And what not to do. He found the closed door to the hall and felt it carefully. It wasn't hot, so he opened it. He hesitated, knowing he couldn't afford to make any mistakes. He didn't have time to fall or get lost. Every second counted.

The smoke was stronger out here in the hallway, but not yet overpowering. He considered crawling, keeping as low to the ground as possible, just like everyone told you to do. But he could breathe, and after all, his wasn't the normal situation. Whatever action he took would already be slowed by his blindness, by the demand that he make no mistakes in getting to Abby and getting her out of here. And in getting…

Deliberately, he blocked that thought. Denied the words before they could form because he knew he couldn't afford to think about that now. He reached out and touched the newel post, orienting himself. This was no different from anyone else having to move through a dark house at night. As if the power had gone already. No different except he was probably better at this than most people would be. Experienced.

The hall seemed endless, however, and he forced himself

to reach out to touch the next door. Still checking. It was just where he expected it to be, thankfully. No mistakes so far.

Abby's door was closed, and he hesitated. It would be a hell of a note if she thought he was an intruder and shot him. A hell of a note, but logical, given their situation. Given what had happened the other night. He knocked instead, pitching his voice loudly enough that he hoped she would recognize it.

"Abby," he called. "It's Nick. I'm coming in." He waited, however, knowing better than to do that without an acknowledgment that she understood. Her door opened instead.

"What's wrong?" she asked.

"There's smoke. From downstairs, I think." He pushed her back inside and closed the door behind him.

"Smoke? I don't smell anything."

"But I do. I think there's a fire, Abby. Somewhere. I think the smoke is coming up the stairwell. Maybe that means it's at the back of the house. This room's at the front, I know but... Look out your window and see if you can see anything."

He listened as she moved away from him. And then her voice came from across the room. "I don't see a thing, Nick. No smoke. Nothing. Are you sure?"

Was he? he wondered. He hadn't seen the fire, of course. *He* hadn't seen a damn thing. And there had been no heat. Nothing but the scent of smoke. Could he be wrong?

At his hesitation, she moved, coming back to him. "I'm going to look down the stairs," she said.

"Abby." He could hear the uncertainty in his own voice—the doubt—and he hated it. As he hated this situation, which made him totally dependent on her. But she was right, of course. He could be wrong about everything. The fire. The location. And if there was fire, then they had to get out of the house, the quickest and easiest way.

"Come on, Nick," she said. "Stay with me. Stay close so I know exactly where you are."

Knowing he had no choice, despite the building anxiety for her and the baby, he reached out. She took his hand, holding it in her cold fingers instead of putting it on her shoulder as he'd expected her to do.

The journey that had seemed to take him an eternity was a matter of seconds with Abby leading the way. The smoke was much stronger now, so dense it was almost a physical presence in the hallway. He thought she had stopped at the top of the stairs. Looking down them, he supposed. He waited, but this was taking too long. Precious seconds of hesitation.

"Abby?" he asked.

"It's downstairs." Her voice was almost too controlled.

"Can we get to the front door?"

"I don't think so," she said. "There are flames at the foot of the stairs. I don't think we can make it through them."

"Back to your room," he ordered. No hesitation.

"Nick..."

"Move, Abby. Move now."

"But..." she began.

"Do it now, Sterling. The phone's up there. Call your friend the local law."

"He's not my friend."

"You better hope you're wrong about that," he said, almost under his breath. He hadn't liked the guy's "Anytime, Abby," crap. And he liked it even less now that he understood why it had rubbed him the wrong way.

Thankfully, Abby had already begun moving. He turned to follow, but stumbled into the newel post, staggering a little and bumping into her.

"You okay?" she asked, her fingers finding his arm.

"I'm okay," he said, angry with himself. With his blindness. "Come on, Abby. Let's go."

She started down the hall, and he followed, being too

careful now. Slowing them down. And he had no idea of distance. He had lost track of exactly where they were. Inside the bedroom or not?

"Close the door behind us," he warned.

"Okay," she said. "Stay here," she ordered. She moved away from him and then he heard her shut the door. The sound was behind him and to the right. He could hear her moving again. Going to the phone to call the sheriff as he'd told her to do?

"It's dead," she said, fear clear in her voice now. Stark.

"The fire's gotten to the wires," he offered, but that's not what he believed. "Window?" he asked.

"Window?" she repeated. "What for?"

"For going out of, Sterling. Now."

"We're on the second floor, Nick, in case you've forgotten."

"Your window looks out over the veranda, doesn't it?"

"Yes," she said.

"Then we go out it and onto its roof."

"What good will that do?"

"It'll give us a little time. A little distance, maybe. Somebody will see the fire. Somebody will call the authorities. The sheriff. The fire department."

"If there is one."

"All we have to do is get out and wait until help arrives."

"And if it doesn't?"

"You Butch, me Sundance," he said. "Come on, Sterling. Don't go borrowing trouble."

He could feel his own anxiety building, and he fought it. He had to get Abby out of this house. Onto the roof and then down onto the ground. Despite what he had told her, he didn't believe anyone would get out here in time to help them. Not the way the wood in this place would go up.

She touched his arm, and he jumped.

"Sorry, Nick. I should have said something."

"Window," he urged again, instead of explaining.

She took his hand, guiding him. This time her fingers were not only cold against the warmth of his, they were shaking. When she released him, he could hear her struggling to get the sash up. Small grunts of effort.

"I think it's stuck," she said finally. "Damn humidity."

"Let me try." Apparently, she moved aside to do just that. Nick waited, but there was no direction. "A little help from my friends here, Sterling. I can lift the thing, but I damn sure can't find it by myself."

"Sorry," she said again, placing his hand on the window.

"Let's just take the *sorrys* for granted," he suggested.

She made no response, and he supposed he'd ticked her off. At least she wouldn't be thinking about their situation if she was mad at him.

She was right, however, he discovered. The window wouldn't budge, not even for him. "Is that it?" he asked.

"The only one," she agreed.

"Is there a chair in here?" he questioned.

"A small armchair. A lady's chair."

"Take me to it," he ordered, not having any image in his mind that fit those words. When she had obeyed, he found by feel that it was just what she'd said—small. He prayed it would be big enough and he'd be strong enough to break the mullioned window with it.

Which was easier thought up than accomplished. Even he hadn't realized the problems involved in trying to line up blind on the window. Of making sure that the chair hit the center and hit it hard enough to break the wood and the glass.

"Okay," Abby said finally, giving him permission to try it.

"Door closed?" he asked.

"It's closed."

"Cover your face. The glass should all go outward if it breaks, but better to be safe than sorry."

"Okay," she said again.

He swung the chair back as far as he could and connected pretty solidly with the window. He could tell by the sound of breaking glass and splintering wood and the jolt in the muscles of his arms that he'd had some success. It would be up to Abby to determine how much.

"Hit it again," she directed. "Same place."

Following her guiding hands, he did and the resistance he encountered was less. The chair almost went sailing through.

"Enough?" he asked.

It seemed that the smell of the smoke was suddenly stronger. Maybe it was being pulled out of the hall by the opening he'd just made, but it seemed that they'd been up here an eternity while the fire, crackling and climbing, ate the rich cypress below. *Too much time, damn it.*

"Enough, Sterling?" he demanded again, his voice harsher than he'd meant for it to be.

"I think so," she said.

He could tell she was clearing out the opening because of the sounds she was making. Glass falling. She beat at something a moment, probably knocking out the wood. Knocking the remaining mullions out of their way.

"Okay," she said. "I think that's enough. Who goes first?"

It was a good question. One he hadn't decided on yet. "Tell me exactly what's out there. Type of roof. Its slope. Anything you can tell me."

"Nick," she said softly. He could hear her fear. Fear for him, he realized, and he hated it. Hated the picture of him this was creating for her. Replacing whatever had been there before. Replacing the memories of what had once been between them.

"Do it, Sterling," he ordered. "Damn it, don't you go chicken on me now! Talk to me."

"Cypress shingles," she said. Her voice quivered a little, but she kept on, overcoming emotion. "The slope's steep, but the roof over the veranda levels out. There's a decorative parapet around the outer edge of that.''

"Good girl," he said, complimenting her. Sincere.

"I'm not a girl," she answered.

He laughed. "God, Sterling, it's just a figure of speech."

"Maybe to you," she muttered. "I go first. Then once I'm out, I can…" She hesitated, but he knew what she meant.

"Then you can help me," he finished. "It's okay, Sterling. You damn well better help me or we're both liable to go off."

Her turn to laugh. Again the sound of it touched him. It was always spontaneous and open. So full of joy. He had loved to hear her laugh. All of a sudden that was something else he was completely sure of. He had loved her laughter.

"What are you waiting for?" he said softly, fighting memory. Then he listened as she climbed through the shattered opening and out onto the sloping roof of the burning house.

Chapter Ten

"Careful," Abby warned sharply.

The incline of the roof was steeper than Nick had expected, and his foot had slipped on one of the shingles as he climbed out of the window. He slid down a couple of feet before he caught himself with the hand that was holding the sill. He dug his toes in against the rough wood.

"I'm okay," he reassured her, but following her out hadn't been quite as easy as he'd expected it would be, forcing himself to step into a situation that was unseen, unknown.

"Let go and just slide down," Abby advised. "You're only about four or five feet from the roof of the veranda. Its slope isn't nearly this bad. It's almost flat."

"Where are you?" he asked. Her voice was coming from above him, slightly to his right.

"I'm propped against the dormer. In the corner it makes with the roof."

"Then I'm going down. Can you get down there by yourself?"

"I'll slide," she said. "Just like you should do."

Again he fought the fear of the unknown, but he let go of the sill. His feet hit the roof of the veranda, and as soon as they did, he bent his knees, easily retaining his balance.

"Come on, Sterling," he invited. "It's not as bad as it looks. I'll catch you."

She laughed. "If I hit you, Deandro, we're both liable to go over."

He turned to face her, to face the sound of her voice anyway, his back to the edge of the veranda. He put the tips of his fingers against the shingles he'd just slid down, feeling them slope away from him.

"I'm not going to let you fall, Abby, I promise. Trust me. Only...before you let go tell me when and where you're coming."

"Move to your left about a foot," she directed.

Away from the window, he realized. He did what she'd suggested, inching carefully to his left.

"You're not close to the edge, Nick," she said, reassuring him, he knew, because of the tentative nature of his movements. "There's plenty of room behind you. We won't really go off. The worst that can happen will be a few splinters in my backside."

"You ready?" he asked.

"Are you?" she countered.

"Just aim yourself this way, Sterling. I'll stop you."

He had braced himself carefully, legs spread wide, preparing to take her weight. It wasn't necessary. Abby slid down the slope, her feet coming to a stop between his legs, firmly planted on the flatter roof. Her hands reached out to grab his arms.

He had leaned forward to stop the movement of her body with his. Suddenly he realized that he could feel the bulge of the baby she carried against his stomach.

Abby was lying back against the slope, his body over hers. All he had to do was bend his elbows, lowering himself, to bring his mouth down to hers. And he wanted to. Just as he wanted the taut rise of her pregnancy pressing into his body. He wanted to put his arms around her and hold her. Just one more time. To keep her safe.

"Nick," she said. A little breathless. He could feel the soft warmth of the word against his cheek.

"You okay?" he said.

"I'm fine."

Still they didn't move. Not either of them. Despite the fire downstairs. Despite the danger it represented. He didn't think he was capable of moving away from her. Abby's body was once again lying under his, and the rush of need and want was too powerful to deny. Just as it always had been.

And it was eerily familiar, despite his inability to really remember what it had been like between them. This was instinctual. Or maybe simply his body's memory, taking over where his mind had failed him.

"I think maybe we've done something like this a couple of times before, Sterling," he said softly. He lowered his face, pressing his lips into the fragrance of her hair. He turned his head slightly, rubbing his chin against her temple. "You want to tell me I'm wrong about that?"

He waited, his body growing harder as the slow seconds ticked by, despite his knowledge that they didn't have time for this. No time for an excursion into a shared past she apparently didn't want to revisit.

"No," she admitted finally.

He nodded, his cheek moving against her hair. He put his weight on his left hand, holding it off her body, although they were touching all along the length of their torsos, her legs lying between his. His right hand moved, big fingers smoothing, naturally somehow, over the protrusion of his child.

That was his right, he had decided. No matter how she felt about him now, about the man he had become, this baby she was carrying was his child, too. Flesh of his flesh.

There was very little between his hand and the baby. Abby's nightgown had gotten rucked up by her slide, so his palm was against the smoothness of her bare skin, distorted by pregnancy.

Surprisingly, her hand moved to cover his, repositioning it slightly, and then she pressed his more closely against her belly. It took a second for him to realize the reason she had done that. And when he did...

The sensation took his breath. A tiny, shifting movement pushing out against the hardness of her stomach. Arm? Foot? Head? Nick didn't know, but he knew without a doubt what he was feeling.

His baby, moving under his hand. And Abby had allowed him to feel that movement. For some reason she had wanted him to. Something which was much more intimate than anything they had ever shared before.

Again he reacted, his already strong arousal tightening, hardening uncontrollably. Painfully. He closed his eyes, fighting emotions he couldn't afford to feel. Fighting the sting of tears. Nick Deandro wasn't a man who ever cried. Not even against the hand fate had dealt him.

Suddenly, the memory of Abby's face was in his mind. Just the briefest flicker of an image. The way she had looked after they made love, still lying beneath him.

Her mouth slightly open, breath gasping, the delicate bow of her lip dewed with perspiration. Her features were relaxed, softened into bonelessness by what had happened between them.

"Did you feel the baby?" she asked, the present reality of her nearness shattering the forbidden glimpse his brain had given him of their past.

He nodded, unable to trust his voice. It would be full of what he'd just remembered. And full, too, of the wonder of his child's movement. Of what it had meant to him. Too full. Too revealing.

He removed his hand, deliberately putting it back on the roof beside her. Then straightening his elbows, he pushed himself upright. Away from her.

"Come on," he ordered, his voice harsher than he'd intended.

She didn't move. He reached out, finding her arm, gripping it hard, just above the elbow. "Come on, Abby. Move, damn it. We have to get off this roof."

"You said someone would come."

Her voice was suddenly full of fear again, and he didn't blame her. He couldn't see the ground, but he knew as well as she did that it would be too far away. Too far away for a blind guy and a pregnant woman. A very pregnant woman.

"I lied," he admitted grimly. He pulled on her arm, and finally she moved, straightening cautiously away from the sloping roof to stand beside him. "Tell me what's here," he demanded again. "Give me some information that will get us down."

She took a breath. Again audible. Shuddering. "I'll have to go over to the edge."

"Okay," he agreed.

"You stay right here, Nick. Don't move," she ordered.

"I'm not going anywhere, Sterling. I'm not a fool."

He listened again to her movements, trying to follow them in his mind. But he believed he could hear the fire now. Too long, damn it. It had taken them too long to get to this point. And that was all his fault.

"There's a wooden parapet maybe a foot high all around the edge of the gallery," Abby said. "There's about two feet of decorated cornice and then the grillwork columns that support the roof, at the corners and along the front."

"Are the columns strong enough to hold our weight?"

"I don't know. I don't… It doesn't matter, Nick, because I can't get down to them. Whatever you're thinking—"

"I'm thinking we don't have much choice, Sterling. Climb over that parapet and then down one of those metal columns or jump. Or you can stay up here with the fire," he reminded. "You just take your pick."

Silence. He didn't say anything else because there wasn't anything else to say. That was the bottom line. A hell of a choice. But he had only told her the truth, a truth she needed to realize. There was literally nothing else they could do.

"Okay," she said.

Good girl, he thought, but he didn't make the mistake of saying it. Abby Sterling was as brave as any other cop he'd ever known. As tough, mentally at least. She would never have made it as far as she had in NOPD if she weren't.

"You'll go first," he ordered, his voice tight and hard, keeping a rein on all the emotions he couldn't allow himself to feel. Not until they got out of this. *If* they got out of it.

She didn't argue, and he was grateful for that, for not having to explain his reasoning in wanting her down first— just to get her away from the fire he could hear. Besides, he was doing enough second-guessing about his decisions for both of them. He didn't want her to start.

He felt her hand on his arm, guiding again, and he moved where she directed him. "We're at the front corner of the veranda?" he asked. They needed to be as far away from the fire, of course, as the rooftop would allow.

"Yes," she said.

"Look at it carefully and then tell me exactly what you'll have to do to get down."

"Climb over the parapet," she began. "Then, I guess hold on to that until I can get my toes into the grillwork."

"Are there fingerholds in the decorations on the cornice?"

"There's... I don't know, Nick. It's carved. There are indentations. I can feel that from up here, but I can't tell if there's anything really that I could hold on to. I just don't know. I can't tell that from up here," she said again.

He could feel her confidence unraveling. He was asking a hell of a lot of her, he knew, but there was no other choice. Maybe they should have tried to go down the stairs. Out the front door. Despite the flames she saw, maybe they should have tried. He should have made her be more specific about the fire, about how near to the door it was, how far up the stairs it had reached. He should have—

"Nick?" she questioned softly.

"It's okay," he said, knowing that she couldn't do what

he'd asked her to do. He'd have to go first and discover that information by feel. He was both stronger and taller. And then, once he knew the situation, he'd try to guide her down. "I'll go first, Abby. Then I'll tell you exactly what to do."

"I can see the fire, Nick. Through the bedroom window."

He ignored that because there was nothing he could do about it. Not now. The choices had all been made, right or wrong, and now they had to live with them. Or die with them.

"When I get over the cornice, I can help you," he said. "I won't let you fall, Abby. I swear to you. I'm not going to let anything happen to you or the baby. You hear me?"

"I hear you," she whispered.

"Okay," he said. "You show me where I need to go over."

If he'd thought climbing out the window was bad, a leap of faith, he knew when he lowered himself over the parapet how wrong he had been. He held on, feeling the strain on his arms, while he felt with his toes for the iron grillwork, which he knew had to be somewhere below him.

And then, once he'd made contact with the metal, cold and hard, he felt for some kind of secure toehold in it. Something that would take his weight, allowing him to maintain his precarious balance, his body pushed as tightly as he could manage against the outer corner of the porch.

When he had, he held on to the top edge of the wooden parapet with the fingers of one hand. His toes were curled around the fretwork of the column, the metal cutting against his bare feet, his other hand seeking the next fingerhold in the carved decorations, praying that it would be there. It was, and having found it, he lowered his right foot, feeling in the darkness below him for the next toehold, a little further down the grill.

He had cleared the cornice, his fingers finally threaded through the decorative cast iron, hanging on for dear life, when he heard the distant siren. The sheriff or the fire department? Help, anyway, but it still sounded a hell of a long way off. Too far away to do them much good, judging by the heat and the noise of the fire burning fiercely to his left.

"Nick?" Abby called from above.

Automatically he raised his head, looking upward in the direction of her voice. That was simply habit. He couldn't see Abby, of course, but there was something there against the familiar backdrop of black.

Whatever it was, it wasn't milky as it had been before. This was redder. A glow. Something that seemed... The fire, he realized. He was seeing the light from the fire. It was as indistinct as the other hazy lightness had been, but there was no doubt in his mind that that was what it was. And if he could see it, it must be incredibly close to Abby.

"Nick?" she called again.

"Come on, Sterling. Over the edge. Lower yourself over the parapet and hold on tight. There'll be a hell of a pull on your arms, but you can hold on long enough to find a hold in the grillwork with your toes. You have to."

"Nick, I don't think—"

"*Now,* Sterling. You don't have time to think. The fire's too close. Just do it now. *Baby,* Sterling. Think about that and not the fire. Move. Move right now, damn it."

The tone of his voice was uncompromising. Demanding. What he had just said was an order, and he prayed she'd obey.

Then, having time to think about it, he prayed that she could do what he'd just commanded her to do. He was a big man, his upper-body strength far greater than hers. He knew Abby had been in good shape before her pregnancy. She was an athlete. But he didn't know how long it had been since she'd worked out.

Above him, he heard her moving. Finally. He listened, trying desperately to figure what she was doing, where she was in the process. And he couldn't tell, of course. Not just from the sounds. "Talk to me, Sterling. Tell me what's going on."

"I'm coming over," she said.

"I'm not going to let you fall, Abby," he promised again. He locked both hands on the thick outside edges of the decorative grillwork, curling his toes more firmly around whatever hold they had found, feeling the metal dig painfully into his feet.

It didn't matter, of course. Nothing mattered but the woman climbing out onto the precarious perch he had just left. He stretched his body away from the cast-iron column he was clinging to, his arms rigidly extended.

If Abby fell, he would try to stop the descent of her body. Stop it the only way he could, with his own. There was always the possibility that the force of her body hitting his would knock him off the column, and then they would both fall. He tightened his fingers, wrapping them firmly around the metal.

"Come on, Abby," he said.

"I don't think I can reach the grill," she said.

Her voice was sharp and high. *Beginning to panic?* he wondered. There had been a minute of that for him before he'd touched the ornamental ironwork with his toes. Could she reach it? He was so much taller than she was. Maybe she had been wrong about the distance.

He could almost feel the strain on her hands and arms as she clung to the parapet, struggling to find with her toes the column he was holding on to.

"There," she said finally. Her voice was breathless, but triumphant. Relieved.

"Got it?" There was a pause, and he held his breath.

"Got it," she said. And then, "Now what?"

This had been the hardest part for him. The trickiest. That next step. Finding a new hold in the decorations on the cornice and letting go of the relative safety of his grip on the parapet. "Are your feet as far as you can reach down the column, Abby?"

"I think so. I've got this slight disadvantage," she said. "This...bulge between me and it. Something you didn't have to contend with, Deandro."

The building hysteria that had been in her voice before was gone. She had a toehold and with that, she seemed to be keeping the panic at bay, at least for the moment.

"I'm the one with the disability, Sterling. What you've got's not even a minor inconvenience. At least not according to you," he added. "So quit whining about it."

Above him, he heard her laugh. It was shaky, but it was laughter, and again the sound of it echoed in his head. Memory.

He thought again about just waiting for whoever was coming, because the wail of the siren finally seemed to be growing louder. The only problem with that was his own fingers and toes were beginning to cramp. Hers would, too. And besides, the heat of the fire was also growing stronger, searing against his left cheek and bare shoulder. Soon it would break through the outside wall of the house and then...

"Now you find a fingerhold in the cornice," he ordered, blocking the thought of what would happen when it did. "One of the ledges. Something you can hold on to while you move your feet down to find the next toehold."

Seconds of silence. He knew she was trying to do what he'd said. And because he had already done it, he knew exactly how much he was asking of her.

"There's nothing—"

The sentence was cut off and at the same time her body came crashing into his, sliding those couple of feet down the metal column with more force than he would ever have thought possible, given the shortness of the distance between them.

He fought to maintain his hold, bending his elbows to pull his chest against the grillwork, trying to trap her body between the column and his. One of his feet slipped off, twisting him to the side for a moment before he found control. But his desperate fingers held until she could grab the column. Somehow they held.

He was aware that Abby had cried out as she slipped those two or three feet. It might have been fear or pain. He couldn't be sure. But she hadn't fallen the rest of the way. Neither of them had fallen off, and that was the only important thing. They were both still here, the strain on his arms and curled toes enormous as he held their bodies pressed tightly against the safety of the metal grillwork.

"Toehold, Abby," he gasped out. "Help me, damn it."

He felt her move to obey. She was shaking. Her entire body was trembling like a leaf caught in a tornado, shuddering vibrations running along the length of it. But she did what he'd asked, and when she had pushed her bare toes into the decorative metalwork of the column, taking more of her own weight, the strain eased on his arms and shoulders.

"You okay?" he asked.

"I hit my chin as I came down," she said. "Other than that, I'm...I think I'm okay."

"We go down together. I'm right behind you. I'm not going to let you fall, Abby," he said. He took a step down, carefully finding another toehold and shifting his weight, but she didn't follow him. "Move, Abby," he demanded.

Still shaking, she finally obeyed, descending now within the protective circle of his arms and body. Inch by inch they climbed downward together. He could feel the heat of the fire, could hear it roaring now through the house, a sucking, searing inferno that burned within a few feet of them. But they were almost away....

The vehicle with the siren, whatever it was, screamed into the yard, braking to a stop with a squeal of tires. He had just stepped down on the wooden porch when Nick felt hands on his thighs. Someone helping them. Trying to, anyway.

"You can jump the rest of the way. It's only about three feet from there to the ground."

Nick recognized Blanchard's voice. And he did what the sheriff suggested, another blind act of faith. His feet were almost numb, and he stumbled a little when he hit the ground. A strong hand caught his arm, helping him find his balance.

"You all right?" the parish sheriff asked.

"Abby?" Nick asked. He listened to the sheriff move away from him. Listened to the other sounds that followed, without knowing what was going on. Left again in the dark.

"I've got her," Blanchard said finally. "She's down. Come on," he ordered, taking Nick's arm. "We need to get away from the house."

The intensity of the heat seemed to be increasing exponentially. Nick hurried, half running, the sheriff's hand pulling him through the smoke-filled darkness. And then he realized he couldn't hear Abby running beside them. Panic grabbed at him.

"Abby?" he yelled.

"I'm right here, Nick. Everything's okay. I'm here."

"You sure?" He knew she'd understand.

"I'm sure," she said softly. When the sheriff released his arm, allowing them to stop, Nick felt Abby's hand grip his. He squeezed, trying to express without words what he felt.

"Volunteer fire department will be out as soon as they can. Not that it's gonna do a hell of a lot of good," Blanchard said. "You folks probably need to get in the patrol car."

"No," Nick said, his voice sharp. He hadn't really thought about his reaction. The decision had just been in his head, maybe put there by years of caution, years of being careful about whom to trust.

But he knew they weren't getting into Blanchard's car. He didn't care who saw him out here. Maybe it was even better that the volunteer firemen saw both of them. Then someone would know he and Abby had survived, had gotten out of the inferno that he knew had been designed to kill them.

"Nick?" Abby said, questioning that decision, he supposed.

She trusted this guy Blanchard, he remembered. Even liked him. And that had eaten at his gut. He realized he was jealous of some two-bit backwater sheriff because...

Because he could see, Nick admitted. Because he wasn't stumbling around in front of Abby like some...blind guy. Only he better get used to that, he acknowledged bitterly. He *was* some blind guy, and the other men Abby Sterling would encounter the rest of her life wouldn't be.

"Somebody set that fire," Nick said. It wasn't only his jealousy of Blanchard at work here, so he knew he needed to make her understand what he was thinking.

"You don't know that," Blanchard said reasonably.

"Somebody just tried to kill us, Abby," Nick said, ignoring the sheriff. "Use your head."

"You think *I* had something to do with the fire?" Blanchard asked, his normally calm drawl sharpened with anger.

"I don't know *who* had something to do with it," Nick answered. "That's the problem."

"Well, you tell me why I'd be the first one out here if I'd been the one who just tried to kill you."

"Because it would look real bad if you didn't respond," Nick suggested. "You had no choice, Sheriff. And maybe arriving first would even have been the smart thing to do. Opportunity."

"Okay," the sheriff said, his voice still tight but striving to sound reasoned. "I can understand that. But you need to remember that I helped get you down. I could just as easily have put a bullet into you."

"Then it wouldn't have looked like an accident."

"Mister, in your case nobody's gonna believe *anything* that happens to you is an accident."

That was the truth, Nick realized, logic finally overcoming anger and fear for Abby and the baby. Even if they had been found beside the burned-out shell of the house, their bodies riddled with bullets, no one would have blamed Blanchard. There were too many other people who wanted Nick Deandro dead. The same people who had already tried once to arrange that.

"Why did Maggie leave?" Nick demanded.

He knew that would seem to them to have nothing to do with what was happening now, but it was something else that he hadn't been able to fit into this puzzle—why Maggie had left so suddenly. So conveniently right before this happened. Nick didn't believe in coincidences. That was something else he'd learned through the years. Like learning to listen to his instincts.

He should have done that this time, except his perceptions had all been skewed by what had happened to him. By the amnesia. His blindness. By his dreams of Abby. By a jealousy that he hadn't even been aware he harbored until tonight.

"You think Maggie's got something to do with all this?" the sheriff asked, his incredulity clear.

"Maggie didn't like you," Abby said. "Or at least…she didn't seem to trust you."

Her voice was calm and controlled, and Nick was relieved to realize that. Relieved to hear her participating in this discussion. Apparently Abby hadn't lied to him. Apparently she *was* okay. The baby was all right. If anything had been wrong, Abby wouldn't sound like this, wouldn't sound that focused on what Nick was trying to find out.

"They were using the bayou behind the house to bring the stuff in," the sheriff said, sounding reluctant to explain. "I don't know that Maggie was helping them. I can't believe she would, but she had to have known what was going on."

"Her son?" Nick asked, putting it together with what he already knew. Maggie's son had been bringing drugs into this parish, apparently through the backwaters. Landing them out here in this safe isolation and then distributing them at his leisure.

"I guess maybe when he got out, it had started up again. If that was the case, as I suspect, she sure as hell didn't want me out here snooping around."

"And you hadn't been," Abby realized. "Not until I came."

"I couldn't understand what Andrews was thinking about, sending somebody like you out here," the sheriff admitted.

"Someone like me?" Abby repeated, the question full of what Nick had heard in her voice so often before. Resentment that someone thought she couldn't do a job because she was female.

"You have to admit a...real pregnant lady is a pretty strange choice of bodyguard for a government witness," Blanchard said, apparently taking care over his choice of words.

"I guess that depends on the woman," Nick suggested, fighting his amusement, despite the situation. Let Blanchard figure out Abby's pet hobbyhorse for himself. He had had to. The hard way.

"Maggie knew you well enough to know you'd keep coming out here to check on me," Abby said. "And she knew that if you did, eventually you'd see or hear something that would make you suspicious."

"My guess is she called her boy and warned him."

"Then why would she leave?" Abby asked.

"Maybe he didn't listen," Nick said. "So she took matters into her own hands. Leaving was the quickest way she could figure out to get rid of us. And it worked."

It made sense, he thought. It all made sense. All that had been going on out here had been a little local enterprise. Some homegrown drug-running. Nothing to do with him.

"It could have been Maggie that night," Abby said softly, apparently realizing something he hadn't yet. "Our intruder, I mean. I turned those alarms on. I knew I did.

But Maggie knew how everything worked. Maybe she was trying to spook me. To get rid of us. Trying to scare us off without doing any real harm.''

"Somebody did a hell of a lot of harm tonight," Nick reminded her. That was something that didn't fit—Maggie trying to kill them. He would have bet his life against her being any part of something like that. Instinct again.

"Not Maggie," Blanchard said. "That's one thing I can guarantee. Something I'd be willing to stake my life on," the sheriff added, echoing Nick's own thinking. "Maggie loved this old place. She thought of it as her home. No matter what, she's not gonna set it on fire. I can promise you that. Not even for that worthless kid of hers.''

"The fire may not have been set," Abby reasoned. "Sometimes things happen in a house this old. Faulty wiring—''

"Like hell," Nick jeered.

In the distance he could hear other sirens winding their way through the smoky darkness. The volunteer fire brigade had finally gathered, but judging by the low roar coming from the direction of the house, they would be too late to do any good.

"Will you take us into the city, Sheriff? Take us into New Orleans?" Nick asked.

"Right now?" the sheriff questioned, obviously surprised by the request.

"Before they get here," Nick agreed.

"Where to?" Blanchard asked.

"Just take us there and let us out," Abby suggested softly, "and then... Then I'll take care of the rest.''

Chapter Eleven

The darkness that surrounded him was so familiar. Nick had been aroused since Abby had guided him up the steps and through the back door of her small apartment.

Part of that was the lingering hint of her perfume. It permeated the very air of the rooms, which were warm and close, despite the late-night touch of fall outside. But part of it was in his head as well. Emotional echoes.

Because he had been here before. A lot of times. Here in this same warm, fragrant darkness. Alone with Abby.

"I guess I need to call Rob," she said, coming back into the room where he was sitting.

She had left him in the living room while she went to take a shower and put on some clothes. When she spoke, he had to force his mind back to the present. Away from the too-powerful memories that were bombarding him.

He was finally remembering. Not in any logical kind of order. And not anything earth-shattering. Not unless he counted the memory of Abby's body moving under his— which had always been pretty earth-shattering, now that he thought about it. But still, undeniably, he had been remembering.

"Not yet," he said quietly. "Don't call anybody yet. I think we need to take some time. Do some thinking."

Which wasn't going to be easy for him, he knew. Not here, at least. Not now that he knew this was where they had secretly met. Had made love. Where, together, they had created the child she carried. Here, where the last thing he wanted to think about was who they could trust.

Abby sat down on the arm of the couch next to him. She laid something across his lap, and automatically he reached for it, fingers examining. It was a T-shirt, he realized, the cotton knit soft and warm.

"I thought you might be cold," she explained.

He could smell shampoo and the soap she had used when she showered. But he could also smell smoke from the fire they'd escaped, caught in the fabric of his jeans or in his hair.

"I'm okay," he denied, but he held the shirt because it gave him something to do with his hands. Something other than what they wanted to do.

They ached to pull her down to him. To examine every inch of her skin. To make sure she was telling him the truth. To make sure everything really was all right. To make sure she wasn't lying to protect him from the knowledge that she or the baby had been hurt.

"What time is it?" he asked. Not because he cared, but because it was something safe to ask and because he had no idea. He had lost all track of time in the endless hours of this night.

"About four-thirty. It'll be daylight soon."

The silence that followed was one of those uncomfortable pauses he hated, caused, he knew, by her sudden remembrance of his blindness. He thought about telling her that he had been able to see the fire. He even wondered if telling her that would make any difference in how she felt about him now.

But he knew the diffuse red glow he had seen might not mean anything. The fact that he could distinguish between total darkness and the presence of strong light was about as important as his newfound ability to tell the difference between the front and the back of a jigsaw-puzzle piece.

A real important job skill, Deandro, he mocked himself.

Abby would be proud of that. And maybe one day he could tell their kid whether it was night or day. Maybe. And then again, maybe not.

"You want to try to get some sleep?" Abby asked softly.

Her voice was concerned. Concerned for him, and that wasn't the way it was supposed to be. Concern for him was not anything he had ever wanted to hear in Abby's voice.

She was the one who had been forced to go through this difficult pregnancy alone. The one who had had to climb off the roof of a burning house tonight. The one who had slipped and fallen—

"How's your chin?" he asked, finally remembering what she'd told him, her voice making light of the injury.

"It's okay. I look like the victim of a little domestic violence, but it's nothing serious. Just another bruise."

"*Another* bruise?" Maybe from climbing out the window?

"It doesn't matter," she said.

"It matters to me, Sterling. Whatever happens to you matters a hell of a lot to me."

"Don't, Nick. Not tonight. I don't think I'm up to talking about this tonight."

"This?"

"About us," she clarified.

Despite what he had known, his stomach lurched. Just from hearing her admit to it. Just hearing her say *us,* her voice full of undercurrents. He nodded, but he couldn't leave it alone. It was too important to him. She was. The baby.

"This is my baby," he said. It was not even a question.

"Yes," she whispered.

"But you weren't planning on telling me about it?"

A long silence. At the end of it she would tell him the truth. He now knew that much about the woman that he had loved enough to have never forgotten her, in spite of everything else he had forgotten.

"I don't know," she said finally.

He nodded again. But her response had hit him like a physical blow. Incredibly hurtful. Devastating in the sense of loss it represented. "You willing to tell me why?" he asked.

"Not tonight," she said, her voice almost pleading. "I told you I don't want to talk about that tonight. I'm really not up to it. Please, Nick, just…"

He waited, but the sentence had faded away, and she never finished it. "Just forget it happened?" he suggested bitterly. "Is that what you want me to do?"

"You already have," she said softly.

And that was accusation, he realized in surprise. He was still able to read her well enough to recognize the bitterness of her tone for what it was. And it was so damned unfair, he thought, fury roiling through him. As if he had wanted to get shot. As if he had wanted to have part of his life destroyed. The most important part of it. As if he had wanted to be robbed of these memories. Of his child.

"What the hell is that supposed to mean, Abby?" he asked, his question cold and angry. "You think I deliberately—"

"I think we're both tired. And I think we've got more important things to think about than hashing over the past."

That hurt, too. She might be right about the more important problems, but again she had relegated him to the past. *Past tense.* He nodded, determined not to beg her. He knew what the problem was, of course, and he didn't blame her for what she was feeling. Not for any of it. He would be the last person in the world to blame her for having difficulty dealing with how much he had changed.

But she needed to understand that he couldn't help what had happened to him. Somehow he'd screwed up, maybe in trying to have this relationship with Abby, and as a result he'd been made. Maybe he'd been careless or stupid, but he couldn't do anything about that now. Nor about the other—about what had happened between them. Which she apparently wanted to forget. And which he had only now begun to remember.

"Why don't you want me to call Rob?" she asked.

"I just think we ought to…lie low for a while. Don't let anybody know where we are."

He had wondered about his motive. Maybe it wasn't just good police work, maybe not just being careful. Maybe it was something else. Something far more personal.

"Blanchard will tell him about the fire," Abby argued. "Somebody will, eventually."

"Let 'em," he said.

"That doesn't make sense, Nick. Rob's my supervisor. I need to let him know you're all right. That I am."

"Can't it just wait until morning, Abby?" he said softly. "Let's sleep on it." Again he felt the discomfort between them, almost palpable. As thick as the smoke had been in the upstairs hallway tonight.

"Okay," she said finally. Reluctantly.

She rose from her perch on the arm of the couch, but he didn't hear her move again. She was still standing there, he realized. Watching him, maybe. Remembering? Just as he had been.

"You can have the bed," she offered finally. "I'll have to put on some clean sheets, but that won't take but a minute. I don't think—"

"Abby." Whatever was in his tone—and even he wasn't sure what was there—stopped the rush of words. She waited, and the uncomfortable silence grew and expanded. "I'll sleep out here," he said. "The couch is fine."

"Except it's a love seat and about two feet shorter than you are," she said. "It won't take a minute to make up the bed." She had already moved, the sound of her shoes on the wooden floor making her direction plain. She was walking away from him.

"I won't sleep in your bed, Abby."

The footsteps stopped. "Why not?" she asked, sounding as if she really didn't know. "The room's a little messy, but I'll clear a path. I'll pick everything up. I'll make sure that—''

"I don't mean I'm refusing to sleep there. I mean…I just won't be able to sleep. Not there."

"Don't, Nick," she said again, her voice softer.

"You can't just make this go away, Sterling. You can't wish it into oblivion. What happened between us happened. And there's nothing you can do to change it."

"I don't need this tonight," she said again.

He waited, listening to the silence fill all the empty space that stretched between them. Listening to his own heartbeat, strong and rapid, pounding in his temples. And even though he tried, determined not to beg, he couldn't prevent the words that came out of his mouth.

"Then I guess that's the difference between me and you. I *do* need it, Abby. I still need you."

"Nick," she whispered.

The sound of his name was full of pain. Maybe even regret. But she said nothing else, and after a long time he heard her move again. Away from him. And then he heard the sound of the closing door.

ABBY CLOSED her eyes, holding them tight against the rush of tears as she leaned back against the safety of her bedroom door. *I guess that's the difference between me and you,* Nick had said. *I do need it, Abby. I still need you.*

She could imagine what it had cost a man like Nick Deandro to make that confession. Physical needs, she understood. She had admitted to those since the first day she had seen him again, standing barefoot in the open door of the old house, looking exactly the same. Except for the dark glasses, a barrier that she couldn't seem to overcome.

And what the hell kind of person did that make her? she wondered, almost hating herself. Hating her fear. How could she walk away from the raw, aching need she had heard in his voice?

She wanted Nick to make love to her as much as he

could possibly want to. She had wanted him for months, dreamed about him touching her again. Dreamed about...

She opened her eyes, and the bed where they had spent so many secret hours was right in front of her. She hadn't made it the morning she'd left. She had been running late, and she knew Rob would be impatient to get out to the safe house and then back into the city. The sheets were tangled and disordered, just as they had been when she'd climbed out of them that morning, leaving the troubling dreams of Nick behind her.

Just as they had always been when Nick left her in this bed alone. Spent. Passion-drained. Satiated with the feel of his body moving above hers in the darkness. His darkness. Why should it matter what kind or degree?

What kind of person was she? she wondered again. What was wrong with her? Why couldn't she bring Nick here, allow him to make love to her again, out of compassion if nothing else.

You got to feel sorry for the guy, Rob had said at the beginning. And Mickey's warning. *If you do, don't do it so he's aware of it. My best advice, Abby. Learned from experience.*

So she wasn't going to invite Nick back into her bed because she was sorry he was blind. He wouldn't want that. He would never forgive her if he figured out that's what she had done.

And he would. If that was all that was left between them, even if that was all that it eventually became, he would know. Nick was too smart, too perceptive, not to figure that out. And he could read her so well. He had always been able to.

So if she invited him back into her bed, it had to be because she wanted him there forever. Because she felt the same way she had felt before. Because she still wanted what they had talked about then. *Rings, mortgages and babies.* Anything less than that was a lie. And it would be cheating. Nick didn't deserve to be cheated.

And right now… Right now she still didn't know if she felt the same way. She had been so afraid of his blindness. Afraid of how it would have changed him. She had been able to admit that finally, after seeing him again.

Now, standing with her back to the door that she had used to shut him out, she deliberately paraded the hated images before her mind's eye. Made herself study them. Let her emotions cringe before their reality.

That sad, half-completed puzzle spread out on the desk. The opaque black lenses, always looking a little to the side of her face. That angry game of blindman's bluff. Nick's groping fingers, unable to find her in the darkness because she wouldn't let him. His hand carefully examining the items she had set out on the table for him.

She closed her eyes again because she couldn't bear to see those images anymore. Or to think about them. They were not any part of the Nick she knew. The Nick she had loved.

She could remind herself of the others, of course. And she had. Standing in the living room beside him after he'd asked her. Standing in the terrible, painful silence.

Thinking about the gentleness of his hand pressed over the movement of his child. About his voice, forcing her out that window when she'd been so afraid. Nick pulling her up when she wouldn't have been able to move on her own. Making her climb over the parapet. Breaking her fall with his own body, knowing all along that they could both go down.

It wouldn't have mattered to him. She knew that, too. Nick would give his life for hers. For this baby. She knew that as surely as she understood any constant in her life. Nick would die for either one of them. Willingly and without hesitation.

Because he loved her. Because that was the kind of man he was. And she…? She was hiding from him in this room because she wasn't sure she could accept the hesitant, searching movement of his hands. An occasional fall. His uncertainty.

What kind of person was she? she wondered again. What kind of woman would do this to the man she loved?

The man she loved. The words repeated, echoing endlessly like a challenge shouted into a cave. The man she loved. Nick Deandro would always be that man. She put her hand on her thickened waist, aware again of the changes in her own body.

And was reminded suddenly that life is made up of endless changes. In our physical bodies. Aging. Illnesses. Changes in circumstances. In emotions. In strengths and weaknesses.

That's why married people lived longer—the bond of a partnership. Working together to deal with whatever life offered. Whatever changes. Ups and downs. And through it all, all the give-and-take, both would change. Grow. Mature. Learn to trust. Learn to believe that love would always be enough. More than enough to overcome whatever happened.

The door opened behind her, and she turned, her vision blurred because of tears she hadn't even been aware were streaming hotly down her face. Nick was standing there, silhouetted against the light she had left burning in the kitchen. A light he couldn't see. Just as he couldn't see her. And might never be able to again. Not able to see his own child.

"Abby?" he said. Questioning. The small note of uncertainty clear and somehow beloved in his voice.

"I'm here," she said. And because she knew it was right, knew it now in the deepest part, the very heart of who she was—and of who he was—she reached out and took Nick's hand. And drew him with her into the room.

HER FINGERS had found the waistband of his jeans. They were trembling so much that pushing the metal buttons through the holes was taking an eternity. When his fingers closed over hers, she thought he intended to finish this for her. To take over the necessary task she had begun.

Instead, he held her hands, stilling the movement of her fingers against the hard, enticing warmth of his stomach. Then, holding both of hers folded within one of his, his other hand lifted to her face, thumb brushing over her wet lashes. It trailed down her cheek, tracing the path her tears had taken.

His big fingers were again gentle, moving like a whisper across her skin. She took a breath, a small intake of air, of sound. In response, his hand shaped her face, its palm warm and roughly masculine against the smoothness of her skin, and then his thumb caressed her lips.

"I heard you crying," he said.

She nodded, knowing he would be able to feel the movement.

"Why, Abby?" he asked. "Why did you change your mind?"

She sniffed, unromantic, but necessary. Gathering control. Trying to think. She had been prepared for his body, for his hands, his touch. Skin moving against skin.

What she had not guarded herself against was his mind. She was not ready for his questions. Not for these that had no simple answers. "I thought men didn't like to talk," she said.

She freed her hands, and they moved back to the job she had undertaken. This time he didn't stop her, but when she had unfastened the last of the buttons, he made no effort to push the jeans off his narrow hips.

Even in the low light spilling through the open bedroom door, she could see him clearly. His body was so familiar. Her eyes traced the arrow of dark hair which disappeared into the V-shaped opening she had just created.

It was shadowed, yet stark against the bronze skin. Above the ridged abdomen that the line of hair bisected, his chest broadened, still hard, despite his injuries. Firmly muscled. Strong. Such a good, strong man.

Her throat closed with love and with need, the same need that flared like summer lightning into her lower body. She reached for him, pressing her fingertips gently against the reddened scar on his shoulders. Then, somehow, they drifted to touch a small pebbled nipple.

She heard the depth of the breath he took. She liked hearing it. She always had. She liked knowing she had this control over him. Everywhere else his strength had always dominated. But not here. Never here.

She flattened her fingers, sliding them downward, over the swell of muscle and to his ribs, tracing along each. Her fingers Brailled his body, as if she were the one who had been tragically blinded. Feeling his breathing expand, become ragged and uneven.

Once his body jerked in reaction to the unintended scoring of her nails, and her hand hesitated. She had been a little startled at the sudden movement, such a contrast to his previous stillness. He was standing so still, just letting her touch him.

Finally she put her hand against his side, palm flattened, and stepped closer. Her breasts, under the thin covering of the shirt she was wearing, brushed against the wall of his chest.

"Nick," she said. He didn't move, didn't respond in any way. "Nick?" The word was questioning, her face lifting at the same time to look at him. His head was unmoving, eyes open and focused on the doorway behind her. Unseeing, she remembered.

She closed her own eyes. There would be no turning back. No retreat. This was her decision, and he was allowing her to make it. Or forcing her to, perhaps, by his very stillness.

Her other hand rose, finding the soft hair at the back of his neck. A little too long. The feel of it unfamiliar. She spread her fingers, pushing them through the black strands, silken and almost curling now. Cupping the back of his skull and urging his mouth down toward hers.

In obedience, his head lowered, eyes closing. That was automatic. Unthinking. Just as was the response that made his lips part and tilt into the perfect alignment to cover hers.

Then his hands closed around her arms, too tightly, pulling her against him. His mouth was hard, and his kiss ravaged. Devoured her.

His was a need born of deprivation. Hunger. It demanded. But nothing that she could not give, she realized. Nothing that she did not want to give him.

His mouth moved, still opened, sliding hot and wet against her cheek. His hands had found the neck of her shirt and were fumbling with the buttons. Too small for his fingers. They were moving too slowly. Everything was too slow.

She pushed away from him, but hungrily his mouth followed, reluctant to release its contact with her skin. She crossed her arms in front of her body and grabbed the hem of the man's shirt she wore, pulling it off in one quick motion.

The sudden spill of air chilled her skin. Goosefleshed it. His hands caught her shoulders again, pulling her back against him. Against his warmth.

His lips moved over her face, her neck, her throat. Lower. His fingers fumbled with the fastenings at the back of her bra and then, when he had succeeded, he pulled it off her arms, dropping it to the floor.

She waited, breathless, and it seemed an eternity until his hands moved again. They slipped under the fullness of her breasts, lifting them, ripened now with the ripening of their child. They were heavy. So heavy. Like the deep inward ache of her body—almost too heavy to bear.

Like the ache of his, revealed in his low groan. Almost sound. Almost sensation. His hand released. Right one. Drifting over the jutting protrusion of her pregnancy, whose swell began just under her breasts.

His breathing had deepened. His hand flattened, fingers turning downward. It moved lower still. Pushed into the loose waistband of her maternity slacks and inside her panties.

She could feel it. Sliding down her distended belly. Palm pressed tightly against her skin. Nick shifted his weight, leaning to reach...

She gasped. His touch was electric, and heat flared along nerve endings that had lain dormant too long. Waiting for him. For his touch. So long. It had been so long. An endless wanting. Nick's hand. Nick's body.

And then it wasn't waiting. It was immediate. Instantaneous. As soon as he began to touch her, the hot aching need released. Scalding in its intensity.

She cried out with it, leaning into his hand, increasing the pressure, giving in to the sweet heat that poured in waves throughout her body.

His left arm moved behind her back, holding her. Supporting the boneless, mindless ecstasy of release. Joy. Her body arching toward his, into his touch. Too hungry to be ashamed of its need. Its passion. And there was no reason to be. This was Nick. Nick. Beloved.

The heat shimmered. Flickered. Smoldered. She remembered to breathe. Finally. Her breasts, damp with perspiration, moved against the hair-roughened skin of his chest. His fingers moved too, and sensation jolted again. Arcing into new current. Burning her up with its heat.

She said his name. Her voice was so hoarse it didn't sound as if it belonged to her. Someone else crying out her loneliness. Such a long loneliness.

When it was finally over, the incremental torment slowly easing, she sagged against him. His hand cupped gently now, only supporting. No longer teasing or tantalizing. Neither promising nor fulfilling. Just holding her, and she lay exhausted, resting against his strength. Drained. Sated.

After a long time, he straightened. Both hands found her waist, tenderly holding the beginning swell of his child. Holding her still.

Her need. Awakened and answered.

His need...

She raised her head. Strands of her hair caught in the sweat that dewed his chest and she brushed them away like spiderwebs. His face was infinitely calm. His lips were set, almost stern. And his eyes were not directed toward her face.

She stepped back, breaking the familiar contact with his body. She had been so safe and warm there. It took an incredible act of will to move away from him. But she did.

"Abby?" he questioned, the raven-wing darkness of his head turning slightly. The light behind her had found his hair, imbuing it with blue highlights.

She didn't answer. Instead, she pushed her slacks and panties down over her hips. She bent, awkwardly slipping them lower until she could step out of them. For a moment her eyes considered her own nudity. Her hand cupped under the child she carried, a gesture that was almost protective.

And then it lifted to find and take his. His fingers closed around her hand, squeezing gently. Hers responded, and again she guided him. This time toward the tumbled bed.

She stood a moment beside it. For the first time she thought about the changes he would find in her. In her ability to respond to him. In the awkwardness of her body.

If they had made love all along, as their child grew and her girth increased, she would never have thought about this. Never have worried. But suddenly, she realized that she was as different as he. More different, here in their darkness.

His hands had touched her, had examined the baby. But that was not the same, of course, as lovemaking. Not the same as her hips arching under the power and force of his. Demanding her response, just as he always had.

"It's all right, Abby," he said. "I understand."

That surprised her. It didn't exactly fit the context of her own hesitation. "Understand?" she questioned.

"I don't know a lot about this. I've never... You said you'd had some trouble."

She didn't know what to say. She had never asked. She had had no reason to question the parameters of this. Of her circumstances. Her "trouble."

Surely, she thought. Surely…

"It's all right," Nick said again. "It doesn't matter."

I guess that's the difference between me and you, he had said. *I do need it, Abby. I still need you.* Need. It had been so raw in his voice. And nothing had changed about that.

This prohibition had not been in the warnings she'd been given. Nothing about sex or about any danger it might represent. If making love was forbidden, surely her doctor would have told her. And she knew that Nick wouldn't hurt her. Nick would never hurt her. Not *this* Nick, who was neither cold nor angry nor groping in frustration.

"Jeans," she suggested softly.

"Are you sure, Abby?" he said. But the need was back. Slipping from his careful control. As raw as it had been before. As aching.

She laughed. "Just exactly what does a girl have to do to get you into bed these days, Deandro? Issue a written invitation?"

Silence. Awkward. Cruel, perhaps, but an unintended cruelty.

"I sure couldn't read it if you did," he said softly. There was no bitterness in his voice. No anger. And the slightest hint of amusement. Self-mockery.

And so, relieved, she laughed again.

"I used to love to hear you laugh," Nick said. "I used to love that so much."

"I know," she said, tears stinging, hot, and demanding release. She blinked, denying them. This was not the time for tears. This was the time for rejoicing. That should be what they were doing. All the important gifts were back. Only her fear had prevented them. Fear that had evaporated in this reality. The reality of the kind of man Nick Deandro still was.

Nick bent to remove his jeans, and when he had, he

reached out behind him, finding the edge of the bed in the darkness. He eased down on it. And this time, his hand drew her down to join him, and there was not a single remaining thread of doubt in her response.

Chapter Twelve

She moved above him in the darkness. Slowly. There was no longer urgency. No longer need. No longer fear.

Her head was thrown back, eyes closed, her breathing deep and shuddering. His strong hands glided over her throat and her breasts. Over their child.

She had once, long ago, wondered how many times she and Nick could make love, given unlimited hours together. Given that there was no secret clock ticking away the precious minutes they had stolen. Given no danger to demand his leaving.

Last night and throughout this long day they finally had opportunity to explore those possibilities. And none of them had been squandered. Six empty months had lain between them. As had injury. Pain. Memory loss. And her fear.

Now nothing was between them. Nothing had separated them during the last twenty-four hours, as one day slipped away again into another night. Their time together had briefly been interrupted by the need for sleep, which had melted again into lovemaking. Once it had been interrupted for food from Abby's meager pantry. Often for whispered confidences and confessions.

And for gentleness. For Nick's fingers to explore the life she had felt growing inside her through those months. To feel again his baby's small, stretching movements. For his ear to strain against the distended skin of her belly, pretending to hear a heartbeat.

The rest had been only lovemaking, enriched by laughter and promises. Sharing dreams she had been afraid were forever dead. And now, again, there was this. Not need, but still desire. Not urgency, but pleasure. Slow heated contact of once more familiar bodies. Minds. Emotions.

"Abby," Nick said softly.

She fought to respond. She tried to lower her head and open her eyes. To look at him. To think about whatever he wanted to say to her. And then he touched her.

Mistake, Nick, she had time to think, before the world dissolved again, reality fading into sensation. Almost as strong, despite the number of times they had made love, as it had been the first time he'd touched her. Almost.

His body arched, responding in kind, hot seed jetting upward, mixing with the heated moisture of her body. "Abby," he whispered again, his voice hoarse and uneven from lack of breath.

But not from lack of her. Never again from that loss, she had promised and then promised again. Silently. Those vows made only with her body.

And when she slipped from her knees, lying down beside him, he drew her close with his arm around her waist. She lay against his chest, the weight of their baby resting on his hipbone.

"We've got to stop meeting like this," Nick said finally. His thumb caressed her bottom, soothing up and then down, from the dimpled base of her spine to the beginning of her thigh.

"Why?" she asked, smiling. She could feel his heartbeat slowing under her cheek, reclaiming its normal rhythm.

"Because I swear you're going to kill me," he whispered. He turned his head, mouth moving against her hair.

"Not if you're a very good boy," she promised softly. "And if you always give me what I want."

"And what's that?" he asked. She could hear his smile.

"You," she said softly. "This. A ring, a mortgage—"

"And a baby," he finished, his hand caressing the swell of her pregnancy. "I'm way ahead of the game in that department."

"And in most others," she said, stretching her legs out to find a more comfortable position. She put the top one over both of his, feeling the hair on his thighs under the smoothness of hers. Her hand rested on his chest, fingers moving through the black mat that covered it.

"Most?" he repeated.

"You can't have everything, Deandro," she said teasingly.

When he didn't respond, when the long seconds crept by without a laughing rejoinder, Abby lifted her head, pushing up on her elbow to look down at his face. "Nick?" she whispered.

His eyes adjusted to the sound of her voice, almost tracking to her face. Almost. His fingers lifted and touched her mouth, thumb sliding across her bottom lip.

"What's wrong?" she asked.

"Can you do this, Abby? Can you really live with this?"

There was no hesitation in her answer. It was the question she had already answered. One she had known she had to decide before she had brought him into this room again.

"Of course," she said simply.

"But that *is* what you were afraid of? That *is* why you didn't tell me about the baby?"

"Yes," she said, because it was the truth.

He nodded, his mouth tightening, revealing a tension his voice had not held.

"You knew that," she said, wondering why they were talking about this now.

"I knew," he agreed. His hand had fallen, and his face moved slightly, blue eyes shifting away from her.

She caught his chin and turned his head back.

"I was afraid," she said. The words were soft, but distinct. "I was afraid of how this would have changed you."

His brow creased, and his chin moved slightly in her fingers, side to side. "Changed me?" he asked.

"In ways that mattered," she tried to explain.

The silence this time was his. Not awkward, but considering. Thinking. "What ways?" he said finally.

"Your strength," she confessed. That was easy. The others would all be harder. "How you treated me. How you viewed yourself."

He laughed, and for the first time in these precious, nearly twenty-four hours they had spent together there was bitterness in the sound. "That sure as hell has changed," he said.

"Maybe. But not in any of the ways that really matter."

"You can't know that," he said.

And she couldn't, of course. She could know only her perceptions of him.

"You aren't afraid of raising a kid with a blind husband who's not going to be a whole lot of help?" he asked when she hesitated.

The essence, maybe, of *his* fear? She supposed they had reached a point where that fear needed to be answered. An answer she knew. "Of course," she agreed.

She watched him swallow, the movement too strong along the strong brown column of his throat. His mouth had tightened again, and she soothed her forefinger over the corner of it, pushing the tension away.

"But I'm more afraid of doing it without you, Nick," she offered. "Far more afraid of that than I am of the other."

She bent, putting her lips where her caressing finger had been. He didn't respond to their gentle pressure, and she could even feel the muscle contract, tighten, under her mouth.

She touched its pulse with her tongue and then slowly moved from there to outline the shape of his lips. The top and then along the bottom. She wasn't finished when they opened under hers, his head lifting, aligning, his tongue invading.

He kissed her a long time. A different need, and she never pulled away, although she wanted desperately to see his face. To judge if he believed her. Because if not, then this was something she knew would always be between them.

Nick, who had never before needed her in any way but physically, needed her for this. To assure him that he would never again be alone in this darkness. And that neither, of course, would she. Because she truly didn't want to be.

Eventually, his mouth released hers. She pushed away again, propping herself on her elbow, to study him. His face seemed relaxed, the tension that had been there before erased.

"You know what I want to do?" he said.

She smiled, trying to think of anything he could possibly want that they hadn't already done. And, given her own creative contributions to this marathon, she couldn't imagine there was anything they hadn't tried that they could try. That had, of course, included nothing that might possibly be uncomfortable for her or that Nick had thought might endanger the baby, a concern that she found both touching and a little amusing.

"I don't have a clue," she said honestly.

"Order out for pizza," he said, his voice sure and decisive. Just as it had always been.

"Pizza?" she repeated, her tone full of disbelief. "How the hell can you think about food at a time like this, Deandro?"

"Do you have any idea how long it's been since I *had* pizza? Any idea at all?" His voice was defensive, pretending to be hurt by her laughter.

"You're Italian. How can you like take-out pizza?"

"Some of my best friends like take-out pizza," Nick said.

"What do you want on it?" she asked resignedly.

She began to push up, preparing to go make the call. The pizza delivery boy would probably be glad they were back. Nick was a good tipper, although she was the one who always answered the door, of course.

Instead of letting her crawl over him, Nick grabbed her and pushed her down beside him. He rolled over almost on top of her, holding his weight on his elbows, and kissed her hard and deep.

In the middle of it, his lips releasing hers just enough to get the words out around his tongue, which was still moving, he whispered, "Sausage." Another involved delay. "Mushrooms." Longer. And she almost had time to forgot the first two, before he added the rest. "And pepperoni. Extra cheese."

He let her go, big fingers unlocking suddenly, but she was too drugged to move. How could she possibly want him to make love to her again, when only minutes before...

"Move it, Sterling," he ordered. He rolled off her and lay back against the pillows, crossing his hands under his head, eyes closed, apparently preparing to wait out the food's arrival.

Abby shook her head, but smiling, she awkwardly scrambled over him and got out of the bed. On her way to the hall she stooped to pick up the shirt she'd discarded last night.

The all-night pizza place, whose number was still written on the message board hanging by the kitchen phone, didn't even ask her for directions. She wondered if the redheaded, freckle-faced delivery boy she had gotten to know so well in the weeks Nick had been part of her life still worked there. If so, she wondered if he'd be the one who would bring their order.

Smiling at the thought, she walked back into the bedroom to find Nick still stretched out, the back of his head resting comfortably in his locked fingers. The muscles in his arms and chest were cleanly delineated by their position. His eyes were open now, and he had pulled the sheet up to his waist.

"I've seen it all, Deandro. Way too late for modesty."

"I miss seeing you, Abby," he said softly. "I miss seeing the way you look when I make love to you."

She nodded, her throat thick again with emotion. "I would miss that, too," she said. "Not being able to see your face."

"That's almost the first thing I remembered. How your face looks then."

"You remembered?" she questioned.

"A lot of things now. The apartment. Glimpses of where I lived down here. A lot of unrelated stuff."

"Anything about…the other?"

"The corruption thing?" He shook his head, lips pursing slightly. "Not yet. At least, I don't think so. Some faces. Impressions. I don't know what they mean. If anything."

"Nothing you could testify to?"

He laughed, without humor.

"But if you begin to remember some things…"

She hesitated, and he finished for her. "Then eventually the rest of it will probably come. *Almost* all of it, anyway. That's what they told me. Just relax and give it time. And when it starts to come…" He shrugged his shoulders. Because of his position, his entire upper body moved.

"Then it will all come back," she whispered.

"That's what they say."

She took a deep breath, fighting reaction. She knew, of course, what that meant. The danger would begin again. The people she once believed had discounted Nick's ability to testify against them would come after him again.

In the peaceful hours they'd spent together, she had even begun to believe again that Nick was wrong about the fire. It was an old house, with lots of opportunities for accidents. The fire didn't have to mean someone was trying to kill him, although Nick had seemed so sure of that. If she had really thought so, she would never have allowed him to be here.

But if Nick began to remember, then it *would* all start over. All of it. And maybe this time…

"I think I'm going to grab a shower," Nick said. Sitting up away from the pillows, his hands still locked by their joined fingers, he stretched his arms high above his head, knuckles cracking. "Think I'll have time before the food arrives?"

"You should have," she said, working to keep the fear out of her voice. "It's the middle of the night, however, so they aren't going to be exactly swamped with orders."

She was congratulating herself on keeping her tone neutral, when Nick shattered that illusion.

"What's wrong, Abby?"

He needed to hear the truth, she knew, selfish though it might be. "It just worries me that you're remembering things."

"Worries you?"

"They'll come after you again, Nick, with everything they've got. We both know that. And they almost succeeded before."

"Then we won't tell anybody," he said comfortingly. "Not for a while. Not until I've remembered something important. Besides making love to you," he added.

She thought about that. There was no reason to report anything to the department. Nick had said that nothing was clear. Nothing that would do the prosecutors any good, that would help with any indictments. So he was right. They didn't have to tell anyone about this—for the time being, at least.

He had swung his long legs off the bed and was sitting on the edge. Blatantly nude, beautifully male, and she couldn't take her eyes off him. Maybe because she had been so afraid that he would never be here with her again. After the shooting, she'd been so afraid he wouldn't make it. And then—

"Abby?"

"I'm right here," she said. "You need some help?"

"Just head me in the right direction. The showering I can manage on my own. Unless you want to scrub my back?"

"And take a chance on missing that good-looking pizza boy?" she teased. She walked across the room and put her hand under his forearm. He didn't stand up immediately, but his hand covered hers, tightening over her fingers.

"Take me to the shower," he said, "old faithful guide." Nick stood up, his body tall and still strong, and put his lips against the top of her head. "Why'd you cut your hair, Abby?"

"Because I missed you," she admitted.

He laughed. "That makes a hell of a lot of sense."

"It did to me," she said. "At the time."

He shook his head. "That's just—"

"Just like a woman?" she questioned, when he stopped abruptly. She had begun leading him toward her tiny bathroom.

"Uh-uh. I'm not touching that one with a—" His voice cut off again, but his grin told her what he had been thinking.

"In your dreams, Deandro," she said sarcastically. But when he laughed, she couldn't help laughing, too.

By that time they were in the black-and-white-tiled room. She led him to the tub and then released his arm to take a clean towel off the stack on the wicker shelf.

"Soap and shampoo are in the rack on the shower wall," she instructed, trying to think of everything she needed to tell him. "Curtain's on your right. Pull it to your left. Be sure to check the hot water before you get under it. I keep meaning to cut the temperature down."

"Okay, Mom," Nick said.

"I'm putting a clean towel on the sink behind you," she went on, ignoring his sarcasm. She laid the towel across the bowl of the lavatory. "Just yell if you need anything else."

"I'll be fine, Sterling. You'll probably be surprised to learn that I've been bathing myself for some years now."

"I'll go get your jeans," she said, knowing that he was right. She was being overprotective.

But he was handling that better than she could ever have expected him to. Maybe because he knew her well enough to know that her concern was only natural—because she loved him. And he was probably used to people trying to do too much for him.

"Thanks," he said.

He reached upward, feeling for the shower curtain and finding it easily. He pulled it around the tub, and then he reached inside the enclosure it had made, turning on the water. She watched him adjust the mixture. She was hovering in the doorway, she realized, almost afraid to leave him alone.

"Jeans and then go away," he ordered, apparently realizing the same thing. He didn't even turn his head as he said it. "I'm not going to cook myself or fall down. And even if I do, Abby, you can't do anything about it. Not all the time, anyway. So…just get used to it," he added softly.

"I know," she said. "I'm sorry," she added, turning away to retrieve his jeans from the bedroom.

"We're considering the *sorrys* already said, remember?"

It was what he had told her during the fire. Something else to add to her list of things *not* to do. *Not* tell him she was sorry every time she screwed up.

"You got it, hotshot," she said instead, "but if you blister your tush, don't you come crying for me to kiss it and make it better."

She turned and determinedly made her way to the bedroom, leaving him to figure out the idiosyncrasies of the plumbing on his own. Because she loved him and because she knew that was just what he wanted her to do.

NICK WAS ALMOST through drying his legs when he heard
the doorbell. His stomach growled, right on cue, and so he
hurried, perfunctorily wiping the moisture from his feet
with the thick towel Abby had given him.

He spread it out across the lavatory to dry, locating the
sink by feel, and pulled on his jeans. The odor of smoke
clung to them, but he didn't have anything else. He'd have
to wear these, at least until after they'd eaten.

Despite his hunger, he felt better than he had in months.
Six of them, to be exact. He had a lot to be thankful for,
and he knew it. First of all for Abby's acceptance of him,
despite her natural fears about dealing with his blindness.
For the baby. For the fact that they had escaped the fire
last night.

That was something he knew he needed to think about,
but not quite yet. They had bought themselves some time
by coming here. No one knew that he and Abby had any
past or even that she'd been assigned as his bodyguard, so
there wasn't much reason for anyone to look for him here.

"I'm getting it," Abby said. Her voice, deliberately low,
came from the hallway that led from the bedroom.

He wondered why she had gone back there after she'd
brought him his jeans. Probably to put on some clothes.
And maybe to do just what she'd promised—clear a path
through the clutter. And that was going to be an adjustment
for them both. One that would probably be a lot harder for
Abby, to whom neatness didn't come naturally.

He opened the door, and he could hear conversation from
the living room. Abby and the friendly kid from the pizza
place. Their voices were too indistinct for him to make out
what they were saying. He hesitated on the threshold of the
bathroom, trying to remember the layout of the apartment,
examining the few pictures that had appeared in his head
after he'd arrived here.

He didn't think now would be such a great time for him
to run into a wall and break his nose or to fall over some
furniture whose location he hadn't remembered. Not too

auspicious a start to their renewed relationship. Despite Abby's claim that she could live with this, he wasn't eager to put her to that kind of test. Not yet, at any rate.

The sound from the front of the house was not loud enough for him to identify it. A bump of some kind. Front door closing? He waited a moment, still listening, but there was nothing else. No more conversation, so he guessed he was right.

"Abby," he called, assuming from the silence that the kid had left. There was no answer, and all at once, the hair on the back of Nick's head crawled upward and his stomach muscles tightened sickeningly.

Whenever he had spoken to Abby, she had always answered him. Immediately. Letting him know where she was. Understanding instinctively the importance of that. Which meant...

His hand felt quickly along the wall beside the door for the light switch. He flicked it downward, and stepped back inside the bathroom, trying to think.

A hundred emotions clamored inside his head. Primary among them was fear. Not for him, but for Abby. Wherever the hell she was, she hadn't answered him. That could mean only one thing—that she couldn't answer him.

Think, he demanded, pushing out of his head the image of Abby lying injured, maybe bleeding, on the floor beside the front door. It hadn't been a gunshot he'd heard, thank God. Not even one fired with a silencer. He would have instantly recognized either of those sounds.

Think, his brain screamed at him again, but he seemed almost numb with fear. How the hell could he fight whoever this was? How the hell could a blind guy—

In all the old movies and TV shows he had ever seen about blind people in this kind of situation, they managed to arrange things so the final showdown was fought on their terms. In the darkness. In a world they were much more familiar with than their opponent.

Only, Nick thought in disgust, that was fantasy, and this

was reality. The stark, unforgiving reality of hit men who would just as soon kill a pregnant woman and a blind guy as spit on the sidewalk. And he had no idea what lights were on in the apartment and no clear layout of its rooms in his mind. That was just another cute fantasy dreamed up by some Hollywood scriptwriter.

There was a gun in the bedroom, he remembered suddenly. The image of the small revolver Abby kept in the top drawer of the bedside table was just there in his head, like a miracle. It wasn't department issue, and he had chided her about it not being big enough to stop somebody, but still it was a gun. She wouldn't have taken it out to the safe house. She would have taken her .38 instead.

He stepped quickly out into the hall, holding his right arm in front of him. He found the open bedroom door easily enough, but he was hurrying too fast, forgetful of the obstacle course that Abby's room would be. He couldn't even know what he had stumbled over, but whatever it was hurt like hell when his bare toes connected with it. It didn't slow him down, however, because the image of that revolver was uppermost in his mind.

He found the corner of the bed, thankfully pretty much where he'd expected it to be, and using his hand, running it along the top of the mattress, he found the bedside table. He eased out the drawer, aware for the first time that his hand was shaking. But he'd feel a lot better with a gun in his hands. Any gun. Even if he *couldn't* see what he was shooting at.

Except…it wasn't there. His fingers searched the drawer from side to side and then all the way to the back. He did it twice, still hurrying, but moving more carefully the second time. Making sure. And then he was. There was no gun.

He turned, again fighting fear, and realized that someone was coming down the hall. Whoever it was was moving stealthily, but they were wearing shoes, and the bare wooden boards of the old apartment's floor were unremittingly revealing.

It wasn't Abby. She had been barefoot. Just out of bed and barefoot. As he was.

He moved quickly and silently, aiming himself toward the back of the bedroom door. He had tried to picture which way it opened, which way it was hung. To the right as you faced it. At least that's what he thought, and if he was right… He put his hand out and found nothing.

The footsteps were getting closer, and his hands searched frantically, sweeping the emptiness before him until finally they encountered what he'd been looking for.

He slid the tips of his fingers around the surface, finally finding the knob. Then, holding that, he put his shoulder against the heavy door, thankful that it wasn't one of the modern, hollow-core jobs. He didn't have much to work with here, and he knew he had to make good use of what he did have or he and Abby were going to end up dead. Very permanently dead.

The footsteps had paused. Maybe looking into the bathroom? Or into this room because he had seen movement? Nick held his breath, waiting and listening. One chance. That's all he'd have. One opportunity, and he knew he had to time it right.

As soon as the guy came through the opening, Nick and the door would both slam into him. Hopefully that would surprise him enough that Nick could get his hands on him. And if he did…

The image he'd had earlier of Abby lying hurt, somewhere in the front of this apartment, was enough to guarantee that if he did get hold of this guy, they would have a chance. Because Nick would kill him with his bare hands. If, he thought, fighting fear again, if his hands could only find the intruder.

Just as Nick's lungs had begun to burn from not allowing himself even to breathe, the quiet movement in the hall began again. Timing, Nick cautioned himself. Timing was everything. Waiting. Waiting. Waiting.

With the passing seconds his ears strained against the darkness. His familiar darkness. Feared and hated, but so familiar.

When the right second came, judged by every unwanted skill Nick Deandro had been forced to learn in the last six months, he jammed the heavy door hard into whoever had just entered Abby's bedroom. And behind that movement was every solid ounce of muscle in his six-foot-two-inch frame.

Chapter Thirteen

The body he hit with the door seemed just as solid. There was sound. A grunt of reaction. Maybe breath released or a gasp of surprise. Nick hadn't stopped to analyze what he'd heard. He had been thinking instead about his next target. Most people were right-handed, so that's where a gun was most likely to be. In this guy's right hand.

Nick knew he had to get hold of that hand. Grab that arm right away and hold on or he was going to get shot, and then he was going to be dead. They both were. Both he and Abby.

It was up to him to do something to prevent that. All up to him. He was the one who had led them here. He had led them straight to Abby and the baby. Because he couldn't leave her alone. He had never been able to. Not from the first.

He charged around the door just as the gun exploded. It seemed to go off in his ear. Right beside his face. The smell was overpowering. As was the report which echoed shockingly in the small room.

The shot checked his forward momentum for a split second, but he hadn't been hit. At least not yet, Nick realized in surprise, so he immediately began moving again. He plunged into the guy, hands flailing, trying to find that right wrist. Trying to connect before he could fire again, maybe with more success.

Nick pressed against the intruder, crowding him, deliberately denying him room to operate, not letting him get the gun between their bodies. Suddenly his fingers found what they'd been looking for. He closed them around a wrist, thick and strong, and pushing it upward, he held on for dear life.

Almost before he could secure his grip, however, the guy began twisting and jerking his arm, attempting to free it. Nick knew then that he'd gotten lucky. Gun hand. If this wasn't the hand holding the gun, then the intruder would already have shoved the muzzle of whatever he was carrying against Nick's side or head and pulled the trigger.

Nick raised his right hand, locking it, too, around the wrist he was already holding high in the air. He knew that would free up the intruder's left hand, but it didn't seem that he had many choices here. Whatever damage the intruder would do with the gun if he got it free would be a lot more permanent than what he could do with his fist.

When the blow crashed into his temple, however, he almost forgot that conclusion. The instinct to throw his right forearm up between them to ward off another hit was strong, and he fought it. He tried to lift his elbow a little anyway, still maintaining his two-handed hold on the guy's gun hand, and at the same time trying to put something between his face and the battering left fist.

It didn't seem to have much effect. The next blow came in over his raised arm and impacted on the side of his nose. Nick not only felt it break, he heard it.

And the pain was much worse, of course, than it had been from the first blow. So intense it caused his eyes to water and the air around his head to thin. Suddenly, against the onslaught of agony, it was hard to draw any of that too-thin air into his lungs.

The third blow struck his ear. The resultant ringing took away one of the few weapons he had gone into this hopeless fight in possession of—his hearing.

He couldn't afford to take many more blows to the head,

he knew. Not with his history. Every head injury leaves its calling card on the brain, and he was probably more susceptible to this kind of trauma than the average Joe.

Pushing the intruder backward, Nick started slamming the hand he held backward also, knowing they couldn't be too far away from the door frame. Or the wall. Away from something.

They weren't. He connected on the third motion, the impact so hard it numbed his fingers, tingling all the way down to the nerves in his elbows. Hard enough that the guy's left wasn't pounding his face any more. It was pulling on his right wrist instead, fingers digging into his skin like talons.

But the adrenaline was roaring through Nick's body now, fueled by his small success and by the knowledge that Abby was lying hurt in the adjoining room. Nick again jerked the gun hand forward and then slammed it back against the wall.

His ears had cleared enough that this time he heard the man's knuckles strike something hard. And then strike again and again as Nick repeatedly pounded the wall with the hand holding the gun.

Finally it worked. The gun hit him on the shoulder as it fell. He heard it land on the wooden floor and skitter off somewhere. He dismissed it from his mind. He would never be able to find it. What he had to do now was make sure that the other guy couldn't, either. And the only way he could do that was to hold on to him, no matter what.

He should have been expecting the knee that slammed into his groin. Maybe instinctively he had, because he had managed to turn his body slightly so that the blow was glancing rather than disabling. It was enough, of course. It turned his knees to water and his fingers into spaghetti. And it nauseated him. The wrist he'd been holding was pulled from his suddenly limp fingers, and he almost didn't care. Almost.

He fought a mental battle to keep from giving in to the

pain. To keep from bending over to protect himself. So far he was getting the worst of the one-sided battle. He didn't know why he had thought he could do this. Fight somebody he couldn't see. A stupid, blindly flailing, one-sided…

Because I don't have any choice, Nick reminded himself fiercely, denying both the self-pity and the fear. He forced his damaged body to lunge forward instead of retreating into the fetal position it wanted to assume. He pushed his assailant through the bedroom doorway, both of them hitting the frame on the right-hand side as they fell through the opening.

Despite his agony, Nick lowered his shoulder, trying to shove it into his opponent's gut. That must have had some success too, because the guy's breath came out suddenly in a whoosh, and he stumbled backward down the hall. Nick heard him hit the wall, and on sound alone, he followed, slamming into him.

Then he got in a good blow, drawing his right fist back and pumping it straight and hard into the guy's solar plexus, just as he'd been taught when he was a kid. Taught by a washed-up boxer in some smelly gym in Queens.

A release of breath again, warm and wet against his face. Whooshing out because the guy's belly was soft. The first sign of weakness—and of hope—that Nick had found in this fight. So he hit him there again. Putting everything he had behind it.

His opponent slumped, bending over Nick's fist, capturing and impeding its movement. Nick used his left hand on the man's shoulder to push him upright, at the same time again drawing his elbow straight back, keeping the motion controlled. Then something exploded against the side of his head. The same side where he'd been shot six months ago.

It shattered with the contact. There was a lot of glass, falling all around them both, shards stinging against his face and neck and bare shoulders. With that much noise, it seemed that whatever it was should have hurt more, but it hadn't. Something light and flat, he knew. Something his opponent had been able to get to, pressed here against the wall. The guy must have grabbed a photograph, Nick realized. Grabbed it right off the wall.

Despite the distraction, his right arm managed to complete the blow it had begun, but it wasn't as solid as the first. During that second's hesitation, his opponent had turned, twisting out of Nick's grasp.

By the time Nick had figured out what was happening, the guy was almost away. He grabbed at him, fingers of his left hand reaching out, desperate to close over something, and they did. Only it was cloth, which he could hear tearing as it was pulled away from him. It had slowed the intruder down enough, however, that Nick got his right arm out also, his fingers catching the guy's shoulder and jerking him around. Trying to.

He swung his left in a wild roundhouse punch and connected with nothing. In the effort of that big swing, he lost his hold on the man's shoulder. He should never have let him go, Nick knew, because the guy was running now. Down the hall and away from him.

Except that didn't make sense. This clown had been sent here to kill him. Why the hell would he be running? It wasn't as if this fight was going all that much Nick's way. He had barely laid a finger on his opponent. Even as he thought it, Nick threw himself after the intruder.

Back toward the living room? Or the kitchen? He had time to wonder that before he hit something and hit it hard, the jolt banging all along his length. He went down, like a cartoon character bouncing off an object that appeared in his path. He didn't even know what he'd hit. It could have been anything. Frame of the living-room doorway? A piece of furniture?

But he could still hear the guy moving, so he scrambled up and went at him again, this time both hands held out in front of him, feeling his way. And as he did, his bare feet making no sound, he was listening. Trying to locate his opponent. By his breathing. Footsteps. Anything.

He heard movement off to his left a fraction of a second before something else came crashing down against his head. That split second's warning was enough that he had gotten his left arm up, partially deflecting the blow. Whatever it was had landed mostly on his forearm and elbow.

The object this time, however, had been heavy enough to do some damage, Nick thought, violently straightening his arm to push whatever it was away. And as he did, he made the identification. A table lamp. He had felt the shade with his fingers.

The son of a bitch was persistent. He'd give him that. Only, so was he. Because he didn't have a choice, he thought again. He swung his right arm, not a blow, but a search, and connected, digging his fingers into whatever he'd touched.

Flesh and cloth. Shirt collar. He had the bastard's neck, Nick realized, elation surging. This was all he had wanted. Just to get his fingers around his throat and squeeze until he was dead. Until he had squeezed the very life out of him and he couldn't hurt them anymore. Not Abby. Not the baby.

He brought his left hand up, clawing fingers finding the other side of the guy's neck. This time he wouldn't let go, Nick decided. No matter what. No matter what the guy did—

But again he hadn't been prepared for the pain, because he hadn't been able to see it coming. It was another one of the classics, taught in a lot of self-defense schools, because of everyone's natural fear and vulnerability.

The intruder's thumbs dug into Nick's eyes, the pressure against his eyeballs almost unbearable. Despite the fact that he was already blind, the fear of having someone gouge out his eyes was still powerful. Sickening in its nightmare force.

He tightened his grip on the guy's throat, trying to cut off the blood flowing through the big carotid arteries that led to his brain. If he could, that would bring on unconsciousness, maybe before he could do some permanent damage to Nick's eyes. And if not, Nick thought, what the hell did it matter?

While they struggled, fighting for dominance, Nick tried to pull his head back, away from those strong thumbs. His opponent was attempting to do the same thing, twisting and turning, trying to tear his neck away from Nick's hold. Bodies joined in an obscene waltz, they staggered into pieces of furniture, each determined to succeed. To outlast the other.

The pressure against Nick's eyes was unbearable, and his fingers ached from the desperate force they were exerting. The whole thing probably lasted less than thirty seconds, but while it was going on, it seemed an eternity.

And then, suddenly, it was over. For a second Nick didn't understand. Had he held long enough that the guy had blacked out? He didn't really understand why the man he held had suddenly slumped against him, a dead weight. Off balance, the movement almost threw Nick down. There had been a gunshot, Nick realized, a little dazed from the abruptness of the end. Someone had shot the guy. And the only person who—

"Abby?" he yelled. He released his opponent, letting the big, limp body slump to the floor.

"I'm here, Nick," she said. "Over here."

"You okay?" he asked.

"I think so," she said. She sounded breathless, but she was talking to him again. Coherent. Making sense.

Reassured by that, he knelt, feeling for the pulse in the guy's neck. He wasn't dead, Nick discovered, but he didn't seem to be moving either. At least the fight had gone out of him. Nick just needed to keep it that way.

He struggled to turn his assailant over enough to get to his necktie and slip it out. When he had, he rolled him back onto his stomach and tied his flaccid hands behind him, operating strictly by feel, hoping that what he was doing would hold.

"You still there, Abby?" he asked. He had begun to wonder why she hadn't come to help him. It would have been far easier for her to do this than for him, and the fact that she hadn't was tightening his gut with anxiety.

"I'm here," she said.

There was something wrong with her voice, he realized, and suddenly the fear in his stomach was alive, an animal, clawing and tearing at him. Leaving the now-trussed intruder, he began to stumble across the room, uncaring of the obstacles that he couldn't avoid. Uncaring of anything but Abby.

"Talk to me, Abby," he ordered. "Give me some direction."

"You're..." The word cut off in a gasp. He heard the intake of her breath and launched himself toward it. Low. She was down. He had been right about that. But he couldn't know how badly hurt she was.

"Abby," he said again, his voice too harsh, too demanding. But that was fear, and she would recognize it and forgive him.

"I'm okay, Nick. I'm okay," she said. "To your left."

"You hit?" he made himself ask.

"No," she denied quickly, but her voice still seemed thin. He could hear her moving, however. Sitting up?

"Good girl," he said, feeling panic subside a little.

"I'm *not* a girl, Deandro." Her tone was reassuring.

He was down now, bent into a crouch, hands extended because he didn't want to step on her. He felt his reaching fingers touch hers, and she took his hand, holding on to him. Her fingers were cold, just as they had been on the roof.

"You hurt, Abby? Talk to me, sweetheart."

"He hit me. I was so stupid, Nick. I went back to get my gun, but I wasn't really ready to use it. I had let my guard down. I never would have believed..." The words faded on an indrawn breath. Audible.

"Where'd he hit you?" he demanded, his fingers searching, only half listening. He had finally found the knot on her skull, touching it gingerly.

"I don't think it's bleeding," she said, adding her own exploring fingers to his. Then she took his hand, the one that had been carefully examining the bump on her skull, and pressed it against her cheek, holding it there. "It just hurts like hell. And I feel like such a fool. So damn incompetent."

"Did it knock you out?" Nick asked, beginning to calm down, to be able to think, now that he knew she was really all right.

"For a little while. I think so, anyway. The next thing I remember, you were both in the room and you were fighting. I tried to get off a shot, but you were so damn close and the light was bad. I was terrified I'd hit you."

"You got him, Abby. It's all over. We're still here. We're okay. A little beat-up, maybe," he said.

Nick was just beginning to realize how beat-up he really was. He hurt in places he couldn't remember being hit in. His hands were shaking. Most of that was reaction, he knew. Shock setting in, now that the physical part was over.

Maybe reaction to his fear about Abby. And thankfully that seemed to be all that was wrong with her, too—shock and a bump on the head. They were so lucky. Lucky to be alive.

"I'm going to call for some backup," he said. "Get us some help. Okay?"

"Okay," she said.

He felt movement against his fingers, which were still touching her face. Nodding the agreement she'd already spoken.

"Can you remember Rob Andrews's home number?" he asked.

There was a long pause, and he supposed she was trying. It could be hard to think after a blow to the head. He was having a little difficulty thinking clearly himself.

He'd just dial 911, he had already decided. It would be

quicker. He didn't even know why he'd asked for the other number, maybe just that lifelong caution about whom to trust. A little worried about which cops might show up out here and recognize him.

"Nick," Abby said softly. "That's…that's who it was, Nick. That's who I shot," she said.

Her voice was still low, and there was something in it that hadn't been there before. Disbelief, maybe, that he hadn't even known who he was fighting? Disbelief at his inability to have figured any of this out?

"Are you sure?" he asked, his own incredulity at his failure probably revealed in the question.

But he had never had any reason to distrust Rob Andrews. Andrews had been in on the original decision to bring Nick into this operation. On the decision to call in the agency. And he'd been in on all the arrangements to put Nick in protection after he'd been hit. And now Abby was telling him—

"I talked to him," she said. "I was even relieved to see the bastard." She laughed a little, full of self-castigation and embarrassment rather than amusement. "And when I turned around to go get you, he must have taken out his gun and hit me. I had time enough to realize what a fool I was before I blacked out. That crooked son of a bitch," she added.

"They bought him."

"Maybe a long time ago," Abby said. "He had too much to lose to let you succeed. For the unit to succeed. He couldn't take a chance on you finding his connections to the people he was in charge of bringing down. I wish I'd killed him when I had the chance," she said. She knew as well as he did what would happen.

"They'll offer him a deal and he'll sing like a canary," Nick said. "Then they'll get them all. The Old Guard's going down." That would be some satisfaction, Nick thought. Some small revenge for all that had happened to them.

"If he does, somebody will kill him."

"*If* they can find him."

"Witness protection," she realized.

"He's really good at protection," Nick said bitterly, thinking about Andrews setting him up. About the fire. About the bastard hitting Abby.

But he was beginning to come down from the adrenaline rush of the fight, beginning to realize that this meant they really were safe. The important thing was that it was over, and they were both safe. At least he was beginning to think that until Abby's breath sucked inward again. A long shuddering inhalation.

"You okay?" he asked, brought back by the sound to the important stuff. He pushed up, slipping his hand under her arm, preparing to help her stand. "Think you're up to making the call? It'll be quicker than me punching in random numbers until I connect with somebody."

He had forced the amusement into his voice because in the back of his mind was the remembrance of Abby's toughness, which belied her apparent fragility. It wasn't like her not to bounce back from something like this. Not like Abby at all, and that scared him. Maybe the lick on the head had been harder than either of them could know, even if it hadn't broken the skin.

"I don't think…" she whispered, taking another deep breath.

Her voice was so low that Nick squatted down beside her again, cupping his palm around her cheek, reassuring. "It's all right," he said. "I'll make the call. I can find the numbers," he promised, smiling at her. "*If* I can just find the phone."

"Nick, I think there's something wrong with the baby."

His heart stopped, but he fought to keep the panic out of his voice. "Wrong?" he repeated.

"I think…" Again she hesitated. "I think I may be in labor. But it's too early. It's way too early."

Her fingers were gripping his again, still cold and now

trembling, her voice filled with anxiety. The thought was even scarier to her now, he knew, because she had put it into words, giving it life. Making it real by telling him about it.

"You're just scared, sweetheart, but it's all over now. Just breathe deep and try to relax. Nothing's going to happen. Nothing's going to happen to you or this baby. I told you that. I *promised* you. Have I ever broken a promise to you, Abby?"

"No," she whispered.

"I'm not going to start now. So just relax, sweetheart. Help's on the way. Everything is going to be all right, I swear to you."

Even as he said it, he was moving. Praying he could find the phone. And when he had, and had made the call, just praying.

Chapter Fourteen

Nick couldn't remember what he had said to the dispatcher after his shaking fingers had finally managed to connect him with the operator. He had identified himself as FBI. He had told her to send the paramedics and a couple of ambulances. He had given her the address and then he had told her there was an officer down, the quickest way, he knew, to round up plenty of cops.

Almost as an afterthought he had also asked her to get hold of Detective Mickey Yates. Although Yates, like Abby, had been handpicked by Rob Andrews, Nick still trusted him. Instinct, he supposed. Nick thought that he might need someone here who knew who he was and who would, without a lot of explanation, understand exactly what had been going on.

Then he had made his way back to Abby and had held her as the sirens again shrieked toward them through the night. He couldn't even remember the order in which they had all shown up, but thankfully the paramedics had been almost as quick as the cops, with Mickey not too far behind.

He didn't think the uniforms would have believed what he was telling them without Abby to back him up. Nick had no ID, of course, and Rob Andrews had been highly respected in the New Orleans police department.

Before their initial questions were satisfied, he'd had to release Abby to the medics. Mickey hadn't arrived yet, and the cops were still verifying his credentials with the Bureau, so they wouldn't let him even ride to the hospital with her.

Letting her go had been the toughest thing he'd faced tonight, but Nick knew he had done all *he* could. For both of them. The rest of it…the rest of it would be out of his control. And Nick Deandro had never liked things he couldn't control. He sure as hell hadn't liked that.

"They say you can see her now," Mickey said, his voice coming from the doorway of the examination room. He'd gone to check on Abby while the emergency-room doctor examined Nick.

He knew he wasn't hurt, at least nothing serious, but they weren't listening to his opinion, and he had been forced to admit that he wouldn't have been able to find Abby anyway. Not without some help. To save time, he had sent Mickey off to do that and resigned himself to their poking and prodding while he waited.

He got up off the end of the examination table, hurrying too fast, and felt his head swim. Unexpectedly, his knees began to buckle. Luckily, someone was close enough to grab his arm and keep him from going down. "Wheelchair," the doctor ordered.

"Like hell," Nick said savagely, jerking his arm away. Enough was enough. He'd already made an exhibition of himself tonight. "Mickey?" he commanded, gripping the big detective's arm like a lifeline when Yates responded. He and Yates had had a good relationship, mutually respectful. He hoped they still did.

"I got you, man," Mickey said under his breath. "I got it covered, Doc," he said aloud, already guiding Nick out of the examination room.

Thankfully Mickey also had sense enough to disappear as soon as they got to Abby's cubicle. "I'll be waiting in the hall," he'd mumbled, putting Nick's hand into hers.

"You okay?" Nick asked her softly, when the sound of Mickey's size thirteens had faded.

"I'm fine, Nick. I promise I am."

"What'd they say about...?" Somehow he couldn't complete the question, his throat closing, hard and tight, so that the words got stuck.

"They gave me something," Abby said. Her fingers smoothed over the back of his hand, over raw scrapes and some bruises he hadn't even been aware of until she'd touched them. "Are *you* okay?" she asked, her voice again filled with concern for him.

"Am I okay?" he repeated unbelievingly. "What the hell kind of question is that, Abby?"

"If you could see your face, you'd know what kind," she said, but she sounded almost relieved that he'd fussed at her.

"Well, I can't," he reminded her. "Just the victim of a little domestic violence, if anybody asks."

She laughed, the sound more subdued than normal, but still he liked hearing it. Felt better hearing it. Better about her. Enough that he took a deep breath and asked the next question. "Will whatever they gave you stop the labor?"

"They think so," she said.

"They think he's all right?" And held his breath, waiting for her reassurance.

"He?" she repeated. Her voice was soft, but he got the message because he was smart. Sometimes even smart about Abby.

"She," he amended. "Maybe," he hedged, feeling his tension relax at her repetition of the pronoun he'd used. Abby wouldn't sound like that if everything wasn't really all right.

"The baby's fine, Nick. As long as she—or he," she amended graciously, "doesn't decide to make an unscheduled appearance."

"So when is the scheduled appearance?"

He couldn't believe he hadn't asked. Or hadn't tried to figure it out. He should be able to. The night this baby was conceived was one he had cause to remember—maybe forever. But he now knew that if nothing else about the consequences of that night ever changed, what he would gain from it might make up for what he'd lost. It would help, at least.

"Christmas," Abby said.

"No kidding?" he said softly.

"Merry Christmas, Nick." He could hear the smile in her voice, and that was almost as good as hearing her laugh. Almost as good as being able to see her face.

It damn well would be good enough, Nick decided. And as he bent to kiss her, he breathed a silent prayer of thanks that all the others he'd prayed tonight had been granted.

FOR SOME REASON he'd imagined that he and Abby would just go home when she was released, just go back to her apartment, and this crap would all be over. Of course, nothing was ever that simple. Not when the government was involved. With his background he should have known that. And he had, he guessed, but it didn't keep him from being any less furious about what they'd done.

The hospital had wanted to keep Abby overnight, and he wanted them to, of course, which meant that he'd ended up with Mickey again. In another safe house whose location he wasn't even sure about. Answering a hell of a lot of questions he didn't give a damn about answering. And worrying about Abby.

But at least during the next few days he began to understand what had been going on, the story filtering down as Andrews did just what Nick had predicted he would— spilled his guts in exchange for protection and a plea bargain.

Maybe such deals weren't right. Nick had had his own doubts about that, but they put people behind bars, closed down protection rackets, drug dealers, and loan shark operations. Little by little they were tearing away what had once been the throat-hold the mob had on some segments of American society.

Deals like this one had worked so well in the past that

few people in power even questioned the ethics of them anymore. Maybe Nick wouldn't have, even in this case, if he hadn't been so personally involved. If he hadn't lost so much in the exchange. And almost lost even more, he thought bitterly.

What Andrews gave the authorities were names. Lots of them. Some of them names Nick recognized. But after Nick had been ambushed, Andrews had claimed to his superiors that Nick hadn't given him any of those names. That he hadn't yet had proof of any officer's involvement with the mob.

And Nick hadn't then been in a position to deny what the captain said. He had reported directly to Andrews, and he couldn't remember what he'd turned up. Of course, they knew now that Nick would never have been allowed to remember. Andrews would have taken care of that. Once Nick started to remember, he would be a dead man.

The shrewdest part of the plan, and still the hardest for Nick to deal with, was that Andrews had sent Abby to him. She was, of course, the one most likely to make Nick remember—if he was ever going to remember—and Andrews had realized that.

If the D.A. had decided not to go forward with the corruption indictments, and there was every indication that was the decision they were coming to, then the Bureau would probably refuse to expose Nick by letting him testify in any of the other cases, the mob cases, which could just as well be made with only the informant's testimony.

Then Nick would go home, out of Andrews's jurisdiction and out of his control. Andrews couldn't afford to let that happen, but he also knew that it would look pretty suspicious if a government witness was killed while under the protection of the NOPD. On his watch, so to speak.

So he didn't really want to make another attempt on Nick's life. Not if he didn't have to. Not only would Nick's death look bad for the department, an indication of more corruption, but another attempt would be dangerous. Something could go wrong.

And Andrews wouldn't ever have to take that chance if he could be sure the amnesia was permanent, as the doctors were now telling him it was. That was the reason Abby had been assigned to protection duty—one of them, anyway.

It was obvious that Abby's boss must have known she and Nick had been involved. Maybe he had followed Nick to her apartment the night he was shot, the night someone had ambushed him in that dark alley a few blocks away from Abby's. Andrews hadn't yet admitted to doing the shooting or to setting the fire. Maybe he hadn't. There were plenty of people in this town willing to do murder for a couple of hundred bucks.

It was the other reason Rob had been so eager to send Abby out there to play bodyguard that Nick hated. And he wasn't sure he would ever tell her what they now knew about Andrew's motives. He never wanted to tell Abby that she had also been selected because Andrews thought she was vulnerable.

He had talked her into taking that assignment not only because she was the final test of the permanency of Nick's amnesia, but also because he thought he could go through her and get to Nick any time he needed to. Any time Abby gave him the news that Nick had begun remembering.

Which must be what had happened before the fire, Nick realized. Abby had told Andrews that he was starting to remember things. She must have said something that made her boss believe he had to act soon or it would all come tumbling down.

Everything would come out—all the dirty secrets. Not only the cops that Nick had tentatively identified as having ties with the mob, but Andrews's own connections. Because if those cops went down, and apparently Andrews had promised them that no one would, it was likely that one of them would take just such a deal as the captain himself had made. And then it would all be over.

It had almost worked. It was only through sheer blind luck, Nick thought, no pun intended, that they had escaped the fire. Andrews somehow found out that they had, maybe through Blanchard, maybe simply by asking that little fire department if there had been any bodies in the ruin.

Then when Abby failed to report in, her supervisor must have believed she suspected him—maybe because of something Nick had remembered. So he had taken a chance that they had come back to the city. Back to Abby's apartment. And he'd gotten lucky.

It must have been a hell of a surprise to Andrews that Abby had been so welcoming when she opened the door. Surprising enough that he maybe hadn't quite figured out what to do, at least until she had turned her back on him, giving him an opportunity he couldn't afford to pass up.

At least, Nick thought, he hadn't shot her. Maybe Rob had not been cold-blooded enough in the face of Abby's friendliness. Or maybe Nick's voice, coming from the back of the apartment at that moment, had made him realize he had another problem to deal with right then.

Maybe that was when he had decided it would be so easy to take care of both of them. Just do it himself and be done with it. After all, all he had to do was take out a blind guy and a very pregnant woman, and then he'd be safe again. No one would ever have known he was crooked.

It might have worked, Nick admitted, if it hadn't been for Abby. If she hadn't been cautious enough to carry her gun to the door. She'd been expecting the pizza boy and had gotten a murderer instead. And apparently in the low lighting, Andrews had never even seen the weapon. She had probably stuck it in the pocket of her slacks as soon as she'd recognized him.

If Abby hadn't been able to get off that shot, accurate enough to put Andrews, a moving target in the darkness, out of commission, it would have all been over. Nick was under no illusions about who had rescued whom that night. He had told anyone who would listen just how it had happened, but he was still getting credit he didn't deserve for the fight.

It must be the way he looked, he had decided. Like somebody had taken after him with a two-by-four, one of the agents said. They had all commented on it, maybe afraid that he didn't really know how battered he appeared.

His nose might never be the same, Nick knew, but then it hadn't been all that great to begin with. At least the swelling had gone down. He could tell that by feel. Mickey had assured him, amusement coloring his voice, that the bruising around his eyes wasn't even black-and-blue anymore. Greenish yellow, Yates had opined.

Nick wondered why he had bothered to ask. If Abby was willing to put up with blindness, she wasn't going to balk at a crooked nose and some discoloration. At least he hoped to hell she wasn't.

He took a breath, fighting his impatience. Mickey had gone way out on a limb for them in arranging this. Nick was still supposed to be in protection, especially now that more and more of what he had lost was beginning to trickle back. Maybe nothing they needed, not with Andrews's testimony, but the D.A. hadn't quite decided that yet, of course. *Lawyers,* Nick thought in disgust.

He sure as hell didn't intend to wait until they made up their minds before he was allowed to see Abby. He had also told that to everyone who would listen. Realistically, he probably wasn't ever going back to work for the Bureau, so he didn't give a damn if they found out about his past relationship with Abby.

It had broken all the rules, and he knew it. He had known it at the time. But he couldn't regret whatever it cost him. No regrets at all. As long as—

"Hey," Abby said softly, interrupting his thinking.

He hadn't heard her come into the room, and his stomach

reacted. Just to the sound of her voice. Just to that one low word.

"Hey, yourself," he said. *Smooth, Deandro. A real show-stopper, conversationally speaking.*

"Mickey said they weren't too happy about this. About my being here."

"Screw 'em," Nick said succinctly. He hadn't gotten off the couch, and he didn't think she'd moved out of the doorway. The blur of paler darkness the opening represented had clouded a little, that cloud almost a shape if he squinted.

She laughed, the sound floating across the distance, so beautiful to him. He'd been hungry to hear her laugh again, and he hadn't even realized it until just now.

"You're not supposed to be that irreverent, Deandro," she said. "These guys are so impressed with themselves, you're supposed to be impressed with them, too. They're the *Feds.*"

Her voice was mocking, especially on the last word. Good-natured insider rivalry maybe, but it made him wonder. "Is that what you thought about me?" he asked.

She laughed again, her voice more relaxed this time, no tension anymore. "Hotshot," she agreed. "Big-time FBI hotshot. Come down to tell all us bumpkins how to do our jobs."

"Is that really how I came across?"

She hesitated, and he knew she was thinking about what she was willing to tell him. "Maybe just to me," she said finally. "But I liked your butt."

"My butt?" he repeated, caught totally off guard.

"I always thought you had a cute butt," she said.

"You're a shallow woman, Detective Sterling," he said, beginning to smile.

"Just unnaturally interested in sex and violence, I guess," she agreed. "What can I tell you, Deandro?"

"That you'll marry me," he suggested softly.

And he waited. The silence stretched, grew, expanded,

and he could hear his heart beating. Too fast. Just as it did when he was faced with something that made him afraid. And her hesitation did. Real afraid.

"Sterling?" he said finally. Nothing else. He had thought this was what she wanted, too. Was it possible that he'd misunderstood that night and the following day? Misunderstood what it had meant? Was he not only blind, but an idiot as well?

"I guess it *is* about time," she said.

He didn't understand what was in her voice. He tilted his head, thinking that if she said anything else, he might get a better read on her tone. Besides, those were too few words for what he'd asked her. A very important question. Or so he had always thought.

"Sometime before this baby gets here," she added.

And for the first time, that possibility hit him. She was right. He *was* arrogant. Because it had never dawned on him that this might be the reason she was willing to marry him. Rings, mortgages, and *then* babies. The way it was supposed to be done.

"Is that the reason, Abby?" he asked.

He almost didn't want her to answer because he knew she would tell him the truth. However painful it might be, Abby Sterling wasn't a woman who ever lied, to herself or to him. That's why Nick had been so sure of her. He knew she would have examined all the realities of his situation— their situation, he amended—before she'd invited him back.

"It's a pretty good one," she admitted softly. "Babies need a daddy. They all do. And the lucky ones get very good fathers like you'll be, Nick. There's never been any doubt in my mind about that. But to be honest…"

Her voice faded and, because he was listening so hard, he could even hear the breath she took before she went on. It was deep, and because of that he was afraid again.

"But to be honest," she repeated, "nothing I do is that unselfish. I wouldn't marry you just to give this baby a name. Or even a daddy. I'll marry you, Nick, because I can't imagine living the rest of my life without you. Can't imagine having to face getting up every day without you there. Can't imagine…''

He knew why the words had stopped. He had heard the tears invade her voice long before they had choked off its low whisper.

"Abby," he said. Comforting. He held out his hand. Invitation or entreaty? He didn't care how she interpreted the gesture. As long as she responded to it.

"I'm right here, Nick," she said.

Suddenly she was. Slim, warm fingers closing over his, and he pulled her into his arms, settling her onto his lap and then crushing her too tightly against him. Crushing both of them.

She turned her head against his cheek, the softness of her hair moving against his face, evoking memories. They had been the first to come back, and they were still the most vivid. The familiar scent of her body seemed like a homecoming.

He put his hand over the baby, fighting emotion. "How's Junior?" he whispered.

She laughed, her breath warm and sweet on his face. "She's fine," she said. She put her palm over the back of his hand, moving it a little. "But she's got a kick like a mule."

"Little girl?" he asked. They could tell those things now. Maybe she had been serious about the pronoun that day.

She shook her head, which was still pressed against his cheek. "I didn't want to know. Old-fashioned."

"You got names picked out?"

"No," she said. "Not yet. I was waiting on you to help." She lifted his hand and held it against her face a moment. Then she turned her head, kissing his palm, before she put it back against her cheek.

"They're not ready to let me go," Nick said. Bad news, but she was a cop. She knew how this worked.

"I know. Mickey told me. But he thinks they will. Soon."

"Yeah. Me, too," Nick said.

"I don't think I want to wait."

He nodded. "That's why I told Mickey to bring the minister's wife along."

"The minister's wife?"

"It takes two witnesses. At least that's what I've always heard. How would you feel about Mickey being your maid of honor?"

"Never mind," Abby said. "I'll furnish my own maid of honor, hotshot."

Her voice had lightened again with the teasing, and she carried Nick's hand from her face to place it over the swell that was his baby.

Epilogue

"You aren't the kind that faints at the sight of a little blood?" the doctor had joked.

"Not unless it's my own," Nick had answered.

He didn't think the rest of them understood why Abby laughed so hard. They probably thought she was high on whatever they had given her. Maybe she was, but still, he had liked the sound of her laughter.

A hell of a lot more than he had liked the sounds that followed it. Maybe because he couldn't see a clock, it seemed as if it all went on for an eternity. They kept telling him she was fine. That she was doing good. That the baby was. Especially after they had figured out that his vision wasn't one hundred percent.

Their voices had changed with the realization, just as they always did, but Nick had ignored that, concentrating on Abby instead. On holding her hand. On talking to her. Breathing with her. Wishing he was the one who was going through this.

Never again, he promised. His mom had said women forgot the pain of childbirth. Maybe so, but he wasn't sure *he* ever would. He didn't like things he couldn't control, and he had so little to do with anything that was happening here that it was frightening and so damn frustrating.

Abby had talked to him. Almost to the end. Reassuring him. She shouldn't have had to do that. Not when she was

the one who was suffering. But at least now he knew that
the next time they decided to do this...

Abby's hand gripped his suddenly, fingernails biting into
his flesh. He welcomed the pain. At least it made him feel
a part of what was going on. Some small part.

"Okay, Abby," Dr. Clarke said. "It's time. Let's do
this."

Abby's hand tightened over his. There were more sound
effects. None of them pleasant.

"Again," the doctor commanded. And then after a little
while. "And again, Abby. You're doing great. Big one,
now."

He wondered how Dr. Clarke could sound so calm, but
of course she did this every day. Delivered somebody's
baby. Somebody's son or daughter. Somebody's—

Abby cried out. It was the first time she had done that,
and it scared the hell out of him. At least until he had heard
what followed. The thin, mewling wail of a newborn, vol-
ume increasing as lungs expanded and it awakened to the
realization that all that warmth and safety had just been
exchanged for bright lights and cold hands.

Welcome to the world, angel, Nick thought, hot tears
unexpectedly burning his eyes. Sweet Christmas angel, he
thought again, listening to her cry.

"Congratulations, Nick," Dr. Clarke said. "You have a
beautiful, healthy son."

"Son?" Nick repeated. Abby had been so certain...
"Are you sure?" he asked.

There was a lot of laughter, spontaneous and natural.
And then it faded as they realized that perhaps their laughter was not appropriate to the situation. To his situation.

"They've been doing this a long time, Nick," Abby said,
amusement still in her voice at least. "I think maybe they'd
know."

"You sorry?" he asked, moving his thumb over the back
of her hand. He was so afraid she'd be disappointed.

"Are you kidding me, Deandro?"

"He might grow up to be just like me," he warned.

"If we're very, very lucky," Abby said softly. There was no doubting the sincerity of that, her voice wiped clean of laughter, and in response he had to fight the burn again.

"Yeah, well…" he said awkwardly. "You might be prejudiced."

"I just might be," she agreed. "You want to hold him?"

"You trust me?" he asked, knowing she would.

"With my life," Abby whispered.

She must have nodded permission to somebody because the next thing he knew they were putting his son into his arms. There was a blanket of some kind around him, but Nick's fingers found the important things. Ten fingers and ten toes. Nose. Chin. Everything he expected.

He looked up at Abby. "At least he looks like you."

"Actually…" she began, amusement creeping into her voice.

"I mean I know he's got blue eyes, but—"

"You can't tell that," she said, laughing. "Quit trying to show off. Besides, all babies have blue eyes."

"And black hair?" Nick said. That much he *could* see.

"A headful," Abby acknowledged.

Nick's fingers drifted over the down-soft fluff, almost afraid to touch the baby's head because he seemed so tiny, at least in contrast with the size of his hands.

"And soon you'll be able to—"

"They said it was okay." Mickey Yates's voice was tentative, seeking verification of the permission someone had given him.

"Hey, Mickey," Abby said.

"They said it was a boy," Mickey said, moving into the room. "I brought you something."

Nick looked up at that, squinting a little. "A Christmas tree?" he said in disbelief. "You brought him a Christmas tree?"

It couldn't be anything else. The shape was right and there were things on it. Primarily red blurs against the green. What he saw was still pretty indistinct, but it was getting better. Day by day. And the doctors who had been so cautious at the beginning were now confident that his vision would be fully restored. He'd even been offered a job in the NOPD when they finally released him. Nick wasn't sure how he would like working under Abby, but he was proud of her promotion. He knew there was no one more capable of running the newly reorganized O.C. unit than Abby.

"Hey, man, it's Christmas," Mickey said, his voice slightly offended. "I just didn't want you guys to forget to celebrate."

Not much chance of that, Nick thought, his gaze dropping back to the oval blur that he knew represented the face of his son. Not much chance of the three of them forgetting to celebrate. Not this particular Christmas, anyway.

And probably not much chance of them forgetting to celebrate the next forty or fifty of them, either. Forty or fifty together if they were very lucky. And apparently, he thought, as Abby's hand closed over his, apparently they really were. Very, very lucky.